D0485208

Praise for the r

"Skillfully balancing susp
gives readers a nonstop breath-holding adventure."
—*Publishers Weekly* on *Going Once*

"Vivid, gripping...this thriller keeps the pages turning."
—*Library Journal* on *Torn Apart*

"Sala's characters are vivid and engaging."
—*Publishers Weekly* on *Cut Throat*

"Sharon Sala is not only a top romance novelist, she is an inspiration for people everywhere who wish to live their dreams."
—John St. Augustine, host, *Power!Talk Radio*
WDBC-AM, Michigan

"Veteran romance writer Sala lives up to her reputation with this well-crafted thriller."
—*Publishers Weekly* on *Remember Me*

"[A] well-written, fast-paced ride."
—*Publishers Weekly* on *Nine Lives*

"Perfect entertainment for those looking for a suspense novel with emotional intensity."
—*Publishers Weekly* on *Out of the Dark*

Also by Sharon Sala

Forces of Nature

GOING GONE
GOING TWICE
GOING ONCE

The Rebel Ridge novels

'TIL DEATH
DON'T CRY FOR ME
NEXT OF KIN

The Searchers

BLOOD TRAILS
BLOOD STAINS
BLOOD TIES

The Storm Front trilogy

SWEPT ASIDE
TORN APART
BLOWN AWAY

THE WARRIOR
BAD PENNY
THE HEALER
CUT THROAT
NINE LIVES
THE CHOSEN
MISSING
WHIPPOORWILL
ON THE EDGE
"Capsized"
DARK WATER
OUT OF THE DARK
SNOWFALL
BUTTERFLY
REMEMBER ME
REUNION
SWEET BABY

Originally published as Dinah McCall

THE RETURN

Look for Sharon Sala's next novel

COLD HEARTS

available soon from MIRA Books

SHARON SALA

WILD HEARTS

If you purchased this book without a cover you should be aware that this book is stolen property. It was reported as "unsold and destroyed" to the publisher, and neither the author nor the publisher has received any payment for this "stripped book."

Recycling programs for this product may not exist in your area.

ISBN-13: 978-0-7783-1816-3

Wild Hearts

Copyright © 2015 by Sharon Sala

All rights reserved. Except for use in any review, the reproduction or utilization of this work in whole or in part in any form by any electronic, mechanical or other means, now known or hereinafter invented, including xerography, photocopying and recording, or in any information storage or retrieval system, is forbidden without the written permission of the publisher, MIRA Books, 225 Duncan Mill Road, Don Mills, Ontario M3B 3K9, Canada.

This is a work of fiction. Names, characters, places and incidents are either the product of the author's imagination or are used fictitiously, and any resemblance to actual persons, living or dead, business establishments, events or locales is entirely coincidental.

® and TM are trademarks of Harlequin Enterprises Limited or its corporate affiliates. Trademarks indicated with ® are registered in the United States Patent and Trademark Office, the Canadian Intellectual Property Office and in other countries.

For questions and comments about the quality of this book, please contact us at CustomerService@Harlequin.com.

www.MIRABooks.com

Printed in U.S.A.

Childhood sweethearts are the first and the best, because the love is new and untainted. Even though most of them do not carry through to adulthood and become the life partner you will have, they all hold a special place in our hearts.

I'm dedicating this book to my first love, my Bobby, who reappeared in my life when I needed him most. I had eight of the most wonderful years of my adult life with him before I lost him to cancer. He was my first love, and he will be my last love.

Some things are impossible to replace.

WILD HEARTS

Prologue

Mystic, West Virginia
May 1980

The sky was as dark as a witch's heart, the smells of whiskey and sex as strong inside the titty-pink Cadillac as the vomit in the floorboard behind the driver. The speedometer was pegged out at a hundred and ten, and still the headlights of the car behind them kept gaining.

Eighteen-year-old Connie Bartlett's fingers were curled around the steering wheel of her brand-new graduation present, her eyes wide and fixed on the white stripe down the middle of the blacktop, and she was screaming at the top of her lungs.

Her boyfriend, Dick Phillips, was on his knees, leaning over the seat and looking out the back window. Like Connie, he could see the headlights coming closer.

"Faster, Connie, faster! He's gonna catch us!"

"It won't go any faster!" she cried.

She swerved toward the right, then swerved back toward the left, tossing her passengers from one side of the car to the other. She was trying to follow the white stripe down the middle of the highway, but she was driving drunk, something her daddy had told her never to do.

In the backseat, Betsy Parr was three beers and most of a fifth of Jack Daniel's drunk, down on her hands and knees in the floorboard, puking up her guts. She always felt carsick in the backseat. Being drunk and dancing with death only made it worse.

Her boyfriend, Paul Jackson, was passed out above her, drunk from the other three beers from Betsy's six-pack and the rest of the bottle of Jack Daniel's, oblivious to the drama and the danger.

Dick was pounding the seat and crying now. "He's gaining! He's gaining! He'll kill us, too. What are we gonna do?"

Betsy groaned as another wave of nausea swept over her, but before she could follow the urge to puke again, the car fishtailed, throwing her against the door at her back. Too scared to look up, she began beating her fists on the back of Connie's seat.

"Oh, my God…Connie, stop, please stop! You're going to kill us."

"We can't!" Dick yelled. "He saw all of us. We have to get to the cops first or he'll finger us for what he did!"

"We're drunk. They'll blame it on us anyway," Betsy moaned.

"Shut up! Shut up!" Connie screamed. "You saw what he did! We all saw it!"

Betsy couldn't believe this was happening. Twelve long years of slogging through an education all the way to their high school graduation, and three hours after getting their diplomas they were going to die. Her only consolation, even though she'd had to get drunk to do it, was that she wouldn't die a virgin.

All of a sudden the car began to slide sideways.

"Connie! Take your foot off the gas!" Dick screamed.

Instead, Connie jerked the wheel in the other direction, and suddenly they were airborne. Her foot was still on the accelerator, the engine was roaring like the backwash from a jet, but the sensation of flying, if only for a moment, was real.

Paul Jackson woke up just as the wheels left the blacktop to find Betsy's foot in the middle of his chest.

"What the hell?" he groaned, and then leaned over and vomited all over the both of them just as the pink Cadillac went nose-first into a tree.

Connie went through the windshield, landing face-down on the hood as steam from the broken radiator rose up around her.

Dick's head slammed against the dash, cutting a gash across his forehead as he slumped down on the floor, pinned between the dash and the seat as it crumpled around him.

Betsy was ejected through the back window onto the trunk and then bounced off onto the ground a short distance away, awash in the exhaust from the tailpipe.

The back door popped open on impact, throwing Paul out against a nearby boulder, breaking his arm and his shoulder, and cracking his skull.

To add insult to injury, a dead limb knocked loose from the impact dropped, landing on Connie's back, although it was overkill. She was already gone.

A few moments later, headlights swept across the scene of the wreck as the driver of the other car finally caught up. He slowed down only long enough to assess the scene and assume they were dead, then disappeared into the night.

Betsy Parr woke up to bright lights and heart-stopping pain. She could hear her mother's voice; the fear in it was palpable. She heard her father, and then the sound of choking and moaning. It took a moment for her to realize she was the one making that noise. She heard her mother cry out, begging them to do something, and then the pain was gone as she sank into unconsciousness.

By midmorning, news of the accident spread through town like wildfire. One of Mystic High School's brand-new graduates was dead, and three more critically injured.

Everyone was in shock, including the driver of the second car, who had been so sure they were dead.

He thought about running. He thought about coming out with a story to lay blame on them first, and then decided to wait and see what happened. They could still die.

And when all the shock and drama was over, and the rush of gossip had long since cleared, waiting was what saved him.

Connie Bartlett took what she knew to the grave, and the three others had been so drunk, and then suffered such critical head wounds, that later on when they were questioned, none of them remembered anything after receiving their diplomas. The ensuing three hours of their lives had been erased.

His future had been saved by a quirk of fate, which made everything else he'd done worth it.

One

The cackle of hens and the occasional squawk of a pissed-off rooster were the beginning to Dick Phillips's day as he went about his morning chores. He opened the coop and began scattering chicken feed, laughing at the rush that ensued as he went in to gather the eggs.

A few years back his wife, Marcy, had got an itch to raise chickens, so he'd built a coop and bought her a few hens to make her happy, and then she died. Afterward, he couldn't bring himself to get rid of them, so they stayed. As time passed, the flock grew, and now, with over forty laying hens, he was selling the surplus to regular customers, who came to the farm to pick up eggs for their family use.

He took the fresh eggs down to the barn to what he called the egg room. He was favoring his right shoulder. He'd taken a bad fall last week and was certain he'd torn something vital. He couldn't lift his arm above his head, and it hurt to carry anything, although there was still work to be done. He stood at the worktable, sorting, cleaning and crating eggs, and then stored them in a small walk-in cooler at the back of the room.

He'd just walked out into the breezeway and was getting ready to feed his cows when he heard a car. He paused in the doorway, absently scratching at the old scar on his forehead, and then raised his hand in greeting when he recognized the driver, then eyed the large sack he was carrying, thinking he was about to make a big sale.

"Hey, how goes it?" he called. "You comin' after eggs?"

"A couple of dozen, please."

Dick turned to get the eggs from the cooler, unaware that the man had reached into the sack and taken out a long braided rope with a noose at the end. Dick heard the footsteps behind him, but before he could turn, the noose was around his neck.

The man gave the rope a hard yank, and Dick fell backward, landing hard on the back of his head, and at the same time reinjuring his shoulder and cutting off his air. Dick was in shock, uncertain what was happening. His ears were ringing and he couldn't think what to do. Unaware of what was happening behind him, he began fumbling with the noose.

The man had tied a weight to the other end of the rope, and when he threw it up, it sailed over the rafter and right back into his hands as if he'd practiced the move for days. Then he took off running toward the loft, and when the rope tightened, Dick was yanked off his feet so hard that he momentarily blacked out.

It was the reprieve the killer needed. He reached the steps leading to the loft and began climbing them hand over fist with the rope in his teeth. He glanced down once, and as he did, his heart skipped a beat. Dick was not only conscious but struggling to get to his feet. With no time to spare, the killer threaded the rope through a step and then jumped.

As he went down, Dick went up, high enough that his feet were dangling almost two feet off the concrete floor below.

Dick was moaning and kicking as the man wrapped the rope once around his waist for added leverage, then pulled Dick even higher as he ran back toward the ladder and tied off the rope.

Now Dick was dangling almost six feet from the ground. His face was turning blue, his eyes were bulging and his arms were flailing as he clawed desperately at the rope, trying to relieve the pressure.

"Die, damn it," the man muttered. And then, in a fit of impatience, he made a run for Dick's legs and jumped. As he did, he grabbed hold of Dick's ankles, and when he came down with all his body weight, Dick's neck broke with a pop.

It was done.

The killer stepped back, looking all around the area to make sure he'd left nothing of himself behind, then pulled out his pocketknife and cut off the weight, taking it with him as he left.

Long after the sound of his car had faded away, the chickens still clucked, the rooster crowed and the cows were still waiting to be fed.

Betsy Jakes had her cookbook out, going down the list of ingredients she needed to make her famous Italian cream cake. Tomorrow was her son Trey's birthday, and it was his favorite dessert. She glanced down at the recipe, writing needed ingredients onto her grocery list, and made a note to stop by Dick's house to buy eggs before she went home.

She had known Dick for most of her life, and in her youth had even survived a deadly crash with him the night they graduated from high school. His girlfriend, Connie, who'd been driving that night, died in the wreck, while Dick, Betsy and her boyfriend, Paul, survived. Even though life had taken them down separate paths, they remained bonded by the past.

Betsy checked out her appearance, making a note to pick up some hair color. Her roots were beginning to show. Then she combed her curly shoulder-length hair and fastened it off at the nape of her neck. There were a few more wrinkles at the corners of her eyes and around her mouth where she smiled, but her brown eyes still danced when she was laughing. Her chin had always been a little too square and with age was beginning to take on a bit of a bulldog look. She frowned, thinking she could lose about ten pounds and get rid of that, and then let the thought go. She was a satisfied widow with no desire to ever marry again. Why bother?

After changing from her work clothes into a clean pair of jeans and a yellow pullover blouse, she made the trip into Mystic in fine fashion. She was listening to her favorite radio station, rockin' to the oldies, when a Bob Seger song came on the radio. Grinning from the memories it evoked, she turned up the volume and sang along.

When she finally drove into Mystic, she glanced toward the police station to see if Trey's cruiser was there. He had been chief for over five years, and she was proud of what he'd become. He reminded her so much of her husband, Beau, and she wished daily that Beau had lived to see his children grow up. But the cruiser was gone, which meant he was out and about. Maybe she would see him before she left town.

She shopped quickly, rejecting an invitation to lunch with one of her friends because she was anxious to get home and start the cake. Still, she took time to pull into the drive-through of a local sandwich shop called the French Fry to get a cold drink on the way home. While she was waiting for her drink she finally saw Trey drive by and wondered what interesting stuff was going on in Mystic, and made a mental note to call him later.

"Here's your Pepsi," the clerk said, and leaned out the window to hand the cup and straw to Betsy.

"Many thanks," Betsy said, and waved as she drove away.

She was sipping on the Pepsi and listening to the Rolling Stones when she remembered the eggs and turned right at the next section-line road.

Dick's farm was small, but it was a beauty, backing up to one of the many mountains that surrounded their little town. She eyed the climbing roses on the trellis against the side of the house, remembering how Dick's wife, Marcy, had loved her flowers. She missed Marcy Phillips. She'd been a good friend.

She parked on the outside of the yard fence and then knocked on the door. When Dick didn't answer, she looked around to make sure his pickup was out back in the garage, which it was. The front door was unlocked, so she opened it a bit and leaned in.

"Dick! Hey, Dick, it's me, Betsy! Are you here?"

With no answer from inside, she looked toward the barn. She could hear the cows bawling and nodded to herself, thinking that was where he would be. Still focused on the long process of making that cake, she ran back down the steps and headed toward the barn with long strides.

The barn had been built over a hundred years earlier, in a style similar to Pennsylvania Dutch. The two-story structure loomed against the landscape with a loft as large as the barn itself. It had a fairly new coat of barn-red paint on the outer walls, while the cross-boards on the old shutters had been painted white. The pasture was fenced off from the house and barnyard and spread out toward the trees ringing the mountain at its back.

"Dick! Dick! It's me, Betsy! Where are you?" she yelled, but got no answer.

She was looking toward the pasture as she hurried along, thinking he would come walking out of the trees any minute. Then she heard a dog bark and frowned. Dick didn't have dogs. She wondered if someone was hunting on his property and turned her head to look.

Her gaze moved past the breezeway that ran straight through the middle of the barn, and as it did, she saw something swinging in the air above the ground. She stopped, then began to stare, trying to focus on what it could possibly be. No longer interested in the pasture, she began moving toward the barn, but at a slower gait, her mind unready to accept the truth.

She was about twenty yards away, so close she could see his clothing and his shoes and the awful angle of his neck, when her knees buckled, refusing to carry her another step. She was on the ground, rocking and moaning. Twice she tried to get up, but her legs wouldn't hold her. She kept trying to make what she was seeing turn into something else instead. But it was Dick Phillips's lifeless body, swinging slowly in the breeze. The sound that came up her throat was more howl than scream, but it was the impetus she needed to get moving.

Trey! She had to call Trey.

She scrambled to her feet and started running back to her car to get her phone, screaming as she went. When she reached the car, she fell into the front seat, grabbing for the cell phone she'd left in the console. Still sobbing and shaking so hard she could barely breathe, she tried to scroll through her contacts and hit three wrong numbers before she finally got through to Trey. The moment she heard his voice, she started screaming again, and this time she couldn't stop.

Trey Jakes was not in a good mood. He and the officer on duty, Earl Redd, had gone to serve an arrest warrant on a guy they had grown up with. The man had turned into a replica of the father who'd raised him: stealing instead of working. Only this time the theft he'd pulled was caught on tape, resulting in a warrant for his arrest. He'd been out of town for almost a week, and this morning the police department had received a tip from a neighbor that he was back. At least when they knocked on his door to serve it, he went with them without a fight.

Trey had just finished the paperwork and was getting up to refill his coffee cup when his cell phone rang. When he saw it was from his mom, he forgot about the coffee. The moment they connected, all he could hear was screaming. The hair stood up on the back of his neck, and he began yelling, trying to get her to calm down enough to talk.

"Mom! Is that you? What's wrong? Where are you? Mom? Mom! For the love of God, what's wrong?"

It was Trey's voice that finally pulled her back.

"I need you. You have to come. Oh, dear Jesus," Betsy moaned, and then got out of the car and dropped to the ground, putting her head between her knees to keep from passing out.

Earl Redd had already come rushing into the room, alerted to the emergency by what Trey was saying.

"Where are you? Are you hurt? What's wrong?" Trey asked, heading for the door on the run.

"Dick Phillips! Come to his farm! Oh, my God, hurry."

"Mom! I need to know what happened so I can dispatch emergency vehicles. Who's hurt? What happened?"

"Dick. He's dead. Oh God, oh God, he's *dead*."

Trey slid to a dead stop on the sidewalk, and Earl stopped right along with him.

"He's dead? Are you sure?" Trey asked.

"Yes, I'm sure. He's hanging from the rafters in his barn."

The moment those words came out of her mouth, she dropped the phone and started screaming again.

Trey clenched his jaw as he made a U-turn and headed back into the office with Earl at his heels. He found his day dispatcher, Avery Jones, cleaning dead flies off the windowsill.

"What's up, Chief?" he asked.

"I need you to get on the phone, not the radio, and tell the county sheriff's office there's a death at Dick Phillips's farm. Give them directions and ask if they want you to notify the coroner or if they're going to do it. Then I need you to call in Carl and Lonnie and tell them I want them on patrol in town until further notice."

Avery's eyes widened, but he didn't question the orders. "Any details you want me to pass on?" he asked.

"Tell the sheriff a man was hanged. We don't know if it's a murder or a suicide and I damn sure don't want that to get out. Dick has a daughter who deserves to know all this first."

"Yes, sir," Avery said, then grabbed the phone and a list of numbers. He began making calls as Trey and Earl left on the run.

"God Almighty," Earl said. "This is awful."

Trey nodded. "Follow me," he said, and jumped into his cruiser and ran hot all the way to the Phillips farm.

His phone was still connected to his mother's call, and he could still hear her screaming, but as he drove the sound became fainter, and then finally it stopped. Even though he kept yelling in the phone for her to pick up, he got nothing.

He was worse than worried. He'd never heard her like that. And even more upsetting, he was going to have to contact the only woman he'd ever loved and tell her that her father was dead. This day just kept getting worse.

Ten minutes later he arrived at the Phillips farm to find his mother in the fetal position next to her car, her hands over her head as if trying to ward off a blow. He knew what she'd seen was shocking, but this reaction was not like the woman he knew. He got out on the run, then scooped her up into his arms and sat her on the hood of her car.

"Mom! Talk to me. Are you okay?"

She was limp, her eyes wide and fixed, and when he spoke, she didn't respond. He shook her, then put his arms around her waist and pulled her close.

"Mom, Momma, it's me, Trey. I'm here. I need you to talk to me now."

He felt her shudder, then take a slow, deep breath. Relief washed over him when her arms snaked around his neck. She was back.

"Mom?"

She pointed toward the barn.

"He's in there," she said. "I saw him. Why would he do that? Oh, my God, why would he do that?"

He could hear Earl's siren.

"I don't know, but I need you to wait here. Since you're the one who found the body, you can't leave. The sheriff will want to talk to you."

She blinked. "I need to go home. Tomorrow is your birthday. I wanted to bake—"

"Hey, Momma, you know I love you, right?"

She nodded.

"So don't worry about a cake, okay?"

She clutched the front of his shirt in panic.

She almost looked like a stranger to him.

"Okay, Mom? You have to stay here, understand?"

"Yes. No cake. Stay here." Then her face crumpled as a fresh set of tears began to roll. "Poor Dick. My heart hurts for him."

Trey sighed. "I know, but here's the deal. No need to hurt for him. He's past concern. You need to be feeling sorry for Dallas. She's the one who's been left to suffer."

And just like that, the mother in Betsy stepped in. "Oh, Lord, Dallas. I didn't even think."

Trey turned around, wondering what had taken Earl so long, and how much of the crime scene his mother might have disturbed.

"Here comes Earl. We're going down to the barn, and I need you to stay here, remember?"

"Yes, of course I remember," she said shortly, and combed her hands through her hair. The hysteria was gone, and she was digging out a tissue to wipe her eyes and blow her nose.

"I need to ask you something," he said.

"Ask."

"Did you drive your car down to the barn?"

"No. I was heading toward the trees, looking for him, when I passed and saw him. I didn't even go all the way in."

"Okay, good," Trey said, and then added, "Oh, don't call anyone. I don't want any locals out here in the middle of this investigation."

"I won't. I understand," she said, and then slid off the hood, stumbled up to the house and sat down on the porch in the shade.

Trey frowned. He should have told her to go wait in the car, but it was too late now.

"Hey, Mom, don't go in the house, just stay on the porch. I don't want anything else disturbed."

"Oh, I'm sorry, I didn't think," she said.

"It's my fault. Just don't go any farther," he said.

She nodded.

Earl killed the siren and lights as he parked beside Trey, and then they started toward the barn.

"What took you so long?" Trey asked.

Earl looked embarrassed. "Gas gauge was sitting on empty. Had to stop and fuel up."

Trey nodded, and then pointed to the area in front of the barn. "Look for fresh tire tracks or anything off," he said.

Earl's surprise showed. "I thought this was a suicide?"

"Until the investigation is over, nothing is certain. And when you hear sirens, run back to the house and stop the crew from the sheriff's department from driving down here, too. They'll want to see the crime scene intact."

"Yes, sir," Earl said, and followed Trey down to the barn.

Two

Trey's gut knotted as he looked up at Dick Phillips's body. Because of Dallas, he knew this man almost as well as he knew his own family. As his mother had said earlier, it hurt to see him this way.

He eyed the rope tied to the ladder leading up to the loft, then studied Dick's clothing. The back of his shirt was very dirty, as was the back of his jeans, while the front of both was noticeably cleaner. It would take an autopsy to make sense of this.

The floor of the breezeway was concrete, so there weren't going to be any footprints. If more than one person had been in here when this happened, it wouldn't show up that way.

He walked all the way through the breezeway to the back of the barn and saw no sign of any footprints there, then walked back to the front, looking for signs of fresh tire tracks, but the ground was hard and graveled. Then he went into the egg room off to the right.

The shelves and tables were all in place; nothing appeared to have been moved. There was no sign of a fight or a disturbance of any kind. The deep sink where Dick cleaned the fresh eggs before sorting was clean, and the new cartons yet to be filled were all in place. There were at least a dozen large empty plastic boxes, about the same size as a child's toy box, stored beneath the shelves, with a stack of lids to fit leaning up against the wall. There was nothing out of the ordinary but the body hanging from the rafter. Nothing made sense. He walked farther back into the cooler where Dick kept the eggs, and turned on the light.

There were shelves lined with cartons of eggs, each marked with the date they'd been gathered.

Earl came walking back from checking the perimeter.

"Find anything?" Trey asked.

"Well, if he killed himself, he fed the chickens before he did it. There's still some fresh scratch out in the coop, and the eggs have been gathered. However, the cows weren't fed. There's no fresh hay or ground feed in the troughs."

Trey frowned. "That's weird. If he cared enough to feed the chickens before he took his own life, then he would have fed the cows, too."

Earl shrugged. "Unless he counted on them grazing. The grass is a little short, but it's still good."

They began hearing sirens.

"Sheriff's on the way," Earl said, and took off toward the house on the run.

* * *

Betsy watched her son walking down to the barn, then mentally rejected the sight of what she'd seen earlier and looked off toward the mountains for solace. She had always felt a measure of peace in being surrounded by the ancient peaks, but today it wasn't working. Her head was throbbing, her eyes red and swollen from crying, and she felt like she'd been kicked in the gut. She shoved her fingers through her hair, absently rubbing the five-inch scar on the side of her head. Her hair hid its presence, but when she was upset it throbbed with every beat of her heart, and today was no exception. The shock of seeing Dick's body had created a feeling of déjà vu, which made no sense. She'd never seen a traumatic death before.

She stood abruptly, unable to sit still any longer, and began to pace the length of the porch and back, anxious for the sheriff to arrive so she could give her statement and move on.

When her phone began to ring, she glanced at the caller ID and then let it go to voice mail. It was her daughter, Trina, and she would never be able to hide anything from her.

She heard a phone begin to ring inside the house and felt like crying all over again. Someone wanted to talk to Dick. Would they weep when they found out, or would they feel nothing more than a passing moment of regret for a good man gone, then forget he'd ever existed?

When she began hearing sirens, she actually

breathed a sigh of relief. All she wanted to do was go home and be grateful for what she had.

The sirens grew louder, and she saw the officer come running toward the house. She glanced down at her blouse, and when she saw how dirty she was, she began brushing at the dust and grass on her clothes, then wondered if her hair was just as bad. After she took it down and shook it out, and then combed it back with her fingers, she once again fastened it at the nape of her neck. She was as ready as she'd ever be.

Sheriff Dewey Osmond arrived on the scene with a knot in his gut. Dick Phillips was a fishing buddy, and he couldn't believe this had happened. When he saw the police officer waving for him to stop, he braked and rolled down the window.

"What?" he asked.

"Chief Jakes figured you would want to park up around the house so as not to mess up any tracks or stuff you might find on-site."

Osmond nodded, wheeled up beside the city patrol car and killed the engine. He saw the woman on the porch when he got out.

"Who's she?" he asked.

"Betsy Jakes, Chief's mother. She came to buy eggs and found the body in the barn."

Dewey broke out in a sweat. He was going to have to go down there, and he was dreading it in the worst way. He decided the best way to begin this investigation was to take the witness's statement.

Unfortunately, as fate would have it, she had next to nothing to say that was going to help them figure this out. He took down her information and said for her to call him if she remembered anything else.

"Am I free to go?" Betsy asked.

"Yes, ma'am, and thank you for your help."

Betsy shuddered. "I would give anything to have never seen that," she said. "Will you tell my son I'm leaving now?"

"Yes, ma'am," he said, and headed for the barn as Betsy got in her car and drove back to town for eggs.

Trey watched the sheriff's team work the crime scene without comment. It wasn't his case and he didn't want to step on toes, but he had a personal request, and as soon as the sheriff stepped outside of the barn to take a call, Trey followed him. He approached after the sheriff disconnected.

"Hey, Dewey, I need a favor," Trey said.

Dewey turned around, eyeing him curiously. Dick had talked about Trey Jakes like he was family. He wondered if Trey felt as gutted as he did.

"Like what?" Dewey asked.

"Notifying the next of kin. I'd like to do that, if you wouldn't mind. Dick's daughter, Dallas, and I go back a long way, and this is going to hit her hard."

Ah, the daughter. So that's where the connection came in.

"I don't mind," Dewey said. "That's the worst part of the job, isn't it?"

Trey nodded. “I know the autopsy and your investigation will all play into the cause of death, but how do you want me to state it to her? Apparent suicide?”

“Yes, that’s how I read it, but make sure she knows the final ruling will depend on the autopsy. The coroner is on the way to claim the body. He should be here shortly.”

“I’ll give her your contact information if she has further questions, okay?”

“Yes, and give her my condolences. Dick and I were good friends. I can’t believe he did this. I don’t want to believe he did this,” he muttered.

“Are your men through inside the house?”

Osmond nodded. “There was no suicide note. The coffeepot was still on, and as usual, the house was spick-and-span.”

“Then it’s okay if I go inside?”

“Yeah, but why?” Osmond asked.

“I need to get a new contact number for Dallas. I haven’t talked to her in several years, not since she moved to Charleston.”

“Okay,” Osmond said, and then wiped sweat off his forehead and headed back into the barn as Trey went to the house.

Trey entered through the back door of the utility room and, out of habit, cleaned his feet on the throw rug at the threshold. The layout was exactly as he remembered, and he headed straight through into the kitchen, then into the living room to the landline by the recliner. He could picture Dick kicked back in that chair and talking on the phone with the television on mute. He'd seen him do it a hundred times. He wondered if Dallas would keep the place. It had been in the Phillips family for over a hundred and fifty years. It would be a shame for that heritage to be lost.

He sat down in the recliner to use Dick's phone book and turned to the back page where special numbers were listed. Dallas's number was the first one.

He started to call her from that phone, then added it to his cell phone instead and left the house. It didn't seem right to call the daughter on her daddy's phone and then tell her he was dead.

He got in his cruiser, reached for the radio and told Avery he would be back in town shortly, then put in a call to his mom to make sure she was okay. He drove away while waiting for her to answer, and when she did she sounded breathless.

"Hello?"

"Hey, Mom, I'm just checking in with you. How are you doing?"

"Honey, I'm fine. There's a big knot in my stomach, and I wish to God I hadn't been the one to find him, but it happened. It's over. I'll be sad for him and life will go on. I'm on my way home now. I went back to town to get eggs."

"Okay, and don't feel bad for freaking out. It rattled me, too, and don't think it didn't. I thought a lot of Dick, and I'm having a really hard time believing this happened."

"Me, too," Betsy said. "It's unlike the man I thought

I knew. Look, I haven't said a word to anyone, and I'm not going to, but has anyone notified Dallas yet?"

"No, and that's on me. Sheriff just gave me the green light, and I stopped in at the house to get her number. I'll talk to you later."

"I'm still making Italian cream cake for your birthday tomorrow," she said.

Trey smiled. "In case I don't tell you often enough, I think you're the best mom ever, and I love you."

He heard her giggle, which made him smile.

"Thank you, honey. I love you, too," she said, and disconnected.

Trey topped a hill and drove up on an old man driving an equally old tractor in the middle of the blacktop. He couldn't pass, so he took this as the opportunity to pull off the road to call Dallas.

Dallas Phillips left for the television station to begin her day in her favorite black slacks, white blouse and a black-and-white jacket. She enjoyed her work, particularly since she'd become one of WOML Charleston's hottest on-the-spot reporters.

She was still in traffic when she got a phone call from the station to meet up with the film crew at the site of a twelve-car pileup on the I-90 outside the city.

Change of plans.

She took the next exit, and then drove under the freeway and headed back out of town.

She met up with the film crew a good quarter of a mile away from the pileup and, despite a stiff wind and thick smoke from the burning cars, began gathering information to go on air. When they signaled to her to get ready, she grabbed the mike, inserted her earpiece and took her stance, waiting for her cue. When it came, she shifted from Dallas the woman to the on-air personality she'd become, and began relaying what had happened with an urgent and somber mien.

"To date, fifteen people have been taken to local hospitals. The northbound lanes of I-90 will be closed indefinitely. Authorities are asking travelers to please take alternate routes. This is Dallas Phillips for WOML Charleston."

"And cut!" her cameraman said. "Great shot with that smoke billowing up behind your head."

Dallas frowned. "More like a shot of hell. Hard to believe it started with twelve cars and at last count there were twenty-five. This is a nightmare. There are people who will never make it home."

"You didn't cause it. You just report," he said.

What a way to start a day, she thought, her shoulders slumping, and then her phone began to ring as she followed the crew back toward where the news van and her car were parked. She glanced down at the caller ID, but it just registered Out of Area.

"Dallas Phillips," she said.

"Dallas, this is Trey."

She closed her eyes, remembering the look on his face when she'd driven away. It was shocking to realize that it hurt just as much now as it had back then.

Then she took a deep breath and turned on her on-camera charm.

"Trey! Wow! I haven't heard from you in ages. How are you? How's Betsy?"

"Honey, are you where you can talk?"

A chill of foreboding swept through her as she remembered he was the chief of police, a person who dealt with death and crimes as she did, but in a different way.

"What's wrong?"

"It's your dad. Get somewhere so we can talk."

"I'm alone now, damn it! What's wrong?"

"I'm so sorry to have to tell you this, but he's dead."

She started crying, weak, helpless sobs of disbelief.

"No! Oh, God, no! What happened? Was there an accident?"

Trey hesitated. This was the part that was going to gut her.

"The sheriff is calling it an apparent suicide, but it will hinge on the autopsy."

Dallas began to scream. "What? No! You're wrong! You're wrong! He would never do that, never! Do you hear me, Trey Jakes? Don't say that! Don't you *ever* say that to me again!"

Trey felt like crying with her.

"I'm sorry, Dallas, as sorry as I can be. At first glance, it was pretty obvious."

"Why? What was obvious? I'm an investigative reporter, remember? What the fuck makes you think it was suicide?"

"Mom found him, Dallas. She stopped off at the farm this morning to buy eggs and found him hanging from a rafter in the barn."

Breath caught in the back of Dallas's throat as shock rolled through her.

"I'm coming home," she said, and disconnected.

Trey ended the call, and then leaned back against the seat and closed his eyes. He couldn't imagine what she was feeling, but she was coming back to Mystic. If only it weren't under such tragic circumstances.

Dallas alternated between numbness and uncontrollable sobs for the two-and-a-half-hour drive from Charleston to Mystic. Once she left the I-79 and turned west, she was surrounded by mountains and enveloped in a green so lush it made her homesick. It wouldn't be long before the cold nights of fall would turn the trees to vivid shades of yellows, oranges and reds. Even though she'd left Mystic for the bright lights of the big city, she'd never completely weaned herself away.

She couldn't believe her father was gone. It was unimaginable. How had this happened? *Why* had this happened? Over halfway there she stopped for gas and a bathroom break, and had to wipe her face and get her act together before she dared get out of the car. Her eyes were swollen, her nose was red from blowing and wiping, and she was sick to her stomach.

She filled up the car and then went into the truck stop to go to the bathroom. She stood out in her city clothes and her shiny red nails, and when she walked, she moved with a stride born of confidence rather than an awareness of her sex.

More than one man looked in appreciation until they saw the tearstained eyes, and then they looked away in embarrassment, as if they'd accidentally walked in on her while she was undressed. It was the naked pain on her face that said she'd been dealt a hard blow.

When she came out of the bathroom she stopped to get a cold drink and a bag of pretzels. She hadn't eaten since her Pop-Tarts this morning and wasn't sure any of this would stay down. Still, she had to try. Being light-headed while driving was not a wise decision, and after the major pileup she'd seen this morning, she didn't want to become another statistic for the evening news.

When she went up to pay, the woman behind the counter kept staring, even as Dallas swiped her card and signed for her purchases. When the lady saw the name, her eyebrows shot up and she broke into a wide, happy grin.

"I knew you looked familiar! You're Dallas Phillips, from WOML Charleston, aren't you? I see you on TV when I go visit my mother. You're really good."

"Thank you," Dallas said.

"Say, can I have your autograph?" the lady asked. "I mean, besides the one you just signed for your credit card."

"Sure," Dallas said. "What's your name?"

"My name is Coralee. I really appreciate this."

Dallas tried to smile but couldn't make it happen as she slid the autographed paper back across the counter.

"Thanks again, and have a nice trip," Coralee said.

Dallas shuddered. "Yeah, thanks," she said, and then she was gone.

She took a big drink of the cold Dr Pepper, then opened the bag of pretzels and set it in the console so they wouldn't spill as she took off down the road. She glanced at the clock on the dash and guessed she would be home around five. And the minute the thought went through her head, she cried again.

Home wasn't there anymore, just the house that had sheltered her. She hated the thought of going into that place tonight worse than anything she had ever had to do. Daddy's presence would be everywhere, but Daddy was gone.

The coroner left the crime scene with Dick Phillips's body just after 1:00 p.m., and by late afternoon nearly everyone in Mystic knew Dick Phillips had hanged himself. The shock wave sparked all kinds of suppositions, none of which made any sense to the people who'd known him, but not a one considered it could be murder.

Trey had nothing to argue the point except his own personal belief that Dick had never struck him as the kind of man who would just quit. The only unexplainable thing he'd seen at the whole crime scene was that Dick's clothes had dirt all over the back but none on the front. He didn't know what to make of that. Mostly, though, he just didn't want to consider that a friend he'd known all his life had become that despondent and no one had seen it coming.

Along about three, his sister, Trina, came running into the police station, bypassing the dispatcher as she burst into his office with her red hair flying and her eyes wide with shock.

"Trey! Is it true? Did Mom find Dick Phillips's body?"

"Come in and shut the door," he said.

Trina was shaking as she dropped into a chair on the other side of his desk.

"You want something to drink?" he asked.

She rolled her eyes. "Not unless there's liquor in it. Is it true? Did Mom find him?"

He nodded.

"Oh, my God," she moaned, and then started to cry. "They were in the same graduating class, remember? Mom and Dick and Paul Jackson were in that wreck together the night they graduated."

Trey frowned. "I'd almost forgotten about that. One girl died, right?"

Trina nodded. "A girl named Connie Bartlett. Mom had her picture circled in the yearbook with a heart beside it."

"How do you remember all that?" Trey asked.

"I was the only girl in the family, that's how. I played with Mom's makeup and went through all of her stuff while you and Sam were out trailing after

Daddy. Is Mom okay? I tried to call her earlier this morning but she didn't answer."

"I told her not to tell anyone anything, so she probably just didn't answer any of her calls. We couldn't have locals crawling all over the place out of curiosity, and Dallas had the right to be notified first."

Trina gasped. "Dallas. Oh, my God! I'd completely forgotten about her. This is going to break her heart. I guess she's on her way home?"

Trey frowned. He already had the same fears but wasn't going to let on.

"Yes."

She shuddered. "I can't imagine staying in that house by myself after what happened."

"It's still her home, Trina, and don't go making it into something bad."

"But her dad killed himself there."

"Technically, he died in the barn, but I happen to know that both her paternal grandparents died in that house in their time. In the old days, generations of people lived on in the family home long after the elders were gone. Death doesn't taint a place. People do."

Trina slumped. "Yeah, okay, I get it. Sorry. I'm just overwhelmed by Mom's involvement, however minimal." She took a tissue, wiped her eyes and blew her nose, and then wadded it up in her hands with the bad news as she shifted to a conversation she could handle. "So, I'm on the way home. You're still coming to supper tomorrow evening, right? It's our family tradition, coming home on your birthday to all of your favorite things to eat."

"Yes, I know and I'm coming," Trey said. "And whatever cake isn't eaten tomorrow night is going home with me."

"Hey! Italian cream cake is *my* favorite, too."

"So tell Mom to make one on your birthday, too. Stop whining."

Trina grinned. "Yeah, whatever. Give Dallas my love and condolences when you see her."

"What makes you think I'll see her?" he asked.

Trina rolled her eyes. "Puh…leese. Don't even go there with me, okay?"

Trey changed the subject.

"Are you still dating that Lee guy?"

"Lee Daniels is his name and you know it, and yes, I'm still seeing him, so leave him alone."

She blew him a kiss and flounced out.

Trey shook his head and then glanced at his watch. He wanted to call Dallas and check on her whereabouts, but she would probably view that as stepping over a line. The relationship they'd once had was over, and she was already angry at him for what he'd told her. He'd heard it in her voice and understood. Until the coroner said the words, he wasn't fully buying Dick's suicide, either.

Three

Dallas always knew the trip home was almost over when she could see the burned-out shell of Herman Wagner's cabin sitting on the promontory of the cliff outside Mystic. After that, it was a matter of navigating the big S curve and then seeing a small green sign: Mystic, WV—Population 6,788.

Usually it made her heart skip a beat, knowing she was almost home. Today she got physically sick to her stomach. There was a moment when she thought she was going to have to pull over, but a couple of deep breaths helped the nausea pass. This was an ugly, horrifying trip for many reasons, not the least of which were funeral arrangements. But she knew enough about unattended deaths to realize they might not release her father's body as quickly as she would hope, and there was no way to know when to plan the service until they were through.

It was just after 5:00 p.m., and she began thinking

of all the chores that would need to be done out on the farm: checking on the cows, putting up the chickens. But she wasn't going any farther through town until she found out where they were with the case. She didn't believe for a minute that her father had killed himself, and it frightened her to think someone would want him dead. Whether she liked it or not, she needed to talk to Trey, so when she got to the first stoplight she took a right and drove straight to the police station.

Trey was on the phone when he heard her voice up at the front desk.

"Listen, I need to call you back," he said, and hurried out of the office, only to meet her coming down the hall. "Hey, did you have any trouble on the drive down?"

"Can I talk to you?" she asked.

"Sure," he said, and led her back into his office and then shut the door. "Can I get you anything? Something cold to drink? I have Dr Pepper."

It was the sympathy on his face, and the fact that he remembered what she liked to drink, that did her in. She had so many questions, but all she could think to do was cry.

"I'm sorry. I'm so, so sorry," he said, and took her in his arms.

Everything she'd been holding back buckled beneath the weight of her grief. She wrapped her arms around his waist and buried her face against his chest.

"Oh my God, oh my God, I cannot believe this is happening," she said, the tears coming faster.

There was nothing to say, nothing to do that would make this better. All Trey *could* do was be there for her in any way she needed, and right now she just needed to know she wasn't in this alone.

Dallas cried until her heart was racing and her head felt like it was going to explode. When Trey reached around behind her and grabbed a handful of tissues from his desk, she took them.

"Thank you," she mumbled, and began wiping away mascara and blowing her nose.

"What can I do? How can I help?" Trey asked.

She looked up. "What can you tell me?"

"Come sit," he said, and led her to a sofa against the wall. As soon as she settled, he took a notepad from his desk and began writing, then tore off the sheet and handed it to her. "Sheriff Osmond is handling the case. This is his contact info."

"Thanks," she said, and dropped it in her pocket. "I don't suppose you know when they're doing the autopsy?"

"No, I'm sorry. That's all being handled at the county level."

"I guessed as much, and just so you know, I still do not believe he committed suicide."

"I find it hard to believe myself. When was the last time you talked to him?" Trey asked.

"Three days ago. We talk at least two times a week, sometimes more. We stayed close, Trey. He never sounded upset. He never seemed down or depressed. I know my father, damn it!"

He reached for her hand, but she yanked it back.

"I want to see his body."

Suddenly Trey was all business.

"No. No, you don't. You do not want that to be your last memory of him. Do you hear me?"

She shuddered, vulnerable all over again.

"Was it that bad?"

"Yes."

Her shoulders slumped. "Oh, my God, this feels like a horrible nightmare. I…I should be going. I need to get the chores done before it gets dark. Sundown comes early in the mountains this time of year. Not that I need to tell you that."

"I can do them for you," he offered.

"No, but thank you. I do them all the time when I'm home. I know where everything is."

He didn't push the issue. And then it hit him.

"Are you going to be all right at the house by yourself?"

Her eyes narrowed sharply.

"Why would you ask that? Do you think I'm in danger? Do you think whoever killed Dad wants to harm me, too?"

"I didn't ask because I think there's a killer on the loose. I asked because you suffered a horrific shock today and you're going to be on your own there."

"I'm not afraid of ghosts, if that's what you're getting at."

"Damn it, Dallas. I'm not trying to pick a fight with you. I'm offering help in any way you need, whether it's doing chores or sleeping on your couch so you'll feel easy in the night."

"I know I'm being defensive, but I feel like I'm in this corner all by myself. Everyone thinks Dad committed suicide but me. Did he have a run-in with someone recently? Did anything happen out at the farm, like a theft? Was he being threatened?"

"I haven't heard about anything like that, and he didn't report trouble of any kind."

"I'll get answers," she said, and then slipped the strap of her purse across her shoulder. "If you hear anything, I would appreciate a call."

Trey resented the brush-off.

"I'll be calling whether there's anything new or not. You're not going through this by yourself. I've known you my whole life, and regardless of how we parted company, that history gives me the right to say this. Understand?"

Her vision blurred all over again, but she refused to cry.

"I hear you. I'm going home."

He frowned. "I'll call you before I go to bed tonight, so if you don't answer the damn phone, you can expect me on your doorstep to find out why."

She left the office without looking back.

He shut the door behind her without watching her leave.

Even in the midst of sadness, the spark between them was still there, and it sucked.

Dallas drove home with a knot in her belly, and she wasn't entirely sure it was completely to do with her father's death. Seeing Trey again… Damn that man. She'd been in love with him for so long that when they'd finally broken up, it had taken her over a year to realize it was final. He wanted nothing to do with city life, and she couldn't put farm life behind her fast enough. Every time she'd come home to visit, she'd made a point of avoiding him. Most times she'd been successful. But this time it wasn't going to work that way.

By the time she turned off the blacktop and headed toward the house, she was shaking. This was going to be a nightmare. All she had to do was remember that nightmares eventually come to an end.

Rocks crunched beneath the tires as she drove through the tunnel of trees, and when she drove out, she was home. As luck would have it, the first thing she saw was yellow crime-scene tape flapping in the wind down at the barn.

"God help me," she whispered, as she parked in her usual spot by the front gate.

It was habit that made her look up toward the porch. She half expected to see her father coming out the front door with that big smile on his face. When she got out, the utter silence made the hair stand up on the back of her neck. She could see the chickens, but they weren't making a sound, and the cows were nowhere in sight. It was as if they, too, knew he was gone.

"One thing at a time," she muttered, then took a deep breath, got her suitcase out of the trunk and headed for the house.

She had her key out, ready to go inside, but when she realized the place was unlocked, her heart skipped a beat. She pushed the door inward and then stood on the threshold, looking and listening for something out of place.

The hall clock was still ticking, and the living room looked like her dad had just stepped away and would be back any second.

The way she figured it, she had two choices. She could stomp her way in and maybe be okay, or she could call Trey and ask him if the door was unlocked when they left. It was too soon to subject herself to his presence again, so she opted for stomping.

She slammed the door behind her as she entered and began tromping loudly through the house, checking every room, under every bed and in every closet, then made a quick check of the basement before she was satisfied she was alone.

She locked the front and back doors, and then paused in the central hallway, trying to think if there was something she'd missed, but the house was so quiet it was unnerving.

"Daddy, if you can hear me, I need an answer. You know me. I'm not leaving this place until I get it."

When the hall clock began to strike the hour, she

jumped. It was already six o'clock, past time to do chores. She hurried into her bedroom and dug out work clothes from the stash she kept there, and then changed. On the way through the kitchen she noticed the cold coffee still in the pot, poured it out and started a fresh pot brewing before she went through the utility room and out the back door.

The wind was moving the cane-back rockers. If she was of a mind to go there, she could imagine her parents sitting on the porch, watching the storm she could see was approaching. But she'd already told Trey she didn't believe in ghosts, and the chairs were as empty as she felt. However, the chickens had heard the squeaky hinges on the back door, and were fussing and clucking and looking toward the house.

"I see you, and I'm coming," she said, and jumped off the back porch.

The quickest way to get the chickens to go in was to feed and water them in the coop. While they were eating, she gathered the eggs and shut the hens up safely for the night. She sat the egg basket down to fasten the gate and then paused outside the chicken house, staring toward the barn. The yellow tape was still flapping in the breeze, reminding her of the horror that had happened beyond it. There was no getting out of taking that walk. She picked up the eggs and started down the path as she had countless times before.

The wind was rising, making the tape pop.

Flap, flap, flap.

She looked up at the gathering clouds. It was going to rain. She hastened her steps, anxious to finish this and get back inside before the storm hit, but the tape was like a guard dog, warning her, blocking her path.

A big gray heron suddenly lifted off from the pond out behind the barn. It knew the storm was coming, too.

Flap, flap, flap.

Now the tape was telling her, *Hurry, hurry, hurry.*

She couldn't run with a basket full of eggs.

Flap, flap, flap.

This is the place. Come see, come see.

"Shut up," Dallas said aloud, wondering what her dad had been thinking this morning when he'd walked this way. What had he been planning to do? Who was lurking in the shadows when he'd walked into the barn?

Flap, flap, flap.

"I said I'm not afraid of ghosts."

Flap, flap, flap.

"I'm not afraid of you!" she screamed, but her vision was blurring, and the smell of imminent rain was in the air.

She stared at the tape for a few seconds more, then set the basket down and started running. She broke through the tape like the winner at the finish line, then turned on one heel and began gathering it up hand over fist, crying and cursing at the top of her voice until it was in her arms and spilling down around her ankles.

She carried it to the burn barrel where they burned the household trash, and threw it inside. Considering her blurred vision and the state of her emotions, it was like looking into a pit of yellow snakes. She wanted to burn it—to watch it melt and take the pain of her loss with it, but she didn't have anything to start the fire, and it was too windy to be burning anything anyway. She dropped her head and went back for the eggs.

Stepping into the barn moments later gave her a momentary feeling of shelter, and then she hurried into the egg room, where she set the eggs in the cooler. She would clean and sort them tomorrow, when there was more time.

The wind was rattling something on the outside of the barn as she walked back out into the breezeway. She paused, giving all the familiar objects a careful inspection. Nothing seemed to be missing—except her dad.

Don't look up. Don't look up.

She heard the voices, but she had to face the fear to get past it, so she tilted her head back, distraught but defiant.

Immediately her eye was drawn to the raw place on the fourth rafter down, where the rope had cleaned the grime of a hundred plus years from the wood, and in that moment the weight of grief was too much. Trey had told her she didn't need to see the body, but in her mind's eye she already had.

She threw back her head and screamed until she

ran out of breath, and then dropped to her knees and wept until she was choking.

The rain hit hard, splattering the first drops onto the hard dry ground, but the dust soon turned to mud. It wasn't until the wind began to blow rain in where she was kneeling that she came to herself enough to get up. If nothing else, she had to get back to the house to take Trey's call or he would come looking for her. She couldn't be vulnerable around him. It was too dangerous for her sanity.

The moment she walked out of the breezeway, she doubled up her fists and shook them at the sky, screaming her every word.

"I'm not afraid of ghosts! Do you hear me, goddamn it? I am not afraid of ghosts!"

With her head up and her shoulders back, she started walking toward the house with a long, steady stride while the rain poured down around her.

Betsy Jakes had just finished Trey's cake when the storm finally hit. She dropped the spatula back into the icing bowl and began walking through the house, closing windows as she went.

"Trina! Shut the windows upstairs!" she yelled.

"I already did," Trina said, as she came hurrying down the stairs, then followed her mother into the kitchen. "Gosh, that cake looks good. Is there any icing left?"

Betsy started to answer, and then grinned when

she saw Trina already licking the spatula and scraping bits from the sides of the bowl.

Betsy covered the cake and then carried it to the extra refrigerator in the attached garage.

Lightning flashed, making the house lights flicker just as she came back inside. Trina had abandoned the spatula for her finger and was licking off icing as Betsy walked in. She smiled and shook her head. Some things never changed.

"Hey, honey, what do you want for supper…besides icing?" Betsy asked.

Trina shrugged. "Scrambled eggs and toast?"

Suddenly her smile felt weird, as if she had just laughed at a funeral, but she managed to hide the jolt. Eggs. For a few minutes she'd almost forgotten. "And maybe some sausage links?" she added.

"Sure, sounds good," Trina said, and then carried the icing bowl to the sink, rinsed it and put it in the dishwasher. "I'll clean up the cake mess if you do supper, okay?"

"Deal," Betsy said, and both women were soon involved in preparations for their evening meal.

Trey picked up an order of sliced brisket and French fries from Jonny's Ribs to take back to his place. The smell of the food was so good he grabbed a couple of fries from the sack and ate them as he drove.

The rain hit just as he entered his apartment. If he was really lucky, he wouldn't be called out tonight, but just in case, he'd learned not to waste time when it came to hot food. He washed up, then transferred the food to a plate and began to eat. A cold beer would have been good, but he was on call, so no dice.

He thought about Dallas, wondering how she was doing. One thing about her hadn't changed. She was still as headstrong as ever. It probably served her well as an investigative reporter. Him, not so much.

He turned on the television as he ate, waiting for the weather report to see if this storm front was going to move through or hang around. Still fidgeting, he glanced at the clock. It was nearly seven. He would give Dallas two more hours and then he was calling.

Freshly showered and in clean, dry clothes, Dallas went to the kitchen for the coffee she'd made. The thought of food made her sick, but she felt lightheaded, almost weak. She hadn't had anything but junk or fast food since noon the day before and knew she couldn't do what she needed to do if she were sick. Finally she settled for an omelet, an old standby for supper, and had it ready in minutes. She added buttered toast to the plate and carried it and her coffee into the living room to eat.

It was almost dark, so she went around the room drawing shades and pulling curtains until she felt safe, then sat down, turned on the television and ate.

Even though it was virtually tasteless, she felt better when the food was in her stomach. Settling in to finish her coffee, she pulled her feet up beneath her, and as she did, her gaze went straight to the recliner where her dad would have been sitting. A wave of loss washed through her so fast it left her shaking. She blinked away tears and turned up the volume. Trey would be calling, and she didn't want him to hear the tears in her voice.

Trina's boyfriend, Lee, had come by to take her to a movie, leaving Betsy with the house to herself. The thought of a long soak in the tub seemed like a good idea, and she headed for her room, ready to put this day to bed.

The tub was nearly full as she poured bath salts into the water and turned off the faucet. She stepped out of her robe and into the tub, easing down into the steamy heat. Water lapped against her breasts and up the back of her neck as she tucked the bath pillow beneath her neck and closed her eyes.

The buoyancy and heat were so soothing that she soon lost track of time. The sound of rainfall on the roof made her feel sleepy. The heat always soothed the ache in her lower back, a remnant from the wreck that had nearly killed her in her teens. The moment she thought of the wreck, she saw Dick Phillips hanging from the rafter. Before she could look away, his face morphed into someone else, someone covered in blood. She sat up with a gasp, splashing water onto the bathroom floor.

"What the hell?" she muttered, chalking it up to the horrendous day.

She wondered if Dallas was back in town yet. She

should call, but since she'd also discovered the body, it made things awkward. She reached down and pulled the plug to let the tub drain.

As school superintendent, one of Will Porter's duties, and there were many, was to attend the monthly school board meetings, and tonight was no exception.

Tonight the school board members, the school principals, the high school secretary and a few interested parents were present as they went through the agenda.

Porter went through the motions, saying all the right things in the right places, but tonight his mind was not on the business at hand. He did what he had to do for his job and his goals in life, but he had bigger problems at home that he didn't know how to handle.

His wife, Rita, was already three-sheets-to-the-wind drunk off her ass when he got home after the meeting, which was really nothing new. But this time she'd used the excuse of grieving for their old classmate Dick Phillips as the reason for her condition, although she no longer needed an excuse to imbibe. All pretense of hiding her addiction was in the past.

Years and added weight had changed his appearance greatly. He looked more like a used-up prizefighter than a school superintendent, but what he wanted didn't require good looks. He had aspirations of greater grandeur than being superintendent of minuscule Mystic and could have cared less if Dick Phillips was dead. Rita had spent a good portion of their married life referring to Dick as the one who got away.

It made no sense to Will. Dick had never left the farm, while he had gone on to graduate school and had a successful professional career. Then one night, in a drunken stupor, she'd taunted him, claiming Dick's cock was bigger and he was better at sex.

That night he'd done an unforgivable thing. That night he'd physically raped his wife. The fortunate part was that she'd been too drunk to remember it. The downside was remembering how much he'd liked it. He'd never thought of himself as a violent man, but he'd learned the hard way that there were times when no other avenue would suffice.

And right now Will Porter's dream of running for State Superintendent of Education was imminent, and the only thing holding him back was the drunk in his bed. Now Rita could whine all she wanted about how she'd let Dick Phillips get away, because he was dead, and Will wasn't a damn bit sorry.

Dallas was sitting in the dark, the television on mute, as she listened to the storm rage on. It fit how she felt, all torn and shattered inside. The thunderstorm hit its zenith just before nine o'clock, rattling windows and pelting the roof with raindrops that sounded more like bullets. Dallas had grown up in this house. She knew every creak and pop the structure could make, but when it thundered, followed by a crack of lightning so close that it lit up the room where she was sitting, she screamed and jumped off the sofa.

"Did that hit the house? I think it hit the house," she gasped, and then realized there was no one to answer.

She bolted through the hall into the kitchen, but the power was still on and she didn't smell smoke. She opened the back door and ran out into the rain to see if the roof was on fire.

From what she could tell, it looked fine. She took shelter again on the back porch, waiting for the next lightning strike to light up the area so she could see if the other structures were okay.

When it came, she saw enough to feel confident her question had been answered. The chicken house was intact. The barn was still there. The security light had been temporarily knocked out, but it was slowly coming back on and from what she could see, she didn't think lightning had struck the pole.

Wind was blowing rain up on her bare feet and legs as she turned around to go inside. Then she heard her phone and locked the door and ran, dripping water as she went.

"Hello?"

"It's me. Is everything okay? You sound like you've been running."

Trey.

"Lightning struck something close by. I was out on the back porch looking the place over when the phone began to ring. I'm fine. Thank you for calling."

"I have a question," he said.

She frowned. "Okay, ask."

"Did your dad feed the cattle every day?"

"There are four cows with calves still nursing. He fed the cows ground feed so they wouldn't lose weight until the calves were weaned. Why?"

"He fed the chickens this morning, but he didn't feed the cows."

Dallas's mind was spinning, trying to see where Trey was going with this, and then it hit her.

"You're wondering why, if he was going to kill himself, would he take time to feed the chickens but not the cows?"

"It crossed my mind."

Her voice began to shake. "You don't think he hanged himself, do you?"

"What I think and what the evidence will show could be two different things."

She started to cry, but softly now, no longer alone in her quest for the truth. "Thank you, Trey."

"For what? I didn't do anything."

"For not taking the easy way out of this."

"You forget, honey. It's not my case. Sheriff Osmond is running the show. He's the man you have to convince to dig deeper. In the meantime, you could go through the house, specifically your father's business records, and see if there's anything there that would help explain what happened."

"I will. I'll do it tomorrow," she said.

Trey hated to hang up, but there was nothing else he could say.

"If you have a question, or if you need help in any

way, call me. Will you do that? Will you let me help you that much?"

She sighed. "Yes. I'll do that. And, Trey, really… thanks for calling."

"Yeah, sure. Try and get some rest."

He disconnected before she could say goodbye, and she told herself it didn't matter, then had to make herself move. All of a sudden the day had caught up with her. She stumbled into the living room, turned off the television and then headed for her room.

She had the bed turned back and was ready to get in when she stopped. She thought about how far it was from here to her nearest neighbor, then about the person who'd killed her dad, and went across the hall to his bedroom to get his shotgun. She checked to see if it was loaded, then put it just under the edge of her bed.

She might not sleep a wink, but it wouldn't be because she was scared. And she didn't believe in ghosts.

Four

Dallas's sleep was fitful, and she was awake before daybreak, sad but determined to find out the truth. Still in her pajamas, she thought even going into the kitchen to make coffee seemed too much to face, but two cups of coffee and a piece of toast later, she got dressed and began to tackle the morning chores.

She walked out on the back porch to a world that appeared to be weeping. Water was dripping from the eaves of the house, from the leaves of the trees, from the crepe myrtle bushes on either side of the back steps. Instead of quiet, she heard the soft patter of the droplets with its own brand of rhythm as she walked away from the house.

The chickens were fussing, ready to be let out of the coop. The cows were bawling inside the corral, waiting to be fed. The normalcy of the morning was somehow comforting, a reminder that some things never changed.

She entered the lean-to against the chicken house, filled a big bucket with feed and a smaller one with what her dad always called “scratch,” part of what chickens ate to help their craw break down and digest their food, and carried them into the pen. She scattered a little bit out on the ground before she opened the coop, and when all the hens raced out to get the feed, she carried the rest of it inside and refilled the troughs. If it rained again, at least they could come in to eat and stay dry. Then she refilled their water, gathered the eggs and headed for the barn.

Remembering the lightning strike, she began looking for signs of what had been hit, hoping none of the cattle had been close. It wouldn’t be the first time they’d lost a cow to lightning, but there were no signs of that. She was almost at the barn when she noticed the burn barrel lying on its side. As she drew closer, she soon realized the entire bottom of it was gone.

That had to be what was hit. She remembered the crime-scene tape and began to look around for where it could have blown. It wasn’t until she started to set the barrel back up that she saw the bottom of it was still there, along with a small wad of what looked like blackened and melted plastic. If it hadn’t been for a tiny tinge of yellow she would never have recognized it as the tape.

“Yes, Lord, I did want that yellow tape burned, and thank you for doing it, but you didn’t have to scare the crap out of me in the process.”

She went back to get the egg basket, knowing she

had last night's and this morning's eggs to clean and put in cartons. The cows were still bawling, so she left the eggs in the cooler and fed them before she went back.

By the time she made it back to the house it was late enough to call the county sheriff's office. She got a cup of coffee, then picked up a pen and notepad and sat down at the kitchen table. As she did, she noticed she'd missed a call from Trey. She would call him back after this, she thought, as she punched in the numbers.

"County sheriff's office."

"This is Dallas Phillips. I need to speak to Sheriff Osmond regarding the death of my father, Dick Phillips."

"One moment, please."

Already the knot in Dallas's stomach was getting tighter. She interviewed law enforcement regarding death and crime on a daily basis, but this was in regard to her own father's death, and she felt as if she were insulting her father's name.

"Hello. Miss Phillips? This is Sheriff Osmond. Your father and I were good fishing buddies. I'm really going to miss him."

"Oh! You're Dewey, aren't you? I didn't get the connection. Please call me Dallas, and thank you for taking my call."

"Of course, and I really am sorry for your loss. How can I help you?"

"As you can imagine, I want to know where you

are on the case. Trey Jakes told me all he knew, and now I want to know what you can tell me."

"Then you probably know as much as I do at the moment. We gathered evidence yesterday as we worked the scene. We found nothing obvious that would lead us to believe his death was anything but a suicide, so I'm waiting on the coroner's findings from the autopsy."

"I want you to know that I will never believe he killed himself. I spoke to him two to three times a week. I came home at least once, sometimes twice, a month to visit. I never saw a hint of trouble or felt as if he had a worry in the world. I knew my father well. I would have known if something was bothering him."

She heard Osmond sigh and resented it, but said nothing.

"I understand and appreciate your feelings, Dallas, and I *will* make note of this conversation in the file, okay? I'm not the kind of man who takes the easy way out to close a case. Okay?"

Now she sighed, and when she did she recognized the action for what it was and understood where he was coming from. Neither one of them had any knowledge that would make this go away. Nothing could do that.

"Yes, I hear you," she said. "Can you tell me when you expect the autopsy to be done?"

"The coroner told me he would have the initial findings within a week, but if there was a need for more extensive tests, the final results would take longer.

However, I promise to let you know when the body will be released."

"Thank you," Dallas said, and gave him the number to her cell phone, then disconnected.

She hadn't learned anything new, but she'd made the first contact to let them know she was here, to make sure they understood someone was paying attention on her father's behalf.

She took a sip of coffee and then finally called Trey.

He answered on the first ring.

"Hello. Are you okay?"

"Good morning to you, too," she said. "I'm as good as I can be, considering."

"I guessed you were outside when I called."

"Yes. I just got off the phone with Sheriff Osmond. The coroner will do the initial autopsy within a week, so I've made the decision to just hold a memorial service for Dad and bury him privately when everything's done."

Trey thought about the condition the body had been in when he'd seen it and knew that she was making a wise decision.

"I think that's a good idea," he said.

"Can you do me a favor as you go about your day?"

"Absolutely. What do you need?"

"Tell people there are still eggs for sale. I can't stop the hens from laying, and I don't want the eggs to go to waste."

"Oh. Right. Life still goes on, doesn't it, honey?"

She laughed, but there was not an ounce of humor in it.

"It damn sure does, whether we like it or not."

"What are you going to do today?"

She glanced up at the calendar on the wall, and as she did, suddenly remembered the significance of the date.

"I'm going to follow your suggestion and go through Dad's things, see if I can find anything that would help explain what happened."

"Let me know if you do," he said.

"I will, and, Trey…"

"Yeah?"

"Happy birthday."

He hurt for the sadness in her voice.

"Thanks. I'm the guest of honor at Mom's for supper tonight. She's going all out on my favorite foods."

"She's the best when it comes to mothering, isn't she?"

"Yes. The whole family will be there…except Sam. I would ask you to join us, but…"

"Oh, no, although thank you for thinking of me. I wouldn't be good company, you know?"

"I figured as much, but would you mind if I came by later tonight and brought you a piece of my birthday cake?"

"Is it going to be Italian cream cake?"

"That's what she said."

"I might let you in the door," she said, and closed her eyes against sudden tears, remembering other birthdays and making out while feeding each other bites of cake.

"That's great. Then I'll see you later tonight, and if I get called back to the office, I'll let you know so you won't stay up waiting on me to show."

"Okay, and have a happy birthday, Trey."

"Thank you, and remember, call if you need me."

And then he was gone. She wished she'd had something else to talk about just to hear his voice a little longer.

She sat at the table while her coffee got cold, thinking about what to do next. She had been in college when her mother died, and by the time she got home, her dad had already made all the decisions and arrangements. It was hard, this business of dying, and when the question of how it happened was unanswered, it was even harder. It was time to call the preacher.

It was almost 11:00 a.m. when Betsy took the chicken potpie out of the oven and set it aside to cool as she finished mixing a marinated salad. When Trey called asking her to spread the word that the Phillips family still had eggs to sell, she'd made a couple of calls to start the ball rolling and took it as the opening she needed to pay Dallas a visit, but she wasn't going empty-handed.

The fact that Dallas was even in her father's room was sad all on its own. It smelled like his aftershave, and the toes of his house shoes were poking out from beneath the side of the bed. Her mother's picture was still hanging on the wall opposite the foot of the bed, the last thing Dick saw at night before he closed his eyes and the first thing he saw when he opened them the next morning.

Salt on an open wound, she thought, and then went to work. Hours later she was still there, sitting cross-legged in the middle of the room, surrounded by the past six months of bills and correspondence that he'd kept in a shoe box in the closet. There were no unpaid bills and no letters of any kind that could be construed as troublesome or threatening. The only thing left to go through was her grandfather's desk, but it was in the living room.

She began putting everything away and was almost done when she thought she heard a car coming up the driveway. She got up quickly, wiping her hands on her jeans as she went down the hall and into the living room. She didn't recognize the car, but she knew the woman getting out. When she saw that she was carrying food, she felt a moment of panic. There had been a death in the family, precipitating an influx of visitors and the bringing of food. She combed her fingers through her hair and hoped she didn't look like she'd been crying.

Betsy's hands were full as she came up the steps, but she didn't have to knock. Dallas was standing in the doorway.

Betsy hesitated. "I hope you don't mind that I came without calling."

Dallas shook her head. "Don't be silly. I'm glad to see you. Come in."

Betsy stepped across the threshold. "Okay if I put this stuff in the kitchen for you?"

"Of course," Dallas said. "Follow me."

"This is chicken potpie, and it's still hot," Betsy said, as she walked over to the stove and put the covered pie plate onto an unlit burner. "This is marinated salad. You'll need to refrigerate it."

Dallas peeked in at the potpie as Betsy set the salad on the counter.

"It looks wonderful. Thank you for thinking of me," Dallas said, and when she looked up, Betsy was crying.

"I'm so sorry," Betsy said, as she put her arms around Dallas and gave her a hug. "I would give anything for this not to have happened."

It was the sympathy that got to her. Dallas dissolved into a fresh set of tears.

"Oh Lord, me, too. I can't believe he's gone," Dallas said. "I'm sorry you were the one who found him."

Betsy shuddered, despite her intent not to go there with Dallas.

"Come sit down with me," Betsy said, as she took a seat at the kitchen table.

Dallas pulled out a chair and joined her.

"Is there anything I can do?" Betsy asked.

"Not unless you know something about Dad that I

don't. I've been going through his things all morning looking for answers, trying to find something that will explain this madness, but so far, nothing."

"How are you going to handle the funeral services? Will you wait for—"

"No waiting," Dallas said. "I've scheduled a memorial service for the day after tomorrow at 10:00 a.m. When they finally release his body, he'll be buried beside Mom without further ceremony."

Betsy nodded. "I think that's a good decision. So, if you're having a morning service, you'll have the family meal here at the house afterward, right?"

"I guess," Dallas said, wiping tears and blowing her nose. "I can't get from one decision to the next without coming undone."

Betsy reached across the table and took her hand. "Will you let me help? You can just be present. Let me deal with the food and the people. Consider me your hostess for the day, okay?"

Dallas squeezed Betsy's hand. "I accept, and gladly. Dad has an elderly aunt in Michigan who won't be attending, but I have to call and let her know. I have a few cousins scattered about the country, but have no idea how many, if any, will come. Mom has two sisters still living. I'll call them and let them notify the rest of the family, but I really don't expect many to show. They're all so far away."

"You could have the service at a later date, so people can plan ahead," Betsy suggested.

Dallas looked away.

"What?" Betsy asked. "What aren't you saying?"

"That I dread seeing them come in the door believing Dad killed himself, because I know the family, and that's exactly what they'll think—especially Mom's side. They always thought she could have done better for herself than marrying a hillbilly farmer."

Betsy frowned. "I'm sorry, honey."

Dallas shrugged. "Doesn't matter. I can't bring him back to life, and I can't change the public assumption that Dad committed suicide until I find out why he was killed and who did it."

Betsy was at a loss as to how to respond to that and went immediately to something else. "In the meantime, we have a memorial service to plan, and you don't want to have some piddly event that says you're not going all out because you believe he killed himself. You're having the 'he was the best man ever' ceremony. Now, have you spoken to the preacher?"

"Yes. I have to write Dad's eulogy, but everything else has been settled. What would you think if, instead of a sermon, the preacher invites anyone who'd like to, to come up to the pulpit and speak about knowing him, or tell a funny story about him, if they want?"

"I think that's a wonderful idea. I wish I could be there, but I think I'd better stay here at the house during the service to receive the food that will be coming. Now, that's enough for today. It's time I get home. I know you probably don't have much appetite, but promise me you'll eat a little. You have to keep up your strength."

"I promise," Dallas said, and gave Betsy a big hug as she stood up to leave.

She walked with her out of the house, and just as Betsy was about to leave, the delivery van from the local flower shop drove up.

Dallas swallowed past the lump in her throat. First the food. Now the flowers.

She waved at Betsy as she drove away, then opened the door for the lady who came carrying bouquets.

"Thank you, dear. Where do you want me to put these?"

"You can put one on that end table and the other on the coffee table," Dallas said.

"Oh, this isn't all. I havc a bunch morc. How about I bring them in and you put them where you want them?"

"All right," Dallas said, and began looking at the cards as the woman hurried out.

One was from their church, the second from Paul Jackson, one of her dad's oldest friends. When the woman finally left, she had delivered a total of six.

Dallas went to get the notepad and started writing down names of the people who'd sent flowers, then started another list of people who'd brought food, with Betsy Jakes at the top.

The scent of the chicken potpie actually made her feel hungry, and it was almost noon. Maybe it was time to take a break. Even though she was anxious to resume her search, she had to start calling the family. After that, a little food.

* * *

She'd only managed to make a few calls before the preacher's secretary called to let her know she'd posted a notice of Dick Phillips's memorial service in the local paper.

Betsy was at home making calls to all of Dick's egg customers about available eggs.

Dallas was getting more help than she could have imagined. One neighbor stopped by with a pie and condolences. Two egg customers came without knowing of the death and were properly horrified. The elderly woman cried, which made Dallas cry with her. The young man with two little kids was saddened by the news, and then embarrassed because his kids wouldn't stop asking where Mr. Phillips was because he always let them pet the hens. Everyone wanted details and then was shocked by her terse answers. Dallas was in tears again by the time the last one left.

It was two hours later before she got a chance to resume her search, and the next place she wanted to look was the old desk. As a child, she'd learned where the secret compartments were and had been fascinated by the idea of finding hidden treasures. Now all she wanted were answers.

She sat down and opened the rolltop. Usually there was a faint layer of dust on the surface because he never used it anymore, but to her surprise it was not only clean, but she could smell the faint scent of furniture polish.

"Weird," she muttered.

In her whole life, she had never known her dad to clean that thoroughly. Then she shrugged it off. Once in a while he *did* have someone come out and clean for him. That was probably what had happened here.

She sat for a moment, looking at all the drawers and slots, and then began opening them one by one. The drawers were empty. All the slots where things could have been filed were squeaky-clean. When she looked in the first hidden drawer she found a penny and then leaned back, her hand shaking as she took it out. The date on it was 1943. She distinctly remembered finding this penny beneath an old brick when she was just a kid. Certain it was worth millions because it was so old, she'd run to the house to show her mother, only to be told it wasn't all that old and it was still only worth a penny. Not to be deterred, Dallas had cleaned it up, then hidden it in the secret drawer to let it get older. She dropped it back into the drawer and pushed it shut with a click.

Only one secret drawer left, and it was at the back of the long drawer. She pulled the drawer out and set it aside, then got down on her knees and pushed. When a second door gave way, she thrust her hand inside, and when she felt a folded piece of paper, her heart actually skipped. She pulled it out, then sat down with her back against the desk to read it.

It took her a few moments to realize what she was looking at, and then she read it again in disbelief.

"What the hell? Why would you do this?" she mumbled, and then noticed the date.

It was the same year that she'd started college. Surely this was no longer valid? But what if it was? And that was when she panicked.

She scrambled to her feet and ran for the phone book, found the number she needed and called it with her fingers shaking so hard she kept misdialing. Finally the call went through.

"First State Bank. How may I direct your call?"

"I need to speak to Mr. Standish. Tell him Dallas Phillips is calling."

"One moment, please."

Dallas groaned. God, but she hated hearing music when she'd been put on hold. The longer she waited, the worse it became, until the tension was making her sick to her stomach. Unable to sit still, she began to pace. When Gregory Standish finally answered, his voice was so forceful it made Dallas flinch.

"Hello, this is Standish."

Dallas opened her mouth and then had to pinch her nose to keep from screaming.

"Mr. Standish, this is Dallas Phillips."

"Dallas, my dear, I was so sorry to hear of your father's passing. You have my sympathy, of course. Now, what can I do for you?"

"I just found the paperwork on an old loan my Dad took out at your bank some years back. I knew nothing about this and wonder if you can tell me when it was paid off."

Standish frowned and then cleared his throat. He had been dreading this conversation, although he hadn't expected it to happen for a few weeks, which was when the balance of the loan, in its entirety, would come due.

"Let me check our records. The computers are slow today, so give me a few moments." She heard the clicking of keys as he checked the computer. "Ah, yes, here we are. Your father did indeed take out a loan some years back. He'd been paying on it regularly until two years back, but I'm afraid he's been in arrears ever since. I believe he and I discussed this briefly earlier in the spring, but I hadn't heard from him since."

"How much does he still owe?" she asked.

Standish cleared his throat again.

"A little over fifty thousand dollars. Interest accrued rather rapidly with the missed payments."

The room was beginning to spin. Dallas dropped down on her knees to keep from falling.

"What did you tell him when you…when you talked in the spring?"

Standish cleared his throat one more time.

"I believe he understood that if the money wasn't paid in full, he would lose the collateral, which was his farm."

Dallas gasped. "The farm? The one that's been in our family for over a hundred and fifty years?"

"Yes."

"What date would that take place?"

"Twenty-seven days from today."

"I'm listed on his checking account. Can you please verify the amount in that account?"

More clicking of keys.

"Seven thousand, five hundred and twelve dollars, and thirty cents."

"And his savings account?" she asked.

"He doesn't have one."

"What? I don't understand. Dad always had—"

"Actually, the amount in his checking account is from a transfer from savings made about six months ago. I'm afraid that's all that's left."

"So my Dad was about to lose the farm?"

"Yes, and I'm sorry to be the one to give you this news."

Stunned, Dallas disconnected without even saying goodbye, then stood and stared out the window at the scene before her. She'd seen it a thousand times before and never thought it remarkable in any way. It was the same pasture, with the same mountain looming behind it. She looked at the barn, built before the house in which she was standing, and then thought of all the people who'd lived here, and the years of toil and hardship they had suffered to keep themselves afloat. Generation after generation had lived and died beneath this roof, and now she was going to lose it because she'd wanted to go to college, and her parents hadn't told her no. They hadn't told her they couldn't afford it. They'd never said, "You need to work your way through if you want to go." They'd just sent her on her merry way, and she'd never thought twice about how they'd made it work, because she'd been so wrapped up in losing Trey and, at the same time, realizing she was about to live her dream.

All of a sudden bile was burning the back of her throat and she was racing to the bathroom. She threw up until her sides were aching and her throat was raw, and then she staggered to her bedroom and collapsed from the weight of her guilt.

Five

One hour passed, and then another, as Dallas wept beneath the shock of what she'd found. Even worse, she knew when this was revealed the authorities would immediately use it as the reason for his suicide and look no further. In her heart, though, despite learning of this debt, she could not believe he would have felt the situation was hopeless.

He already knew Dallas made good money, really good money. She had three times the amount of the outstanding loan in her own savings account and a healthy checking account. All he would have had to do was confess what was happening and she would have given it to him in seconds, and the farm would be saved. This debt was not the kind of "all is lost" incident that would precipitate suicide. He wasn't so vain that he couldn't face what had happened, either. There had to be more to it.

She drifted off to sleep, and when she woke up

it was nearing sundown. Time to do chores all over again.

She got up and washed the tears from her face, changed her shoes and headed outside. The moment she felt the chill in the air she made a U-turn and went back for a jacket. Fall was a fickle time of year in West Virginia, and while she'd been sleeping, the weather had turned. The air was nippy, and the sky was laced with long, thin gray clouds.

The chickens bunched together, clucking almost anxiously. Before she would have chalked the noise up to them trying to get to the feed first, but since her dad's death, nothing was the same. They watched her as she moved around inside the coop, some even following her a bit. She paused to look at them, wondering if they were anxious because some predator had spooked them. She quickly checked the perimeter of the coop, as well as the fenced-in area, but it was secure. When she put out the feed and the scratch, they were around her feet, clucking and pecking but still huddling together, their little squawks and clucks all running together until, in her mind, she imagined they were talking.

Do you see what's happening? Do you see? Do you see? Winter will come. What will become of us? What will become of me?

She paused, her hand in a nest and the warm egg beneath her palm, and had a moment of déjà vu, remembering something from her childhood.

* * *

Dallas was squatting down beside the chicken feeder, petting an old hen, and her mother was standing in the spot where she was standing now. The hen seemed droopy, and Dallas was asking her mother if she might be sick. Her mother said the hen wasn't sick, she was just old.

The moment Dallas heard that, she picked up the hen and started running out of the chicken yard.

"Dallas Ann! Where do you think you're going with that hen?" her mother yelled.

Dallas stopped, her eyes welling with tears.

"I'm saving her life."

Her mother frowned.

"What do you mean, you're saving her life? I told you she wasn't sick."

"But Daddy says you always cook the old ones. She knows you're going to eat her. She's not sick. She's sad, Mommy. She doesn't want to die."

A hen flew off the roost between the door and Dallas's line of sight, startling her back to reality. She put the warm egg in the basket and moved on down the row of nests, taking the memory with her. She had been so shocked by her father's death and the immediate need to prove that he'd been murdered that she hadn't thought about what would happen to this place until today, when she'd come face-to-face with losing it. Would Charleston still hold as much glamour for her, knowing she'd given away her heritage and this way of life for something shiny?

Her heart was heavy as she started toward the barn. The cattle herd, which now consisted of less than twenty head, was at the far end of the pasture near the foot of the mountain. Thankful the grass was still good enough to sustain them, she had to think about what would happen to them, too. Did she want this life to disappear? Where would she go when she longed for the mountains again?

She was halfway to the barn when she heard a car coming up the drive. She waited beneath the oaks as the driver saw her and pulled up to where she was standing.

The old man behind the wheel was a neighbor, as familiar to her as her father.

"Hello, Mr. Woodley. Did you come for eggs?"

"Yeah…yeah I did, girl. That and to tell you how sorry I am for your loss. Dick was my friend. I'm sure gonna miss him."

Dallas's eyes welled. Their shared loss was true and touching.

"How many eggs might you be wanting?" she asked.

"Hazel said get three dozen if you have them to spare."

"We have that and more. Drive on down to the barn. I'm heading that way myself."

The old man eased his pickup past the trees and

parked at the barn. By the time she got there, he was standing in the breezeway waiting.

"Just give me a second and I'll bring your eggs right out," she said.

Woodley was looking up at *that* rafter.

"Is that where they found him?" he asked.

"Yes."

He kept looking and finally shook his head.

"I just can't wrap my mind around him being able to do that."

Dallas set the eggs down. "What do you mean?"

"He wrenched his right shoulder real bad last week. It was paining him something fierce. He even said he was thinking about going into town to see the chiropractor. So I don't see how the hell, excuse my language, he managed to throw a rope over that rafter, then climb those stairs to tie the end off, put the noose over his head and hang on long enough to jump. That's what I mean."

"Oh, my God!" Dallas cried, then threw her arms around his neck and burst into tears. "You think he was murdered, too, don't you?"

Woodley didn't seem to mind her emotional outburst and patted her in a consoling manner.

"Well, I sure don't think he killed himself. Dick Phillips wasn't a quitter."

Dallas fished a tissue out of her pocket and began wiping her eyes.

"Did my dad ever confide in you about money trouble?"

Woodley frowned. "I knew he was struggling financially, but he knew that would happen once he quit growing tobacco."

Dallas was floored, realizing she hadn't known nearly as much about her father as she'd thought.

"I don't think I knew that. When did that happen?"

"A couple of years ago. He woke up one day and said God told him he didn't have any right to be angry that his wife had died, when he'd been partly responsible for making it happen."

Dallas felt like she'd been punched in the chest.

"Oh, my God! Mom's lung cancer! She got lung cancer because she smoked, and she didn't quit even after she was diagnosed."

Woodley nodded. "He said he didn't have the heart to raise tobacco anymore. He didn't want to feel responsible for another death from smoking."

Her mind was racing. Two years. Right when he'd begun missing loan payments.

"Did he worry that he would lose the farm?"

Woodley frowned. "Oh, Lord, no! He said he was coming into big money soon, more than enough to pay off the loan, and his troubles would be over."

Her eyes widened. "Big money? How was that going to happen?"

"He never said, but I believed him. Dick Phillips wasn't a man who lied."

"Thank you, Mr. Woodley. Thank you."

"Why, shoot, girl, I didn't do anything."

"You did. You gave me hope. Hang on a second and

I'll get your eggs." She ran into the cooler for three cartons of eggs and hurried back out.

"Here, and I won't take anything for them. You've given me something far more valuable than money. You tell Hazel I said hello."

He took the eggs and smiled. "I'll do that," he said.

"Oh…I'm having a memorial service for Dad day after tomorrow, 10:00 a.m. at the church. It's not a funeral. It's a celebration of Dad's life, and whoever wants to speak about him will have the floor to do so. I'll be looking for you and Hazel to come here for dinner afterward. It's tradition in these mountains for friends and family to come eat, and I won't take no for an answer."

He smiled again. "We'd be proud to accept."

She watched until he was gone, and then all but raced into the egg room to clean and carton up the ones she'd just gathered. As she was getting new cartons out, she noticed a bunch of large plastic boxes about the size of trunks. They were stashed beneath the lowest shelf, and she was curious as to what her father had been planning to do with them. They weren't meant for anything but storage. She nosed around a little more and found a brand-new padlock and keys still in the packaging, but thought little of it. She wondered what he'd been planning, and then she let go of the thought and put the new eggs to the back to make sure she would use up the older eggs first. When she left, she carried all of the empty egg baskets and dropped them off at the coop on her way back.

She would never have believed that she could feel relief today, but she'd been wrong. The moment she reached the house she called the sheriff's office, hoping he wasn't gone for the day.

A different voice, a man this time, answered the phone.

"Sheriff's office."

"This is Dallas Phillips. Is Sheriff Osmond in?"

"I'm not sure if he's still here. Hold, please."

She waited, thankful there was no music in her ear, and moments later her call was picked up.

"Sheriff Osmond. How can I help you, Miss Phillips?"

"I found out something you need to know."

"I'm listening," he said.

"A neighbor of ours just stopped by to get eggs."

"Eggs?"

"Oh, sorry. Yes, eggs. We sell them, remember? Anyway, he and Dad were really close friends, and when he went with me to the barn, he kept looking up at where Dad was hanged and finally said Dad wouldn't have been physically able to manage it himself. He said Dad wrenched his shoulder pretty badly last week and was still in severe pain, which was something I didn't know. He said Dad had been talking about seeing the chiropractor this week because he was hurting so much."

The silence was telling.

"Sheriff Osmond? Are you there?"

"Yes, ma'am. Could you give me that man's name and phone number?"

"It's Otis Woodley. Just a moment while I get the phone book."

She came back within moments and gave Osmond the information.

"Thank you," he said. "I'll make sure the coroner gets this information and see if he can verify it. If you learn anything else, like someone who might have held a grudge against him, give me a call. I'll do the follow-up investigating on whether there's merit to it or not. I don't want you getting involved in something that could turn out to be dangerous for you."

"Yes, sir, and thank you, Sheriff Osmond."

He almost chuckled. "Thank me for what?"

"For listening. For not blowing me off."

"I've been in law enforcement a long time. Just when I think I've seen and heard it all, something will pop up and make a liar out of me. I never write anything off until I know all the facts there are to know. Take care. I'll be in touch."

Dallas disconnected with a sense of satisfaction. It wasn't a lot to pin her hopes on, since there was no obvious bad guy hovering in the wings, but it was something, and that was more than she'd had when she got up this morning.

Trey's day had been beyond hectic, and having to bring Carly Standish, the local bank president's daughter, into the station for shoplifting had only made it worse. She'd been defensive and then dissolved into tears when confronted with the security tape showing her stuffing a blouse into her oversize purse.

By the time her mother, Gloria, showed up with the family lawyer, he had also received a phone call from her father, Gregory. The call was rude, threatening and brief. When it was over, Trey was happy that he and his family didn't owe that bank a dime. Gregory Standish was not a man who liked to be thwarted.

By the time Trey left town for his mother's house, he had more than food on his mind. All day he'd kept thinking of Dallas. He hadn't heard from her and wondered if she'd found anything in the house that would help the case. If he hadn't stayed so busy at the office, he would have been hard-pressed not to call her just to hear her voice. But the day was over, and tonight he was not on call. He intended to enjoy every minute of the evening, even though the weather was turning nasty.

Halfway to the farm, it began to mist and the sky looked like more was imminent. He stepped on the gas, anxious to get to the house before the weather worsened. He turned on the windshield wipers and turned up the heater, thankful he'd thought to bring a jacket.

By the time he reached the farm, the mist had turned into a drizzle. He jumped out on the run, leaped over the front steps and onto the porch only seconds before the sky opened up.

"That's timing," he said, laughing at himself, and

then opened the door and walked in. “I’m here!” he yelled, and hung his hat and jacket on the hall tree.

“We’re in the kitchen!” Betsy called back.

Trina was at the stove and his mom was at the cabinet when he walked in. Trina’s boyfriend, Lee Daniels, was at the table nursing a beer, and gave him a quick nod and a grin.

“Birthday boy is here,” Lee said.

The women stopped what they were doing to give him a hug.

“Happy birthday, big brother,” Trina said, and kissed him on the right cheek.

“Happy birthday, son,” Betsy said, and kissed his left. “Your presents are on the sideboard.”

Trey grinned. “You shouldn’t have.”

Trina poked him in the ribs. “That’s what I told Mom, but she said I had to.”

“Trina Lee Jakes, that’s uncalled for,” Betsy grumbled.

Trey grinned.

Trina rolled her eyes.

“I always knew you were her favorite,” she said.

“Oh, no way, little sister. Sam is her favorite, and she’ll tell you so herself. Am I right, Mom?”

Betsy looked over her shoulder. “Of course Sam is my favorite. He’s the only one who really left home.”

They all burst into laughter as Trey got himself a beer. Then he picked up his presents and sat down, chose one and began with the card. The first one was from Lee.

"Hey, man, you didn't have to buy me a gift," Trey said.

Lee shrugged. "I heard about what a great meal this was going to be. I thought if I sweetened the pot a little it might get me some seconds."

Trey opened the package and found a half dozen of his favorite fishing lures.

"These are really nice! Thanks a lot."

"You're welcome. Trina put the bug in my ear."

"She's my favorite sister," Trey said.

"I'm your *only* sister," Trina muttered.

Trey arched an eyebrow and picked up the second package. It was from Trina.

"Since we're home and she's standing within spitting distance of me, I'm gonna assume it's not rigged to blow."

Trina giggled.

Trey opened the box and pulled out a new wallet.

"Trina! Thanks, honey. I needed this," he said.

"Yeah, we know. You sewed your old one back together with fishing line."

Trey grinned. "I'm into recycling. What can I say?" He was still smiling when he picked up the last one. "And this one is from Mom."

"Hurry up and open it," Trina begged. "She wouldn't tell me what it was, and I want to see, too."

Betsy was standing with her arms folded across her breasts, listening to all the teasing and wishing their father were still alive to see what great people they'd grown up to be.

Trey winked at his mom as he tore into the package, then he opened the lid and froze.

"Oh, hell. Oh, Mom."

Lee leaned over and looked in the box. "Damn, that's a Colt .45. Is that pearl inlay on the handle?"

Trina was in tears. "It was Daddy's. I haven't seen it in years."

Betsy wrapped her arms around Trey's neck and gave him a big hug.

"He would want you to have this, Trey. Happy birthday, son."

Trey turned and hugged her close.

"Thank you so much, but you know Sam's not gonna be happy about this."

"Sam already knows. It was his idea," Betsy said.

"This means a lot to me," Trey said softly.

"Your dad would be really proud, knowing you turned to law enforcement, too," Betsy said.

For a moment the room was silent, all of them thinking about Beau Jakes, an eighteen-year veteran with the West Virginia Highway Patrol, who'd been shot and killed beneath an overpass when he'd stopped to write up a speeder.

A loud ding sounded behind them.

"That's the casserole," Betsy said. "Your birthday supper is officially ready. Trina, help me get food on the table. Lee, you're assigned to putting ice in the glasses for sweet tea. Trey, please clean the wrapping paper off the table and grab that big metal trivet and put it in the middle."

No one argued. They were used to taking orders from Betsy Jakes.

It wasn't until they got to dessert that Trey brought up Dallas's name.

"Hey, Mom, while you're cutting the cake, would you please cut a big slice and wrap it up? I promised Dallas I'd bring her some before I went home tonight."

Betsy smiled. "I sure will, and that's real sweet of you, honey. I went to see her today. I took her some chicken potpie and that marinated salad she always liked."

Trey stifled a pang of jealousy that his mom could go see her so much more easily than he could.

"How was she?"

"Oh, about like you'd think. We both had ourselves a cry and probably felt better for it afterward. I dreaded going. It still feels to me like I'm somehow attached to what happened to her father."

Trey frowned, remembering what shape she'd been in yesterday. She'd gone from screaming uncontrollably to almost comatose by the time he'd found her.

"No, Mom. No. You found him. You did not kill him."

Betsy sighed. "I know, but I can't describe how blue I feel. It's the same sad I had after Connie died. I know they said she was driving, but I was there—we were all there—only we lived and she died. Just like now. Dick is dead, and I was there. He's dead, and I'm still alive. There's a tragic connection between the four of us that will never go away."

Lee frowned.

"Who's Connie?"

"Oh, right. I forgot you wouldn't know anything about my sordid past," Betsy said.

Trey and Trina both yelled at her at once, "Mom! Your past is *not* sordid."

Lee looked embarrassed. "Sorry. I didn't mean to—"

Betsy shook her head. "Oh, Lee, don't worry. You didn't do anything, and it's not really a secret. You're just too young to remember. It happened the night I graduated high school. All through school there were four of us kids who hung out. At first we were just friends. Dick and Paul were buddies. Connie and I were best friends. As we got older, we sort of paired up into boyfriend-girlfriend. Dick Phillips was sweet on Connie Bartlett. I was sweet on Paul."

"That's Paul Jackson. Mr. Jackson, who owns Jackson's Auto Repair," Trina added.

Betsy nodded. "Right after our high school graduation, the four of us took off in Connie's brand-new pink Cadillac. What happened after that is still a mystery. They found the car wrecked three hours later. Connie was dead. The three of us were critical. No one expected any of us to survive, but we did. Only we have no memory of where we went or what happened to cause the wreck. They told us our blood alcohol level was off the charts, but we didn't even remember drinking. Now Dick is gone, too, and I'm sorry I got off on such an ugly subject and ruined the party."

"The party isn't ruined," Trey said. "We have you, and we have cake. Nothing bad about that."

Betsy blinked back a few tears, and then laughed. "Four pieces of Italian cream cake, coming up."

"And one for Dallas."

"Yes, and one for Dallas, which reminds me, I offered to stand in as the hostess at her house for the meal. She's set the memorial service for 10:00 a.m. day after tomorrow, so I'm roping all of you into helping move tables and chairs, and anything else that might need doing at the dinner."

Trina nodded. "I can do it, but Lee has to work."

"I'll be there, too," Trey said. "We'll make it happen."

"Thanks, all of you. My life would be very empty without my babies…even if you've all gone and grown up on me."

Dallas was still going through tax receipts and files of farm-related invoices, hoping to find something that would give her a clue as to where her dad's big money was supposed to come from, but so far she'd had no luck.

It had been raining since before seven o'clock, and it was now after nine. She wondered if Trey was still coming by and secretly hoped he was. This would always be home, but it was incredibly lonely in this house without her father.

She'd gone through the last file of receipts and was putting them back when she saw car lights flash across the back wall. Trey was here! She tossed the rest of the stuff in the box, shoved it in a corner and then took the band out of her hair and combed her fingers through it to shake it out. The almost headache she'd been nursing began to dissipate the moment that band was released, and she made a mental note to take her hair down when she wasn't working outside. When she ran to answer the knock moments later, she did it without thinking why she was suddenly so happy he was there.

"Come in," she said. "I was about to give up on you."

"I don't go back on my word," he said, resisting the urge to kiss her. "Here's your cake. Mom says hello and hopes you enjoy it."

Dallas smiled as she took the little bag.

"I love this, and you know it. Will you help me eat it?"

"Oh, Lord, no. I can't eat another bite," he said. "But don't let me stop you. You get a fork. I'll get something to drink and join you."

"I have stuff to tell you," she said, as she grabbed a fork and slid the cake onto a plate.

"Want to sit in here?" he asked, as he got a cold pop from the refrigerator.

"Let's go back to the living room. I have a spot already warmed up on the couch."

He followed with the Dr Pepper, happy with his view of her backside. She was tall and leggy, with a very shapely butt, and he ached, thinking of how good it felt to make love to her.

She sat, took the first bite and rolled her eyes. "Mmm, just as good as I remembered."

Trey watched her for a few moments before it hit him what was different. She wasn't on the verge of tears.

"You said you had stuff to tell me," he prompted.

She took another bite and then set the cake aside. A blast of wind rattled the storm door and made the damper pop inside the fireplace.

"Sounds like that storm is getting worse," she said.

"Are you uneasy here?" he asked.

"Not really. It's lonely here now, but it's still home, and I've learned a lot of new stuff today about Dad. I've already passed the info on to Sheriff Osmond, but I want you to know, too."

"Did you find out something in your Dad's papers?"

"Yes, and I came so close to calling and crying on your shoulders. As it turned out, I'm glad I waited."

He set his pop aside and leaned forward. "Tell me."

"Dad mortgaged the farm to put me through school, and I never knew it."

Trey was shocked. The land had been in the family forever, free and clear. "You're kidding!"

"No, and I wish I were. I would have happily worked my way through college. If they'd only said they couldn't afford it, I would have figured another way to make it happen." She looked at him, and then looked away. "I was so dead set on getting out of Mystic, I didn't pay close enough attention to the people who loved me."

Trey didn't comment. There was nothing he could say that wouldn't start a fight.

"So he owed money on the farm," Trey said. "Lots of people are in debt and don't kill themselves."

"Did you know Dad quit raising tobacco a couple of years ago?"

Trey frowned. "I don't guess I did. That's not something we ever raised, so I wouldn't have necessarily noticed if someone else quit growing it, especially since I didn't come out here anymore."

She wouldn't let herself think why that had happened. She felt guilty enough as it was.

"Well, I didn't know, either, and it's worse on me, because this was home, he was my dad and I was so caught up in my world I never knew how his was changing. I wouldn't have known any of this if Mr. Woodley hadn't come by for eggs this morning."

"So he's the one who told you about the tobacco."

"Yes, but that's not all. I called the bank. Mr. Standish told me that Dad was two years in arrears and we're losing the farm in twenty-seven days."

Trey took a deep breath and then shoved his fingers through his hair in frustration.

"Sweet Lord, Dallas. Are you saying you think that's why—"

"Oh, hell, no," she said. "I make good money, and he knew it. I have three times the amount in my savings account that he would have needed to pay off the loan, and a decent amount in my checking. I would have paid it off with a smile, and he would have known it. He might have been a little embarrassed, but he would never have thought it was the end of the world, or that he'd done something so unforgivable that he had to be too ashamed to face me. He would never have lost the farm."

"Then what? I don't get the big revelation. If anything, the debt makes a stronger case that your dad did commit suicide, despite what you think."

"Mr. Woodley had something else to tell me. He didn't believe Dad killed himself because he said Dad hurt his shoulder pretty badly last week. Badly enough that he was barely able to use it and was talking about going to the chiropractor this week. Mr. Woodley went down to the barn and looked at where Dad's body was found. He said there was no physical way Dad could have hanged himself."

Trey jumped to his feet and began to pace.

"This is exactly the kind of evidence you need to make your case. If the coroner can verify that injury when he does the autopsy, this will pretty much end the supposition that it was suicide."

Dallas nodded. "That's what Osmond said. But there's one more thing. Woodley said Dad wasn't bothered by the loan coming due because he said he was coming into big money very soon, enough to get him completely out of debt, with some to spare."

"Money from where?" Trey asked.

"I don't know. I've been looking through his papers all evening, trying to find something that explains it."

"If you can figure that out, if you can prove that money wasn't an issue for him, and the coroner can verify the shoulder injury, then we can officially say we have a killer in Mystic. The downside of that is that the big money your Dad claimed was coming could be connected to the killer. In a way it makes everything even more mysterious—and maybe more dangerous."

Six

"It also means there's no way this was impulsive. Impulsive is shooting. Beating. Not this. Someone had to bring a rope, someone who knew the layout of the barn and wanted people to think it was a suicide. The question is, why?"

Trey frowned. "In a place this small, it's almost inevitable that your dad knew his killer. The only reason they would have been in the barn together is if your dad believed the killer had come to buy eggs. He doesn't advertise, so the killer has to be a local. Your dad turned his back because he trusted the killer, and that brings up something else I noticed when I first saw him hanging."

"What?" Dallas asked.

"The back of his clothes was dirty, but the front wasn't."

"You mean muddy? Or dusty?"

"Very dusty, but only the back."

Dallas frowned. “So how did that happen?”

“I don’t know… Maybe someone grabbed him from behind. He would have fallen on his back and—”

Dallas moaned. “If his shoulder was bad, he wouldn’t even have been able to fight back. The pain might have even made him black out.”

“Someone could even have thrown the noose over his head from behind and yanked him backward,” Trey said. “He would have choked, maybe been stunned by the blow to the back of his head when he fell.”

“I’m going to be sick,” Dallas mumbled.

She flew down the hall and into the bathroom, and threw up until she was shaking. When she flushed the toilet and turned around, Trey was standing at the sink with a wet cloth in his hand and a look of contrition on his face.

“Damn it, Dallas. I am *so* sorry. I got caught up in trying to figure out the how of it and forgot it was your father we were talking about.”

She took the wet cloth, grateful for the cold shock on her face. Then she rinsed out her mouth and sat down on the closed lid of the commode.

“Don’t apologize, Trey. I’ve already been through the hows and whys of it a hundred times in my head. Once I accepted that he was murdered, I was under no misconception that it was painless. I got carried away with the scenarios myself. The nausea surprised me. I thought the shock had finally passed. I was wrong.”

Trey still felt bad. “Look, I’ve screwed up your night enough. I’m going to leave and let you get some rest. Just be grateful for the fact that your instincts were right."

Dallas didn't think. She just got up and wrapped her arms around his waist.

"I'm grateful for you."

Trey pulled her close, his voice gruff with emotion as he said, "When you hurt, I bleed, and time hasn't changed that. Come on, so you can lock the door behind me."

She followed him into the living room, then stood in the doorway as he walked out into the rainy night.

"Drive safely," she said.

"I'll call you tomorrow," he said.

Dallas caught herself as she was about to say "I love you" and waved instead, then locked up for the night.

She told herself it was just habit, something she'd said to him so many times before their split. She couldn't afford to love him. He didn't fit into her life any better now than he had before.

But later, when she crawled between the covers and closed her eyes, she didn't dream of Charleston and her cosmopolitan lifestyle. She dreamed of the land and the mountains, and Trey Jakes standing at her side.

Silver Hill Plantation was on the outskirts of Mystic, and Marcus Silver was the sixth generation of Silvers to have lived there. The family interests had shifted from farming to industry after the Civil War, and Marcus continued to run the business to this day.

As impressive as his estate and fortune were, Marcus had a yen for something none of his predecessors had considered. He wanted to be in politics. He'd thought about it for years, fostering friends in all the right places in both industry and government. He was serious enough about it that he'd even gone so far as to start interviewing campaign managers to discuss their views of how to proceed and what it would entail.

Divorced for over fifteen years, he had no one but his son, T.J., to consider, and T.J., who had political aspirations of his own, happily envisioned his father becoming senator as a way to give *him* an instant foothold in that world, as well.

After some discussion, they began toying with the idea of holding a fall gala at Silver Hill, inviting all the right people in West Virginia politics to witness him announcing his intent to run for a seat in the state senate.

Then, in the midst of planning, Marcus learned of Dick Phillips's suicide. They had been classmates in high school, and even though they had never traveled in the same social circles, he had always liked Dick. A day or so later gossip began to spread about why Dick had killed himself. People were saying he'd been days away from foreclosure on the land that had been in his family for generations when he died. When Marcus thought of Silver Hill and the idea of losing it, he understood how Dick might have chosen that end, and even mentioned it to T.J. over breakfast the next morning.

The maid was refilling Marcus's coffee as T.J.

forked a waffle onto his plate, liberally dousing it with pure maple syrup. Only the best was served beneath the roof of Silver Hill.

"I can't quit thinking about poor Dick Phillips," Marcus said. "So distraught about losing his heritage that he would take his own life."

T.J. frowned. "What are you talking about?"

"It's not common knowledge, but I heard it straight from Standish at the bank. Dick mortgaged the family farm some years back and was two years in arrears. The bank is foreclosing in less than a month."

T.J. shoved a bite of waffle into his mouth, thinking of Dick Phillips's pretty daughter, Dallas. She'd been a year ahead of him in school, but he'd always thought she was hot.

"So you think that's why he hanged himself?" T.J. asked.

"Why else?" Marcus asked.

T.J. shrugged. "Yeah, I guess that makes sense."

"I feel as if I need to do something," Marcus said. "The memorial service is tomorrow, and people have been invited to speak in memory of him."

T.J. shoved his plate back and put his elbows on the table as he leaned forward.

"How many of your old classmates are still local?" he asked.

Marcus shrugged. "I don't know, maybe twenty or so. Why?"

"So why don't you all stand together at that time, and then each offer a special story you have to share."

Marcus's eyes widened, and then he smiled.

"Son! That's a wonderful idea. I'll have my secretary get right on that."

"Dad, it would be better, more personal, if the calls came from you. You have to be cognizant of these little moments if you plan to run for Congress."

Marcus's smile widened. "You're right! I'll make a list of names and call them from the office. Thank you, T.J. Oh, will you do me a favor? Call the florist and have them send two big arrangements to the church. I want them identical. That way they can stand on either side of the pulpit."

T.J. grinned. "Now you're thinking like a politician. Never miss an opportunity to shake hands or kiss a baby."

Marcus eyed his son proudly, thankful he'd inherited his mother's looks and not his own. There wasn't anything intrinsically ugly about Marcus, but the only remarkable thing he had going for him was a full head of silver-gray, perfectly groomed hair. Bill Clinton had nothing on him.

His son was a different story. He had always been athletic and was Hollywood handsome. He would be a shoo-in to win the female vote should he decide to pursue this path.

It was afternoon when Betsy and Trina showed up at the Phillips farm. Dallas was glad to see Trina, but a little stunned to realize she was all grown-up.

"Trina! In my mind, every time I thought of you,

you were still a teenager, and now look at you! You've turned into a gorgeous young woman."

"Thank you," Trina said, as she gave Dallas a hug. "It's good to see you, but I'm so sorry for the reason."

Betsy was all matter-of-fact. She didn't want their visit to set off another emotional upheaval for Dallas.

"I'm going to put these two pies on the sideboard," she said, and sailed past, carrying her latest handiwork.

Dallas was comforted by noise in the house and the chatter of two people she adored. She followed Betsy into the kitchen.

"I'm not sure how to go about this," Dallas said. "When Mom died, we set up the food buffet-style in here and let people sit anywhere they wanted around the house and out on the front porch and lawn, but it was summer then. I think we're going to have to keep everything inside this time."

Betsy eyed the layout and nodded.

"I agree. Short of setting everything up outside and hoping it doesn't rain, you don't have another option. And this time of year the weather could be too chilly to enjoy sitting outside anyway."

Dallas's shoulders slumped, and her chin began to tremble. "I can't wrap my head around life without Dad. No more holidays in this house. No more anything."

"I know what you mean about losing the anchors to your childhood. I felt the same way when my mom passed," Betsy said. "Of course, I was already married, and Sam and Trey were little, so I wasn't alone. I regret that Trina never knew my parents, though. But if you think about it, you don't have to leave this house. That's your choice."

Dallas heard the rebuke and realized Betsy was right. No one was running her out of this house. It was already hers. If she abandoned it and all it stood for, that was on her. As she listened to Betsy move on to discuss arrangements for the meal, her mind wandered and she began to reminisce, remembering the first time she'd seen Trey Jakes. First grade—first day of school. He was sitting at the desk directly across the aisle from her in Mrs. Simmons's class. He'd had a black eye, a skinned nose and a fat lip, and when she'd stared at him, he'd winked. She'd fallen in love that day and never looked at another man since. She had the occasional dinner date in the city, but they never measured up to the man she'd left behind.

"So I think that about covers it," Betsy said.

Dallas blinked. She'd lost focus and had no idea what Betsy had just said.

"I'm sorry—I was lost in thought," Dallas said. "Forgive me."

Betsy waved away the apology.

"Honey, you have a lot on your plate. Just let me and my family do this for you. All you have to do is be here, eat what you can and field condolences."

"Yes, I can do that, and thank you," Dallas said.

"We're happy to help," Trina said.

"Do you have any other chairs or folding chairs?" Betsy asked.

Dallas nodded. "There are some in the basement. The day I came home the house was unlocked, and it spooked me enough that I had to go through every room and closet to make sure I was alone before I locked myself in."

Betsy frowned. "Oh, that's too bad. I'm sure the sheriff's men were responsible for that. They were still here when I left or I would certainly have known to lock it for you."

"No harm was done, but that's why I know there are chairs in the basement," Dallas said. "I'll help you carry them up."

She turned on the light at the top of the stairs as the three of them went down. She pointed out the stack of folding chairs against the north wall, then got a handful of cleaning rags and they began dusting them off.

Betsy stopped momentarily to give her back a rest and gazed around the basement at the odd assortment of things on the shelves.

"Isn't it strange how we accumulate so much stuff during a lifetime?"

Dallas paused. "Yes, and when you look at it after someone's gone, you wonder why they kept it all."

Trina set the last folding chair back into the stack. "Okay, these are all clean."

"Then let's carry them up," Betsy said, and led the way.

They made two trips before they got them all up, and then left them leaning against a wall in the living room for tomorrow.

Trina grabbed the dust mop and began cleaning up the tracks they'd left in the hall.

Dallas started counting off the necessities for the meal.

"I'll put tablecloths on the tables and hot pads out for you to use as needed. Oh, and I have fancy silverware as well as Mom's set of everyday flatware, but I know it won't be enough."

"I have plastic forks and paper plates," Betsy said. "We are *not* dirtying up everything you own. You have a big coffee urn. I know because Marcy used to bring it to the church now and then when we needed extra. I'll make coffee in that and sweet tea in mine, and we'll be good to go."

The mention of her mother was a reminder of how much Dallas had lost. She was all that was left of her family, and the sadness was overwhelming. She began to lose focus again, but this time Betsy saw it and spoke up.

"Trina, I think we're done here for the day. Dallas, I'll be over around nine o'clock tomorrow morning, and I'll be staying to receive the food that will come in. I let the churches know where the family meal is being served, and speaking of family, how many of your relatives are coming? Do you know?"

Dallas shrugged. "Four for sure. Maybes…about ten more." Then she frowned. "One of Dad's cousins refused to come after hearing how he died. She said, because he killed himself, she wasn't going to celebrate a life that was going straight to hell."

Betsy gasped. "You're not serious!"

"Unfortunately, I am. There's nothing like a 'good Christian woman' to put everything in perspective. She's one of those people who believe it's their duty to judge everyone. I don't care. Never liked her, and it's just as well she won't be here spreading her distaste for Dad's supposed sin."

Betsy hugged her. "I'm so sorry, but don't let it get you down, okay?"

Dallas sighed. "I'm fine. I just want tomorrow over with."

Betsy started gathering up her things as Trina put up the dust mop.

"What are you going to do when the service is over?" Betsy asked. "Are you going straight back to Charleston?"

"No. I'm for certain staying until Dad's name is cleared. It will give me time to figure out what I want to do with the farm. Then I guess I'll go back."

Betsy's smile was polite, but Dallas knew Betsy wanted her to stay. To her credit, she said nothing more about it.

Betsy wiped her hands on the legs of her jeans.

"Okay, I see Trina is finished with the floors. Call if you need anything beforehand. Oh! And don't worry about ice for the guests. Trey is bringing several sacks over to put in the deep freeze, so make sure there's room."

"I will, and thank you again," Dallas said.

She stood on the porch and watched them leave. She'd just started to go back into the house when she heard a gunshot, and then, moments later, a second. They sounded like they were coming from somewhere up the mountain, and while it wasn't unusual to hear gunshots because of hunters, this was an odd time of day to go hunting. It was usually just around daybreak for deer, or after dark for coyotes and foxes that got into people's livestock.

She went back inside, then walked straight through the house and out the back door for a better view of the back of the property, but she saw nothing out of place, and she didn't hear any more shots. Shrugging off her curiosity, she went to change her shoes, get a jacket and do the chores.

The killer was on his way home after a busy day, wondering what dinner was going to be and how his role in the memorial service tomorrow would play out. He had to admit, it was something of a kick to know that he would be mingling with all of Dick Phillips's friends and family, knowing he was the one responsible for the man's death.

Dallas didn't think she would be able to sleep when she went to bed, but she did. The next thing she knew, the chickens were squawking and the cows were bawling, and it was still dark. It took her a few seconds to realize something was at the chicken coop trying to get in.

She stepped into her tennis shoes and grabbed

the shotgun from underneath the bed as she headed through the house in her pajamas. There was a flashlight on the table by the back door, and as she turned on the outside lights, she grabbed the flashlight, too.

The chickens were still in distress as she ran, and she feared whatever was out there would have decimated the flock before she arrived. She swung the bright light of the flashlight into the darkness, sweeping the fenced-off area around the coop, but saw nothing. The double-barreled shotgun was resting in the crook of her arm, her finger on the trigger. All she needed was a look at what was out there and she would raise the weapon and unload. Buckshot scattered far and wide, giving her a good chance of hitting her target.

She darted around to the back side of the coop and caught a brief glimpse of something bigger than a fox. She was thinking coyote when she raced back around the other side, hoping to get off a shot, and then all of a sudden she heard a low growl behind her. She turned and fired.

She had a brief glimpse of a huge head, a dark coat and glowing eyes, and then it was gone. There had been no cry of pain to indicate she'd hit it, and when she ran over to where it had been standing, the size of its tracks startled her. That wasn't a coyote. It was far too big. Maybe someone's dog? What bothered her was that it hadn't run away when she'd first come out. It had turned the tables on her and caught her off guard. She could still hear the growl, and she shuddered. If she hadn't had the gun, it would have attacked.

She swung the flashlight out into the darkness, trying to see if it was still out there, but she couldn't see past the beam of light. The cows had stopped bawling, which told her that whatever it was, it was no longer a threat.

She checked the coop one last time to make sure the gate was secured and the animal hadn't tunneled its way inside, and then shone the flashlight through the window to see if the chickens were okay. Most had gone back to their nests or up onto the roost.

After one last look out into the darkness, she headed back toward the house, and the closer she got, the faster she went. By the time she reached the porch she was running. She slammed and locked the door, and then laid the shotgun down on the floor and dropped to her knees, too shaky to stand.

"Oh my God, oh my God."

She'd never had to do anything like that before, and her hands were shaking and she wanted to cry, but the danger was over, gone in the night just like the animal that had challenged her.

Finally she made herself get up and reload the gun before taking it to her room.

It was just after 4:00 a.m. Her alarm was set for six, but she was too shaky to close her eyes. And then she did burst into tears. If her dad had been alive, he wouldn't have missed that shot and the danger would be over. Instead, now she knew something was out there. Something that made being alone out here frightening after all.

* * *

Betsy and Trina went to bed early, knowing tomorrow was going to be a long, hard day, but the moment the house got quiet, Betsy's thoughts went into rewind.

There's so much sadness in Dallas, and she doesn't even know it, Betsy thought. *She's just like Trey. They're only half-alive without each other.* Fate had played a dirty joke on the both of them, making sure the girl who'd run away didn't want to come home and the boy who'd stayed behind couldn't forget her. She was sad for both of them but there was nothing she could do. They were adults, and they would either work it out or, once again, go their separate ways. When she finally fell asleep it was almost midnight, and even then her sleep was fitful.

Faces moving past her line of sight so fast their features blurred one into the other. Laughter morphing into screams and someone crying, someone praying. The sour smell of vomit, the burning taste of whiskey. More screams. Impact!

Betsy woke up gasping, her face streaked with tears, and just like that, the dream was gone. She moaned, and then rolled over and looked at the clock.

It was almost 6:00 a.m. She wasn't going back to bed after that horrific nightmare, so she got up and headed for the shower. She needed to be at the farm in three hours.

Seven

The telephone was ringing, and Dallas rolled over to answer before she opened her eyes, expecting the call to be from her boss at WOML Charleston. But when she heard Trey's voice, she remembered. Today was about saying goodbye.

"Hello."

"Hey, it's me. I wanted you to know I'm thinking of you, and that I'm coming out with Mom this morning to take you to the service."

"Oh, that's not—"

"Yes, it *is* necessary," Trey said. "You don't go through this alone."

The knot that had filled her belly since she'd heard about her dad eased. "Thank you."

"You're welcome. Is everything all right out there otherwise?"

"Yes, except something tried to get at the chickens last night."

"What was it...coyote? Or a fox?"

"Neither. Way bigger and more aggressive. I think it might be someone's dog. I shot at it when it lunged at me. Of course I missed, but it did run off."

"It attacked you?" The tenderness in Trey's voice was gone.

"It tried."

"Son of a bitch," he muttered. "A year or so ago the sheriff broke up a dogfighting ring somewhere up the mountain. They were tipped off that he was coming and were in the process of disbanding when the authorities rolled up. They'd already let a lot of the dogs loose, and some of the men had already escaped. I've heard people complaining about feral dogs, but I never thought to warn you. Please don't go out in the dark alone again. I'll come up and see if I can find his trail. We both know animals that were tame and have gone feral are far more dangerous than the wild ones, because they aren't afraid of us."

Dallas sighed. "I will be careful. That's all I can promise, because I'm not going to go into hiding. This is still my home, and the animals that are mine have every right to expect food and protection. I'll see you later."

She disconnected before he could comment, knowing he wasn't through arguing his case. Still, she decided to carry the shotgun and her phone when she went out to do chores.

The morning was chilly, the grass heavy with dew. The cows her dad had been feeding were standing in the back of the lot waiting; their calves at their sides were either nursing or lying down nearby.

Before she went into the chicken house, she circled the enclosed yard and coop looking for tracks, and when she saw them in the bright light of day, the skin crawled on the back of her neck. The paw prints were huge. She started to take a couple of pictures of one to show Trey and then stopped, looking for something to put beside it for size comparison, but she didn't have anything with her but the gun and the phone. So she put her foot down beside it and snapped the pictures, then dropped the phone in her pocket and got to work.

She put scattered feed and scratch out in the yard and then opened the coop, grinning when the hens came running. Once they were out, she went inside to refill their water, then began gathering eggs. A couple of old hens had gone broody and were sitting on the nests, reluctant to give up their eggs. Dallas hated to break the news, but without a rooster in the pen, there was no way those eggs were hatching. She slipped her hand beneath the warm feathers of the first hen, took the egg, put it in the bucket and moved on down the row. The second old hen wasn't as amiable. She pecked Dallas's hand as she slipped it under her feathered breast.

"Ouch, dang it," Dallas grumbled as she grabbed the egg. She finished gathering, then headed to the barn.

Just as she was about to step into the egg room, she heard a car coming up the drive and frowned. It was barely 7:00 a.m. But when she saw who it was, she relaxed.

Larry Sherman was their—her—neighbor about five miles over, and she could pretty much guess why he was making an early call. The man and his wife had six kids, and her dad used to say they came by for eggs so often that the kids must be going through them like a plague of grasshoppers.

She stepped out into the breezeway and waved. He honked when he saw her and headed down to the barn instead. The tall, skinny redhead who emerged from the truck didn't look like the forty-something man she knew he was.

"Dallas! I'm glad I caught you. I expect you know why I'm here."

"You need eggs for breakfast."

"Yes, ma'am, I do," Larry said. "And the wife and I want to tell you how sorry we are for your daddy's passing. We are sure gonna miss him."

"Thank you, Larry, so will I. How many eggs do you want?"

"Do you have six dozen to spare?"

"Yes, and as long as I'm here at the farm, the eggs will be, too, okay? So don't hesitate to come again when you need them."

He smiled. "That's real good to know. This place just wouldn't be the same without a Phillips on the land."

Dallas hurried into the cooler to get the eggs, then waved as he drove away, but long after he was gone, she kept thinking about what he'd said about having a Phillips on the land. She hated the position she was in. She didn't want to be the person who abandoned what her ancestors had fought so hard to keep.

After going back to the house, she finished off the piece of cake from last night and called it breakfast, chasing it with a cup of coffee and two aspirin because her head was throbbing. By the time she was dressed, the pain had dulled enough to cope, and she was putting tablecloths on the kitchen and dining room tables when she heard more cars. That would be Trey and Betsy, she thought, and she was right.

Trey headed for the house carrying three bags of ice. She opened the door for him and then ran to the back room to open the deep freeze, as well.

"You look beautiful," he said, as he dumped the ice and then kissed her on the forehead. "I have more. Be right back."

She stood by the freezer, waiting to lift the lid again and thinking about that throwaway kiss. As she waited, she watched Betsy taking charge. Their presence was all she needed to get through this day.

Trey came back with four more bags. "That's it. If it's not enough, they can drink cold tap water."

Then he paused, frowned and cupped her cheeks.

"Oooh, your cold hands feel good," Dallas said.

"Are you sick?" he asked.

"No, just a bad headache. I took something. It's getting better."

"Did you eat?" he asked.

"Cake."

His eyes narrowed thoughtfully as he noticed the dark circles beneath her eyes.

"And that is exactly what I would have prescribed. You'll do, girl. I know how tough you are."

Betsy's voice calling from the other room shifted their focus and the moment was gone. All too soon it was time for Dallas to leave, and she found herself struggling against an urge to cry. She was going to have to face everyone, including the distant family members, and she had no intention of explaining to a one of them what she and Trey already knew: that her dad had not killed himself. That would come with the coroner's official report. This day wasn't for dissent. It was for remembering the wonderful man he had been.

She was standing in the living room, looking down the hall at her father's bedroom and half expecting to see him come running out, yelling that they were all going to be late, when Trey came up behind her. Unaware that he was there, she jumped when he cupped her elbow.

"Oh, I'm sorry, honey. I didn't mean to scare you, but it's time to go."

Dallas took a deep breath and turned around. "I'm ready."

Trey hated the sadness in her face. He wanted the right to kiss her, to be that person who put joy in her life, but that wasn't likely to happen.

Betsy came out of the kitchen, wiping her hands on a towel.

"You look stunning, Dallas. That is a beautiful dress. Navy blue does wonders for your blue eyes. And I love the way it flares just above the knees. It has long sleeves, but will you need a jacket?"

"Since we won't be at the cemetery, I'll be fine."

Betsy gave her a quick kiss on the cheek, and then patted her son's arm.

"Take good care of our girl. I'll be here when you two get back."

"Yes, ma'am," Trey said, and escorted Dallas out to her car. As soon as she was buckled into the passenger seat, they drove off.

Trey wanted to distract her, if only for the drive into Mystic, and brought up the subject of the wild dog.

"So tell me again me about that dog. Could you see what color it was, or tell what breed it might have been?"

"It was too dark. I saw a brief glimpse of it as I swung the flashlight around to shoot, but mostly all I can remember are glowing eyes and big teeth as it snarled."

"I sure don't like knowing we've got something like that roaming the area. I need to talk to the locals and see if they've seen it, too."

"The other day I heard two gunshots somewhere on the back side of the pasture, like high up the mountain. I didn't see or hear anything more, but maybe other people are having the same trouble I am and shooting at strays. I did take a picture of the paw print this morning. Want to see it?"

"Yes," Trey said, and when she pulled the picture up on her phone and handed it to him, he slowed down for a better look. "Is that your shoe?"

She nodded.

"Damn it, Dallas! That dog must be huge. Its paw is wider than your foot."

"I know. I wish my aim had been better."

Trey handed the phone back.

"It might take a while, but an animal like that has to be taken out of circulation."

She put the phone on vibrate and dropped it in her purse.

"Maybe because I shot at it, it won't come back. Maybe it's on another mountain by now."

Trey frowned. "I don't trust maybes to keep you safe."

"I've been taking care of myself for years now," she said.

A muscle jerked at the side of his jaw, but he didn't comment. It would only cause a fight, and today was not a day for discord.

Dallas knew the moment she'd said it that it would hurt him, and yet she'd done it. Why? Was she so afraid of her own weakness where he was concerned that she wanted him to be mad at her, because he was easier to deal with that way?

Coward. That's what you are, Dallas Ann. You are a coward.

She took a deep breath and looked at him. "I'm sorry. I shouldn't have said that."

Trey shrugged. "You always say what you think. I expect no less. Besides, it's not news how you feel."

Dallas felt sick, like she'd failed him all over again. God, would she ever get this right? Why were the choices in life so difficult?

After that, the ride into Mystic was mostly silent. When they drove up to the church and she saw the number of cars already there, her stomach rolled. "That's a lot of people."

"Your dad was born and raised here. He lived here all his life, and everyone loved him. I'm not surprised."

Dallas couldn't help but think of what had passed her by while she'd been chasing dreams.

Sunlight bounced off the hood and into her eyes as Trey parked. She turned away from the glare to unfasten her seat belt, and then Trey was at her door, helping her out. She stood for a moment to get her bearings, then slung the strap of her purse across her shoulder and instinctively reached for Trey's hand.

"You can do this," he said softly.

"Thank you for being here."

"I'm always here for you," he said, and together they walked into the church.

The pastor was watching for them. He expressed his condolences and then led them into a classroom that had been set aside for family to gather. As soon as they walked in, Dallas was surprised by the number of family members who'd come.

Trey stepped aside as she began to greet them, although he knew who most of them were. By the time they started into the sanctuary, the church was packed, and there were more than twenty family members accompanying Dallas and Trey.

As soon as she sat, Trey scooted close, just as she'd known he would, and put his arm across the back of the seat behind her. She *would* get through this with the comfort of his presence.

When the pastor began to read the eulogy, Dallas zoned out. She couldn't believe this was happening again. First her mom, now her dad, and all she could think was, why? Someone sang a song, and while the voice was familiar, she couldn't remember who it was. She'd been gone too long.

Then she heard the pastor announce that they were opening the floor up to the congregation and anyone who wanted to say a few words about Dick Phillips was welcome to do so.

She was curious as to who would choose to speak, and was stunned when two entire rows of people got up and walked together to the front of the room.

Marcus Silver was the first to speak, quickly explaining their presence.

"We're all members of the graduating class of 1980. We grew up with Dick, and we want you to know him as we did, so this is my first memory of him. In first grade, they lined us up alphabetically every time we left the room, which was fine, except I didn't know my alphabet that well. I soon realized that if I could find where Dickie Phillips was standing, all I had to do was get in line two kids behind him and I would be in the right place. You know…*P* for Phillips, *S* for Silver. I told this to Dick once after we were grown, and he started laughing. I asked him what was funny, and he said that he hadn't known *his* alphabet, either, and was just following the cute little blonde from the front row."

It wasn't the story so much as the sound of laughter that made Dallas smile. Her dad would have loved this.

One by one, the others told their own stories, which ranged from trapping a skunk to dissecting frogs in science class. One woman talked about how she'd been driving home during a heavy rain and had got a flat. She said the first person to come by was Dick, and he bailed out of his truck in the downpour and changed it for her. But, she said, no sooner had he finished than it became apparent the spare was also going flat, so even though he was soaking wet, he followed her home to make sure she wasn't stranded again.

One after another, classmates and friends stood to tell their stories, and by the time the service was over, there wasn't a person in the church who wasn't smiling, and few, if any, tears had been shed.

Just when Dallas thought the last person had spoken, Trey suddenly gave her hand a quick squeeze, and then stood up and walked to the front. She didn't know what he was going to say, but it wouldn't matter. She was already crying.

Trey took a deep breath. This was going to be hard, but he needed to get this said.

"Dick Phillips was smart and funny, always ready

to help a friend. I never heard him begrudge anything to anyone. But when I was eleven, he became my confidant. I was standing in line at the concession stand during a high school football game when I realized who was behind me. I turned around, introduced myself and told him I loved his daughter. He smiled, shook my hand and said he loved her, too."

Dallas heard the laughter behind her, but she was in shock. She had never heard this story.

Trey was baring his heart and couldn't look at Dallas for fear of the rejection he would see.

"After that, every time he saw me, he'd ask if I was being good to his girl, and of course I always said yes, at which time he would thank me and we'd go our separate ways. The year we graduated high school, he stopped by the farm one day and asked me to take a ride with him, which I did. We didn't go anywhere in particular. He just needed to talk. He said his girl was going away to college, and he was worried. He said he'd counted on me all those years to take care of her when he wasn't around, but now she was going to be on her own, and he was scared for her."

Dallas was stunned. She'd been unaware that her father had been troubled by her leaving, and she was also in disbelief that he and Trey had shared such a close relationship and she'd never known.

"Anyway, I listened to him talk as we drove up and down the mountain, and finally, as we headed home, he got real quiet. I didn't really know what to say to make him feel better, except to tell him the truth. I told him that the truth about Dallas Ann was that she didn't need anyone to take care of her, and that he shouldn't worry when she left, because she would never forget the way home."

Dallas choked on a sob, and Trey heard it.

"Dick Phillips was a good man and a good father, and I called him my friend. We are all better for having known him, and he is going to be missed."

He sat back down beside Dallas and took her hand without looking at her. The preacher was talking, informing those in attendance that a meal would be served at the Phillips farm and that anyone who didn't know where it was should just follow the line of cars heading out of town. But Trey was barely listening. His heart was pounding so hard he thought it might burst. He'd bared his soul in front of the town in honor of a man who'd meant the world to him, even knowing full well Dallas would reject him again.

When the preacher stepped down from the pulpit, he stopped at the first pew, waiting for Dallas and the family to get up and follow him out. Still holding her hand, Trey went with her.

Dallas was silent as he escorted her to the car. As soon as he got in and started in the direction of her farm, he began talking—saying anything to keep from having *that* talk.

"I think the idea to hold a memorial service was brilliant, honey. That will be what people remember when they think of him, and not how he died. It was amazing how his classmates joined together like that.

It was a thumbnail sketch of his life from the age of six and all through their years together in school. What you need to remember is how people thought of him, what they thought of him. It was all good stuff."

Before Dallas could speak, Trey's cell phone rang.

"Damn it. It's the police station. I told them not to call unless the place was on fire."

He was negotiating a particularly narrow part of the road and put the phone on speaker because he needed both hands to drive.

"Hello?"

The dispatcher's voice was frantic, and both Trey and Dallas were immediately alarmed.

Trey had to interrupt twice to get the man to calm down enough for them to understand what he was saying.

"Now...say that again. Did you say someone broke into the jail?"

"No, no," the dispatcher said. "I said a skunk got into the jail. I think Dwight left the back door open while he was carrying out garbage yesterday evening. The skunk came in and spent the night. We just arrested Dooley again for public intoxication, and when they went to lock him up, the skunk objected."

"Oh, for God's sake," Trey said. "Did he spray everything?"

"No. The moment that tail went up, we all hightailed it out of there. We just took Dooley home and put him to bed. I don't smell no fumes, so I guess we missed that bomb, but he's still there. What do we do?"

"Go unlock the back door and leave it open. Maybe he'll leave the same way he got in. Find something skunks like to eat and put it just outside the door. Make sure it's close enough that he can smell it, but not so close that you can't get the door shut once he leaves."

"Yeah, okay… Uh, wait, Chief. What do skunks like?"

"The hell if I know, Avery. Look it up on Google. And whatever you do, don't upset him. We don't want to smell that for the next six months."

"Right, right, we're on it, Chief. Sorry to bother you."

Trey ended the call, looked at Dallas and burst out laughing.

"I'll bet stuff like that doesn't happen in Charleston," he said, and threw back his head and laughed some more.

Dallas was charmed by his reaction and for a moment forgot the revelation he'd laid at her feet in church. By the time she thought about bringing it up, they were pulling into the driveway.

At that point she sighed, wishing she didn't have to face a crowd all over again.

Trey saw the white line around her mouth and could only guess at what she was feeling. As soon as he parked he reached for her hand.

"You've got this. You celebrated Dick's life with great stories, now try and think of this as sharing a meal with all of his best friends."

"And the family," she added, rolling her eyes.

Trey laughed again, which made her smile.

"They aren't so bad, but if they cause any trouble, I'll take them back to town with me and lock them up with my skunk."

Dallas laughed, and then was shocked by the moment of joy.

"You always were my knight in shining armor," she said.

He stifled the pain in his chest and made himself smile. "Still am, always will be. Let's go inside. Even if the day is chilly, I'm ready for a big glass of sweet iced tea."

Betsy was watching from the living room window, and when she saw Dallas and Trey coming toward the house hand in hand, she said a quick prayer, and then met them at the door.

"How was the service? Did very many people speak?" she asked.

"Let me put my things up and make a quick trip to the bathroom before everyone gets here, and then I'll tell you all about it," Dallas said.

As soon as she left, Betsy pinned Trey with a look.

"Did you speak?"

"Yes."

"Did she cry?"

He nodded.

"Then there's hope for you yet," she said.

Trey shrugged. "Don't get your hopes up, Mom.

She cried when she left me the first time, but it didn't stop her."

Betsy frowned. "I don't understand. When people love each other like you two do, there should be a way to make it work."

Then they heard footsteps coming up the hall, and Trey followed his mother into the kitchen for that tea.

"Ooh, would you pour some for me?" Dallas said, when she saw what he was doing.

"Absolutely," he said.

Dallas looked at Betsy. "Did he tell you?" she asked.

Betsy looked startled and then glanced at Trey. He felt equally anxious, afraid she might have overheard part of their conversation.

"Tell me what?" Betsy asked.

"About the skunk!" Dallas said.

"Oh, that," Trey said. "I was just about to." He gave Betsy the story, blow-by-blow, and she was still laughing when the first guests began to arrive.

Trey pointed toward the living room.

"Dallas, go find a comfortable seat, and don't get up or you'll lose it. I'll get the door."

She took her tea into the living room and claimed her dad's recliner. It wasn't much, but if she closed her eyes, she could almost imagine she was a little girl again and sitting in his lap.

The killer could see that the turnout was good when he arrived at the farm. There were so many cars parked around the house that he had to drive toward the barn to find a spot.

"How's this?' he asked, but didn't wait for an okay from his passenger before he got out.

He glanced down toward the barn, remembering he was the one who'd caused all this ruckus, then he locked the car door and joined the others walking toward the house.

Inside, Betsy Jakes was in her element—directing people to the buffet-style setup for food, and to the dining room table for dessert and drinks.

Trina had arrived with the first wave of people from the church, and was keeping food on the tables and ice in the glasses.

Trey mingled his way through the crowd with an eye on Dallas, just in case someone decided to criticize Dick's exit from this world.

Almost all the people from Dick's class had come out to the house and were sitting around sharing even more stories, which kept the energy light, instead of the darkness that came with grief.

When the front door opened again and another wave of friends walked in, Trey saw his mother take them in hand. He smiled. She would have made one hell of an event planner.

It took him a while to notice that Dallas hadn't got a thing to eat but her glass of iced tea was empty. He walked up behind her chair and, when there was a pause in the conversation, leaned down and whispered in her ear.

"I'm getting you a refill of iced tea. Will you let me bring you something to eat?"

She leaned back and looked up, straight into the eyes of love. He'd pretty much announced his intentions to her father at the age of eleven, and she'd still turned her back on the two people who loved her most. What he'd said today had stunned her. She was ashamed and didn't exactly know why, but the unabashed way he had of loving her, knowing full well she wouldn't reciprocate, hurt her heart.

"Yes, maybe I should, but don't bring much, Trey."

"Don't worry, I know what you like," he said, and strode through the crowd on a mission.

I know what you like.

That had never mattered before, but today it felt like a gift she'd been given in the midst of all this pain.

"Dallas, honey. Have you decided what you're going to do with the family farm?"

She turned to see who was asking. It was Georgia Wakefield, her second—or maybe it was her third—cousin once removed.

"I have plans," she said, and left it hanging. She didn't know what the hell she was going to do, but she wasn't going to discuss it here, or with family members she hadn't seen in years.

"It's such a beautiful place," Georgia said. "I remember coming out here with my granny and granddaddy when I was little. I used to play in that big old barn and—"

Her expression froze into a half-assed smile as she realized what she'd just said, but Dallas picked up without missing a beat.

"I did, too. Every spring I climbed into the loft looking for new kittens. The barn cat had a penchant for having babies as high off the ground as she could get. I used to ask Dad why, and he would laugh and say, 'I guess she thinks they'll grow feathers and fly.'"

The ensuing laughter saved Georgia from embarrassment. She mouthed, *I'm sorry*, but Dallas just smiled and shook her head, and the moment passed.

Trey appeared just then, easing things even further. "Here you go, honey. Some of your favorites," he said, and handed her the plate and fork, then presented a paper napkin with a flourish. "For the parts that don't reach your mouth."

"You know me so well," she said.

"I do, don't I?" he said, then touched the crown of her head before walking away. He came back shortly with a new glass of iced tea, set it nearby and left her to it.

She actually ate the small servings that he'd chosen and even enjoyed them as she fielded condolences and listened to more stories about her father's giving ways.

Betsy was in the kitchen when she heard a voice behind her.

"Hey, Bets."

Only one person had ever called her that. She

turned around to see Paul Jackson standing in the doorway, looking at her with a strange expression on his face.

"Hi, Paul. Did you get some food yet?"

Finally he shook his head as he came closer.

"No, I just got here. When I didn't see you at the service, I was afraid you were sick. Then I get here and find out you're running the whole shebang. I should have known."

She smiled. Old boyfriends had their place. Just not at the head of the table.

"Dallas didn't have any family close by, and she's been part of mine for most of her life. It only seemed fitting I handle things for her."

"And you'd be right. You always were thoughtful of others. It's one of the things I admire about you most. Anyway, just wanted to say hi. I'll let you get back to work. I'll grab a bite to eat and go say a few words to Dallas."

He started to walk out and then paused.

"I'm damn sorry you were the one to find him. It's almost like fate wanted someone who mattered to him to do the finding. There's just two of us now. Feels weird, doesn't it?"

Betsy's lips trembled. "It feels wrong," she said.

He gave her another long, studied look, seemed about to say something more, then visibly changed his mind. "Sorry. I didn't mean to make you cry."

"I've been crying off and on for days. The whole thing is just so tragically sad."

Betsy watched Paul leave and then went back to work. She didn't want to think about the past. It was already intruding into her sleep. She didn't want to relive it in the bright light of day, too.

Eight

Marcus Silver saw Paul getting food at the buffet and walked over.

"Thanks for joining us this morning. I think it meant a lot to Dallas to hear all the stories about her dad."

"Good that you thought to get us all together," Paul said.

Before Marcus could answer, his son, T.J., was at his elbow.

"Dad, you have a phone call. Someone's been trying to get in touch with you and finally called me," T.J. said.

"Is there a problem?" Marcus asked.

"No, but—"

"Tell them I'm at a funeral and take a message. Tell them I'll call them tonight."

"Sure thing," T.J. said, and hurried away, heading

outside where it was quieter, so he could pass on the message.

"Nice kid," Paul said, as he watched T.J. politely moving through the crowd.

Marcus beamed. "He's the light of my life. Don't know what I'd do without him."

Paul nodded. "I feel the same way about my son, Mack."

"What's he up to these days?" Marcus asked.

"He owns the lumberyard in Summerton, and he's doing quite well for himself."

"That's great. Any grandchildren?"

Paul shook his head. "No, Mack's not married."

Marcus glanced toward the open front door. He could see his son standing out in the yard, still talking on the phone.

"T.J. shows no signs of settling down, either, but he's young. Listen, I'll leave you to your food. Good to see you."

Paul forgot Marcus almost as soon as he left. The two of them hadn't been close friends in high school and they didn't exactly run in the same social circles now. Still, he seemed like a decent man, and Paul wasn't one for envy.

It was almost four o'clock before the last guests left. Betsy was cleaning out the coffee urns, and Trey was carrying folding chairs back to the basement. Dallas had changed back into blue jeans and a sweatshirt, and was putting tablecloths and dish towels into the washing machine. Trina was, once again, running the dust mop over the hardwood floors.

Dallas came back into the kitchen, grabbed a cold pop from the refrigerator and sat down at the table as Betsy was packing her coffee urn away.

"Betsy, I am so grateful for everything. You know I couldn't have done this without you guys."

"Oh, honey, you're welcome," Betsy said. "It was a wonderful turnout, wasn't it? Said a lot for how much Dick meant to everyone."

"Yes, it did. I heard more stories about him today than I'd heard in my whole life. I have a much bigger picture of what he was like besides being my father."

"Have you heard anything more about the coroner's report from the sheriff?" Trina asked, as she put the dust mop back in the kitchen closet.

"No."

"Are you going to stay a few days, or do you have to go back to work right away?" Trina asked.

"I'm staying until Dad's name is cleared. I can't think beyond that," Dallas said, and then looked up and saw Trey standing in the doorway. The look on his face broke her heart. Once again, he'd been given a deadline to be with her, although she hadn't meant that for his ears.

"I think we've got your house put back together," he said. "I just got another call from Avery. He's going off duty, and Dwight Thomas, the night dispatcher, refuses to be in the same building with a skunk. I have to go see if I can straighten this mess out."

"Wait," Dallas said, and started to get up. "I'll walk you out."

"Don't bother," he said. "I'll call you later to make sure you're safely back inside, and don't do chores without taking your gun."

Betsy gasped. "Gun? What on earth?"

"She'll explain. Duty calls."

He left so fast Dallas knew he was hurt by what she'd said, but she didn't know what to do about it.

"I'm listening," Betsy said, her hands on her hips in a defiant stance.

"Last night something tried to get at the chickens. I went out with Dad's shotgun, thinking it was probably a coyote or a fox, but it was a dog…a really big feral dog. It snuck up on me. I shot and missed but it ran away."

"Oh, dear Lord!" Betsy said, and pointed at Trina. "See! I told you I've been seeing a wild dog in the area. It's from that dogfighting ring they broke up. It has to be."

Dallas pulled the picture of the paw print up on her phone and handed it to Trina.

"That's a picture I took early this morning when I was doing chores."

"Dallas! His paw is wider than your boot."

"Let me see that," Betsy insisted, and then stared at the picture in disbelief. "Honey, a dog that big could kill you. Please be careful, and whatever you do, if you see it again, don't try to hunt it down. You get somewhere safe."

Their concern made Dallas that much more uneasy, but she wouldn't let on.

"I'll be fine," she said. "There's buckshot in Dad's shotgun, and it sprays everywhere. If there's a next time, I won't miss. Now, I'm assuming you had the good sense to take home something to eat. There's no way I want all that food left here."

"There are a couple of dishes in the refrigerator for you, and I put a few containers of leftovers in your deep freeze. They're labeled, so you'll know what's what. I sent food home with some of your more elderly neighbors, and a lot of it home with the Shermans. They have all those kids, you know."

"Thank you. I can't think of a better use for the extra," Dallas said.

Betsy gave her a kiss, and Trina hugged her goodbye. Moments later they were on their way.

Dallas glanced around the yard as they drove away. The sky was cloudy, the air already getting cold. She didn't want to be doing chores after dark and hurried back inside, changed into old shoes and a jacket, and headed out the back door with the gun and her phone.

Even though she was leery the whole time she was working, nothing happened, and she made sure every chicken was safely inside for the night before she headed for the house. The cows would be up in the morning, bawling for hay, but not at night. She was walking up the back steps when she caught a glimpse of lights up on the northernmost side of the mountain. They were there, and then moments later gone, hidden by the trees. She watched for a few moments longer, making sure they didn't come onto her land, which lay in the opposite direction, and when she didn't see them again, she went inside and locked the door behind her. It wasn't until she walked into the kitchen and let the comfort of home envelop her that she realized how territorial she'd felt.

Her land. Her home. Whether she wanted the responsibility or not.

Trey got to the police HQ just in time to see the skunk waddling down an alley between the station and the next building over.

"Hey, I see you got the skunk out," he said, as he walked inside.

Dwight, the night dispatcher, nodded. "Avery did it. He found an app on his phone that played a recording of hounds baying. He turned it on and shoved it under the door next to the cells. Sent old stinky butt flying out the back door so fast it was funny."

Trey grinned. "Brilliant."

Dwight nodded. "I'm sorry about letting it in last night. I never saw it."

"No harm done," Trey said. "But keep a watch next time."

"Have no fear," Dwight said. "Stupid once, to be expected. Stupid twice, shame on me, or something to that effect."

Trey laughed. Dwight was a character in his own

right. "Okay, I'm heading to my apartment. Have a nice night."

"Thanks, Chief. Sleep well," Dwight said.

Trey went back to his truck, grateful to be going home. He was tired and heartsick, and needed some alone time to lick his wounds. Hearing Dallas talking about leaving again, even if it was at some indefinite time, was hard, but nothing he hadn't expected. But once inside the apartment, he was struck by the empty feeling of the place. It had all his stuff: pictures from hunting trips, a couple of trophies from high school, a commendation for rescuing an entire family from a burning car and his diploma from the police academy. It memorialized what he'd done but not who he was. There were no pictures of Dallas left on the walls. He'd taken them down when she hadn't come home from college. Except for his mother and his sister, no other woman had set foot inside his place. He loved a woman who wanted more than he could give her. It was a sad, sad fact.

Trina went to bed early with a headache and a stuffy nose, hoping she could sleep off the beginnings of a cold.

Betsy paced from kitchen to living room and back again until almost midnight, so weary she could barely put one foot in front of the other, but afraid to go to bed and close her eyes. The dreams she'd been having since finding Dick's body were frightening. She kept dreaming of being chased, of being so sick she couldn't stand up. Paul was in the dream, but then he wasn't, and she could see Dick's face. He was screaming, but she could never hear what he was saying.

Finally she gave in to exhaustion, took a hot shower and crawled into bed. It felt so good to slide between those cool, crisp sheets. She grabbed the extra pillow and hugged it close as she shut her eyes. It was almost like having Beau beside her again. The wind outside was rising. She could hear the leaves as they began to rattle. It wouldn't be long before fall came to the mountain. She loved fall. It was her favorite time of year.

"Bets, Bets, please don't cry. I'm sorry that hurt. The next time it won't. I promise."

"Did you see that? He fell. No. Someone pushed him!"

More crying. Head swimming. "I'm going to throw up."

"He saw us! Get in the car! Get in the car!"

"Faster, drive faster!"

"We're gonna die! We're all gonna die!"

A scream, loud and long.

Silence.

The killer lit his pot-laced cigarette and leaned back in his recliner as he took his first puff. He'd been wound so tight all day that it felt like his body was humming, high on his own proximity to Dick Phillips's friends and family. He inhaled and held his breath as long as he could, then exhaled slowly, feeling the love as his body began to relax.

"This is some good shit," he mumbled, and then reached for the remote and turned on the TV. He could hear footsteps in the hall outside the door, but no one would bother him in here.

He took another puff, repeated the process and exhaled with a smile, then proceeded to get higher than a kite all alone.

Dallas rechecked the shotgun, making sure it was loaded before she went to bed, and then crawled between the covers and turned out the lights. She felt a sense of satisfaction, knowing she'd honored her father's memory today, one of the things she'd come home to do. There was still the business of laying his body to rest, but that she would do alone.

But the moment she closed her eyes, Trey's face slid through her mind. She saw him standing up in front of everyone at the church, professing a lifelong love for a girl who didn't want him, saw the pain on his face before he left. She hated the trick fate had played on them, giving soul mates two different paths in life and watching them squirm. Cosmic injustice to the max.

She cried herself to sleep, but despite an expectation of being disturbed in the night, she woke up only minutes before daybreak.

"Oh, Lord," she mumbled as she threw back the covers and got out of bed.

The floor was cold beneath her feet as she went

across the hall to the bathroom. After a quick shower, she dressed and headed to the kitchen for coffee. She drank a cup standing on the back porch, watching daylight come to the land, and wondered how many of her ancestors had stood in this very same place, watching another day dawn.

Had they been ready to welcome the day, happy about a good crop, or had they been worried about the weather and praying for rain? Was a family member ill or dying? Were they as torn as she was, wondering if this life was where they belonged?

She emptied her cup and set it aside, felt her pants pocket to make sure she had her phone, then started down the steps. As she did, the chickens began to cluck and squawk, as if sensing her approach. About five feet from the porch, she remembered the shotgun and ran back to get it.

By the time she got to the coop, the chickens sounded like they were in dire straits.

Dallas smiled as she got the feed and scratch, and then headed into the pen, scattered everything for them, then opened the door to the coop. The hens came out in high indignation, which made her laugh.

"Fuss all you want, ladies. I do the best I can," she said, and began filling up the water troughs. She was getting ready to gather eggs when she saw one hen huddling down beneath the roost. She frowned. It was either hurt or sick. Damn, she didn't want it to die.

"What's wrong here, little lady," she said softly, as she squatted down and reached for her.

The fact that the hen didn't fuss or try to get away made her anxious. It was going to die. She knew it. It clucked when she picked it up, and then she saw the slight tear in the comb and the egg beneath it, and sighed with relief. This was that same broody hen she'd dealt with yesterday.

"Poor little girl," Dallas said. "You want to nest, and no one is paying attention. I can fix that." She got up and opened the door of a small cabinet by the door, took out one of the ceramic nesting eggs her Dad kept, and slipped it into a nesting box and the hen along with it. The hen settled down on the familiar shape with a cluck and pecked Dallas's arm again, stating her disapproval of being moved.

"Ouch, damn it. I'm trying to help." She bent back down to get the egg on the floor of the coop, then gathered up the rest to go with it.

She was halfway to the barn with the shotgun in one hand and the egg basket in the other when she realized the cows weren't waiting in the pen for their ground feed.

She paused to glance out across the pasture but didn't see the herd anywhere. She frowned. This wasn't normal. She hurried on down to the cooler to put up the eggs, and then went out the back side of the breezeway for a closer look, but she still saw nothing. It was early, though, and they would surely come in sometime this morning, so she went ahead and put out the ground feed and hay, then headed back to the house. She was planning what she would do today when she noticed the hens were no longer in the yard.

Out of habit, she looked up at the sky. Sometimes when a hawk was flying over, the hens would run for cover back in the coop, but she didn't see a bird of any kind anywhere. And the moment she thought that, she realized she didn't hear anything, not even the squirrel that wintered in the big oak. The hair stood up on the back of her neck as she swung the shotgun up and started walking. The closer she got to the house, the more nervous she became. It was too damn quiet. She was about to take another step when she caught movement from the corner of her eye, and then the dog was coming toward her, less than two yards to her left.

His size alone stopped her heart. His head was down, and the snarl coming up his throat was all the warning she would get. The barn was too far away, and he was standing between her and the house. She had nowhere to run. It was fight or die.

She fired the first barrel as he leaped, but was a second too slow. He hit her chest high and knocked her flat on her back, the gun still in her hands. Now he was standing over her, straddling her body as she struggled to catch her breath.

The pain of the first bite on her shoulder caught her off guard, but then she remembered the gun in her hands and shoved the side of the barrel against his head as he lunged for her throat, making him miss. He kept lunging and snapping as the pain in her shoulder grew so intense she was afraid she would pass out. She was screaming and jabbing at him, trying to angle the gun for one more try. When he lunged yet again she shoved the gun barrel up as hard as she could push with one hand, ramming it hard against his jaw, then pulled the trigger with the other.

The shot was so loud it hurt her ears. Blood flew. The weight of the dog knocked the air out of her lungs as it collapsed on her chest. The last thing she remembered was the complete absence of sound.

If Hazel Woodley hadn't stumbled over her house cat and dropped the bowl of eggs she was carrying, then Otis wouldn't have been sent back to the Phillips farm for more eggs quite so soon.

Otis was irked with Hazel and cussing George Strait, their house cat, as he drove up to the Phillips place. Almost instantly he saw a huge dog down by the chicken house and quickly drove that way to run it off.

He realized two things upon arrival. First, the dog was dead, and second, Dallas Phillips was lying beneath it, unmoving and covered in blood.

"Lord, Lord, Lord!" he cried as he grabbed a pistol from his glove box and jumped out, scared to death of what he would find.

The dog was missing part of its head and obviously dead. He couldn't tell what shape Dallas was in, only that she was covered in blood.

"Oh Lord, help me, Lord," he kept praying, as he dropped to his knees beside her and felt for a pulse.

When he felt it beating steadily, he went weak with

relief, and even though she was unconscious, he patted her head.

"Hang on, honey! I'll get you some help."

He ran back to the truck, frantically fumbling in the seat for his cell phone to call the police.

Trey was at his desk when he heard a call come in to the dispatcher. The panic he heard in Avery's voice brought him to his feet. He was moving out of his office into the hall when he heard Avery paging the ambulance, and then everything became a nightmare.

All he heard was an ambulance being dispatched to Dick Phillips's farm, something about a bloody woman and a dead dog. Trey couldn't get out of the building fast enough.

He drove hot out of Mystic with the siren screaming in a way he couldn't, and he didn't slow down until he had to make the turn leading down the driveway.

He didn't realize he'd beaten the ambulance there until he saw Otis Woodley's pickup and Otis on his knees. It took Trey a few moments to realize what he was seeing, and then he slid the cruiser to a stop and got out on the run.

Otis looked up at him. He was crying.

"I couldn't move the dog. I couldn't get it off her 'cause I'm too damn old. She keeps coming to and then passing out. I know she's having trouble breathing."

Trey was speechless. There was so much blood on Dallas's face that he couldn't even tell where she was hurt, and he was afraid to drag the dog off for fear of making other wounds worse. And then training kicked in, and he heard a voice in his head.

Don't look at her. Focus on what has to be done.

She needed oxygen? Move the dog.

Trey leaned over, grabbed the dog around the belly and lifted it straight up, then threw it aside.

Otis shook his head in disbelief.

"Lord, Trey. That was amazing."

Almost instantly, Dallas's chest began to heave as she drew much-needed oxygen into her lungs. At the same time, her eyelids began to flutter.

Trey heard an approaching siren. "That's the ambulance," he said.

Otis jumped to his feet and ran to wave them over.

Trey leaned over Dallas's body, one hand on the crown of her head, the other with a finger on her pulse.

Her whole body jerked as she opened her eyes, and then she frantically grabbed at his wrist.

"Trey?"

"Thank you, Jesus," he whispered. "Yes, baby, it's me. The ambulance is here. You're going to be fine. Can you tell me where he bit you?"

"I can't hear you," she said.

Trey blinked. "You're covered in blood."

She saw his lips moving, but still couldn't hear. She touched her ear.

"Are they bleeding? I can't hear."

Trey looked. "I can't tell whose blood is whose," he said.

She shook her head. "He was on top of me. The…

gun was between us. I jammed the barrel against his jaw and fired."

Trey nodded without speaking. The percussion of the shot was what had deafened her. All he could do was hope to God it was temporary.

And then the paramedics were coming toward them, so Trey stood up and stepped back. One of them saw all the blood all over Trey and stopped.

"Are you injured, Chief?"

"No, it's theirs," he said, pointing to Dallas and the dog. "She can't hear you. The gun went off too close to her head."

Otis came up behind him as the paramedics began assessing her condition.

"It's a miracle she's alive," Otis said. "I never saw a dog that big."

Trey eyed the carcass, stunned that Dallas had fought the thing and lived. "It could be a mixed breed, but it looks like a mastiff. It's certainly as big as one. From the look of all the old scars, it's for sure one of the dogs they were fighting. It's no wonder it went feral after they turned it into a killer. Dallas is lucky to be alive."

Reassured she was in good hands, he ran to the house to look for her purse, knowing it would have medical information they might need. When he found it, he went through the house, turning out lights, shutting off the coffeepot, then locking the doors behind him as he left.

* * *

It didn't take long for word of what had happened to sweep through Mystic, and with a few more phone calls, the horror of it spread up and down the mountain, sending panic through the families living there. Women scattered, calling their children in from play, running along the creeks behind their houses in a frantic race to find their teenagers, ringing the bells on their back porches to call in family, all in a panic to be safe should another wild dog appear.

What had happened to Dallas Phillips was the straw that had needed to break. People had been shooting at wild dogs off and on for months, running them off their cattle, losing geese, turkeys and chickens to them, even their hogs right out of the lots.

But once they learned the size of the animal that attacked Dallas, a large group of men headed to the Phillips farm to see for themselves. The monster shocked them. It was all the impetus they needed to act.

One man offered his pickup truck to bring the dead dog to the vet to check for rabies. The rest of the men formed hunting parties on the spot and took off in four different directions from the Phillips farm, determined to eradicate the danger from the mountain.

Nine

Dallas woke as they were moving her from the paramedics' gurney onto an exam table in the ER. The silence in her head was frightening. She could see people scrambling. The horror on their faces was obvious, but she could only imagine how bad she looked. When they began to pull at her clothing, her anxiety grew. She wanted Trey and called his name.

When she didn't see him, her voice rose an octave. "Trey."

A nurse leaned over her, talking.

Dear God, was she going to be deaf forever?

Panic hit her, and the next time she spoke his name she was screaming. "Trey!"

Within seconds he was standing at the foot of the exam table in her line of vision. His clothes were bloody and his expression grim as he grabbed her ankle. Then she read his lips.

I love you.

She hadn't heard his voice, and she couldn't hear her own, but this was not the time to evade the truth.

"I love you, too," she said, watching as quiet joy spread over his face.

Two nurses were cleaning the blood off her face, while another was cutting off her clothes. A doctor she didn't recognize was standing near her elbow. She could see him talking and guessed he was asking her questions. She pointed to her ears and shook her head.

Trey intervened.

"She can't hear," he said. "The gun was between her and the dog. When she pulled the trigger, it went off just above her head."

"Okay, good to know," the doctor said. "As soon as they get her cleaned up, I'll check that out and get some X-rays, as well."

At that point they had all her clothing except her underwear cut away from her body. The bite marks on her shoulder were horrible, but they seemed to be the worst of it.

Trey breathed a little easier.

The doctor leaned down for a closer examination of the wound.

"Good thing she had that jacket on. I think it saved the flesh from much tearing, although there are close to thirty different puncture wounds. We'll clean this up and get her started on some high-powered antibiotics to prevent infection. The dog is dead, correct?"

"Yes," Trey said.

"Get it to a vet to check for rabies."

"I got a phone call a few minutes ago that someone picked it up from the farm and took it straight to the vet for testing."

"Good," the doctor said, and then began examining the rest of her body to make sure there were no other wounds. Then he looked up at the two nurses. "Help me roll her over onto her right side. I want to check for wounds on her back."

Dallas moaned when they rolled her over. "That hurts!" she cried.

"Damn it. Her ribs. I didn't even think. The dog was lying on her," Trey said.

The doctor frowned. "How big a dog are we talking about here?"

"About the size of a mastiff," Trey said.

The medical staff stopped what they were doing and looked up, shocked that a dog of that size had been running wild in their area, and then looked at Dallas, surprised that this woman had brought it down.

The doctor wasn't happy. "Get the portable X-ray in here, stat! We need to make sure moving her didn't puncture a lung."

And just like that, Trey's fear was back, and he didn't breathe easy until he got confirmation that her ribs were only bruised, not broken.

Dallas woke up in pain. It hurt to breathe, and her left shoulder was throbbing. Betsy was sitting in a chair by her bed. She looked around for Trey and saw him blocking the door to her room, and guessed he was arguing with what looked like a news crew. She recognized the cameraman and groaned. That was a crew from WOML Charleston. Damn it to hell, she had become a segment on her own evening news. Watching them argue without being able to hear what they said was an ugly reminder that she was still deaf. She touched her ears, then closed her eyes as tears rolled out from beneath the lids.

Betsy stood up and brushed the hair away from Dallas's forehead as she called to her son, "Trey! She's awake."

Trey shut the door in the news crew's faces and hurried to her bed. The moment his hand cupped her cheek, she opened her eyes and started sobbing.

"Ah, sweetheart…you're breaking my heart," he said softly. "I can't pick you up for fear of hurting your ribs or your shoulder. I know you can't hear me, but you're going to be fine."

"What did the news crew want?" Betsy asked.

"What do you think?" Trey said. "One of their own became news. They want the exclusive. Someone wants to tie it to a story about the dangers of dogfighting. Someone else wants to do a story on her father's death. They're like vultures, picking at people's lives for thirty seconds of news time."

"What did you tell them?"

"That she couldn't do interviews because she can't hear. That the hearing loss is temporary and when she's better she can make the choice for herself. In the meantime, get the hell away from her room."

Dallas came up off the pillow as she grabbed Trey's hand, her tear-filled gaze fixed on his face.

"They were from WOML, weren't they?"

He nodded.

"Don't let them in," she begged.

He gave her a thumbs-up.

"Still my knight in shining armor," she said, as she eased back against the pillow and closed her eyes.

Gregory Standish was about to leave the bank for a Lions Club lunch when he learned what had happened to Dallas Phillips. It suddenly occurred to him how he would be perceived once the bank claimed the Phillips farm in bankruptcy. After the tragedy of Dick's passing, and now Dallas being attacked and mauled by some feral dog, public sympathy would be on her side. He'd been thinking seriously about running for mayor, but that would be a waste of time and money in the circumstances.

"How the hell did my life get so out of whack?" he muttered, and punched his fist into the wall.

When his cell phone rang, he almost didn't answer it, but then he noticed it was from his wife, Gloria, and picked up. "Hello."

"Gregory, it's me, darling. Carly and I are going shopping in Summerton. We won't be back in time to get your dinner, and I wanted you to know so you could pick something up for yourself on your way home."

His heart began to pound.

"Shopping? Carly is still grounded for stealing, or don't you remember? And what the hell are you going to do with more clothes? You both have more now than you'll ever wear, and you're spending more than I make."

"Oh, Gregory, don't be silly. You're president of the bank, and we have a reputation to maintain. You'll figure something out, and Carly said she's sorry. Love you," she said, and disconnected before he could argue.

Rage swept through him so fast he felt the heat on the back of his neck.

"Stupid bitch," he muttered, and set the phone down before he followed through on the impulse to throw it across the room.

The pain meds finally knocked Dallas out. She was asleep, and his mother was getting ready to leave, when Trey was called out to a wreck.

"Mom, will you stay with Dallas until I get back? There's been an accident just inside the city limits. Pickup truck and a school bus. I don't think there are any serious injuries, but I need to be there."

"Of course I'll stay," she said.

Trey left on the run, his mind in cop mode, sorting through who he needed to contact and what had to be done. Wreckers had already been dispatched, and the rest would have to wait until he assessed the scene. He jumped into his police cruiser and drove through town with his usual haste.

The killer watched from the window as a police car sped past. This had certainly been a day for drama. Dallas Phillips had been mauled by some stray dog, and now this, whatever it was.

His cell phone was ringing. He glanced at the caller ID and then turned away. Let it ring. He wasn't in the mood.

When Dallas woke up again it was dark, a nurse was at her bedside, and Trey and Betsy were gone. As soon as the nurse finished taking her blood pressure and temperature, she patted Dallas's arm and gave her a thumbs-up before leaving the room. It appeared word was getting around that she couldn't hear, Dallas thought.

She raised the head of her bed enough to see out the window, and then pushed the hair away from her face. It felt damp. She thought she'd dreamed people were washing her hair, but that must have actually happened. She could only imagine what she must have looked like before, covered in blood and dirt and dog.

She looked up at the dark screen of the television and sighed. She could watch, but it didn't seem worth it, since she couldn't hear. Then she noticed a folded piece of paper with her name on it beneath the corner of the phone and picked it up.

Dallas,
Mom went home. I'm out at your house doing chores. I'll be back soon.
Love you,
Trey

"I love you, too," she said, and then was haunted by the fact that although she'd finally admitted that twice today, she could no longer hear the words.

Was this punishment for turning her back on something as rare as true love? If it was, it hurt her heart too much to think about it now. She needed to focus on something else, like the fact that the farm was going into foreclosure if she didn't step up. As soon as she was able, she would get to the bank and pay off the debt. No matter what she decided, she needed to know that the family home was still secure.

She took a deep breath and closed her eyes, and as she did, she had a vague memory of Otis Woodley hovering over her, praying. She frowned. Why had Otis been praying? Oh. The dog. He couldn't get it off her chest. Thank God he'd come to get eggs. She might still have been lying there if he hadn't. She remembered that Otis had said Dad was coming into money, but so far she'd seen no sign of that being real.

She felt the bed move, and when she opened her eyes, Trey was sitting beside her, his hand on her knee.

"I got your note," she said. "I have to say this, even if I can't hear my own words. I love you, too, but then you've always known that."

Trey's eyes darkened with emotion—then he touched her shoulder and chest, as if asking how she felt.

"Throbbing and sore, but nothing unbearable." She touched her ear. "What about my ears?"

He pulled a pen and paper out of his jacket pocket and began to write, then handed it to her: "Doctor said no damage to your inner ears. Your hearing should return, but there's no way to say when."

"Thank God," she said.

He nodded.

"Can I go home?" she asked.

"Tomorrow. I'll take you," Trey wrote.

"Good. I just want to be home."

He wrote on the paper and handed it back: "I'm staying with you. Don't argue. Just until you can use your arm okay. I won't attack you, but I might stalk you."

She laughed out loud, and then felt like weeping. She couldn't hear her own laughter.

Trey grinned, unaware of her inner turmoil.

He took the pad and wrote again, then handed it back: "The food is less than tasty here. What do you want for supper?"

She remembered Trey bringing her food at the funeral. *I know what you like*, he'd said.

"You know what I like. Surprise me."

Trey's gaze locked on her face. He got up, then leaned down and kissed her. The kiss was long and hungry, and when he pulled back, he made no apology.

Instead, he tapped his watch, indicating he'd be back soon, and walked out without looking back.

Dallas was trying to process the fact that earlier today she'd been certain she was going to die, and just now, with only one kiss, it felt good to be alive. She touched her lips to see if they were as hot as she felt, then winced as the movement pulled the wounds on her shoulder.

Trey wheeled into the graveled parking lot of Charlie's Burgers and got out. As he was walking toward the café he noticed an out-of-state tag on a dirty black SUV. It was low to the ground, as if there were a heavy load in the back, but when he looked in the rear window, all he saw was a suitcase and a wadded-up blanket. On instinct, he went back to his patrol car and ran the tag. It came back belonging to a man named David Judd, aka Mutt, who had four outstanding warrants. Two were federal warrants for intent to distribute drugs, and the other two were for assault with a deadly weapon. As a bonus, the report came with a mug shot.

He made a quick call to dispatch for backup, specifying that it should come silent. Within a couple of minutes Earl Redd showed up, and Lonnie Doyle was right behind him.

"What's up, Chief?" Earl said.

"The guy driving that black SUV has four outstanding warrants on him. Two are federal for intent to distribute, and two are for assault with a deadly weapon, so consider him armed and dangerous. I don't know if he's alone, but we know what he looks like." He pulled the mug shot up on the screen but didn't bother with a printout. "Lonnie, you go inside and order two burgers with everything, and a large order of fries to go."

Lonnie grinned. "Seriously?"

"Seriously," Trey said. "That's supper for me and Dallas. I think when he sees your uniform he'll make a point of exiting as quickly as possible. We'll take him down outside."

"Mustard or mayo?" Lonnie asked.

Trey grinned. "Mustard only, no ketchup on either one. Now hurry up. I want to get this over with. I have a bedside dinner date I don't want to miss."

Lonnie opened the door wide, letting it swing shut behind him as he strode into the café. The only stranger in the place looked up and then froze as Lonnie teased a waitress nearby before going up to the counter to place his order.

"Hey, Charlie, I need two burgers with mustard, no ketchup, and everything else on them, plus a large order of fries, and would you make it to go?"

"You got it," Charlie said, as he slid a plate of food onto the pickup window. "Order up!" he yelled.

Lonnie slid onto a stool at the front counter to wait for his order, then glanced over his shoulder just as the stranger left his table and headed for the door. An elderly couple was about to get up from the booth where they'd been sitting, and the moment the stranger walked outside, Lonnie bolted past them.

"Stay inside!" he said quickly, and ran.

Trey was standing beside the door, and the minute the man came out, he grabbed his wrist, twisted his arm behind his back and pushed him up against the building to handcuff him, then began to pat him down. He pulled a knife out of the man's boot and a gun from underneath the back of his shirt.

"What the hell's goin' on?" the man yelled.

"What's your name?" Trey asked.

"David Judd. Come on, Officer. What did I do, park in the wrong spot?"

Trey read him his rights, loaded him up into the cruiser and then handed Lonnie twenty dollars.

"Do you mind picking up that order for me and bringing it to the precinct? I don't want it stone-cold before I get it to Dallas."

"Since this means you get the paperwork, I'm happy to help," Lonnie said, and took the money.

Trey radioed dispatch as he headed to jail with the pissed-off prisoner cursing him soundly.

"Hey, Dwight, fluff the towels and turn back the bed. I'm bringing you a guest. And make sure we don't have any skunks in there tonight, okay?" Trey said.

Judd choked on a "damn it to hell, motherfucker" and gasped. "Skunk? What's up with that? You can't put me in no stinky cell. I got rights."

"I already read you your rights," Trey said. "Did

you hear me say I was going to put you in with a skunk?"

"No, but—"

Trey turned on the siren just for the hell of it and drowned out the sound of his prisoner's wrath.

By the time he had Judd processed and locked in a cell, he was sure the burgers were going to be cold. He notified the proper authorities about the arrest and was hanging up the phone when Lonnie came into his office.

"Hot off the grill. Should still be warm by the time you get to the hospital," Lonnie said, and handed him the sackful of food.

Trey felt the bottom of the bag.

"How did you keep it hot?"

"Oh, I ate the first order while waiting on this one for you."

Trey grinned. "Thanks, Lonnie. I owe you. The prisoner's in lockup. He doesn't need supper. Call if you need me. I'll be at the hospital with Dallas."

"You got it." Then Lonnie added, "She's one tough lady."

"Yes, she is," Trey said, and headed for his car.

Dallas was just beginning to worry when Trey finally came back. He had a sack in one hand and two cans of pop from the machine in the waiting room.

She sniffed. "Burgers from Charlie's?"

He nodded.

"And fries?"

Another nod.

"Oh, wow," she said, then grabbed the bed control and moved herself to a sitting position.

Trey pushed the tray table across her lap and started unloading their food. He tucked a paper napkin in the neck of her hospital gown and then popped the top on a Coke.

"We share the fries, right?" Dallas asked.

He nodded.

"This must make you crazy, having to figure out how to answer me. I'm sorry I can't hear you," she said.

He frowned, pulled the pad and pen out of his jacket, and wrote quickly: "I went crazy when I thought you were dead. Eat your fries or I will."

She sighed. "Okay. Point taken." She put a French fry in her mouth, chewing slowly to savor the salt and grease. It wasn't anywhere near healthy, but it tasted wonderful.

Trey watched, and when she tried to pick up the burger with one hand and it began to fall apart, he wrapped the paper tightly around the bottom half and handed it to her again, then smiled with satisfaction when she began to eat.

Even though it was the first meal they'd shared in six years, being together felt so natural that the gap didn't register.

Dallas watched Trey plowing through his burger and stifled a smile. He ate like a man who'd had too many meals interrupted to waste time, which made her think about his job. She wanted to talk, but the conversation would be stilted, considering he had to write down all his answers. Still, the curiosity of an investigative reporter made her try.

"Do you like being the chief of police?" she asked.

He thought about the arrest they'd just made and nodded.

"Do you love it?" she added.

He grabbed the pen and paper: "It makes me feel good to know I help keep Mystic safe."

She read it, then handed back the pad.

"You were always good at taking care of people," she said.

He wrote again: "It's easy when they matter. Do you like your job?"

"Yes."

"Do you love your job?" he asked on the notepad.

She read it and frowned. "Most of the time."

"What don't you like?"

"It's nearly all sad or bad. We don't do nearly enough feel-good stories, or at least *I* don't get to do them. I'm not perky enough."

He laughed.

She wished to God she could hear it. The thought of never hearing Trey's voice again made her sick.

"Did the doctor really say my ears weren't permanently damaged?"

He nodded vehemently, and wrote: "Have I ever lied to you?"

Her eyes welled. "No."

"Okay, then."

She reached for her Coke and then winced as the muscles pulled across her belly.

He immediately pushed the can closer.

"Thank you, Trey."

He winked.

"I'm sure glad you thought to do this. Charlie makes the best burgers, but you were gone so long I was beginning to worry."

He took the pad and wrote again: "Had to make an arrest and process the perp. Outstanding warrants, etc."

"Really? Where did that happen?"

He grinned and pointed at her burger.

"You arrested a bad guy at Charlie's?"

He nodded.

"Was it a local?"

He shook his head.

"Then how did you know someone eating at Charlie's was a criminal?"

He focused on the notepad: "Out-of-state tag, altered SUV for running drugs. Ran the tag. Owner came up with outstanding warrants. Me, Lonnie and Earl took him down without a fuss. Put him in the skunk cell."

Dallas burst out laughing, then handed him the rest of her burger. "Here. You deserve this more than me."

He downed it in a few bites, then cleaned up all the trash and tossed it in the wastebasket. When he pulled a Hershey bar out of his pocket, her heart skipped a beat. She glanced up at him and noticed he was watching to see her reaction.

When she stayed silent he took it as permission, and unwrapped the candy bar and broke it in half. When it came apart, he heard her sigh.

Then he took one half and began to break apart all the tiny blocks of chocolate, stacking them individually, one on top of the other. He pushed the pile toward her, then went through the same process with his half.

Together, they took the top blocks from their stacks and put them into their mouths, and the moment the chocolate began to melt on Dallas's tongue, her hands began to shake. They'd done this together for as long as she could remember. She couldn't look at him without crying.

They ate the chocolate, one small block at a time, in unison, and when they were down to the last one apiece, Trey kissed his block and held it to her mouth.

Her heart was pounding. This ritual was taking them down a path that had got overgrown in the intervening years, but maybe it was time to walk it again.

She picked up her last piece of chocolate, kissed it, and then held it to his lips.

They opened their mouths at the same time and in went the candy, then Trey leaned forward until his lips were only inches from hers.

Dallas hesitated briefly, then moved just enough for their lips to meet.

Chocolate was on their lips and sex was on their

minds, because the next step after the kiss was when they stripped.

She moaned.

Trey heard her and pulled back, took the pad and wrote one last line: “Hold that thought.”

Ten

Trey dozed in the chair by her bed, but every time he heard her moan or shift position, he was awake. The room was quiet, although not the corridor outside her door. Voices waxed and waned as people walked up and down the hall, and every so often he heard a flurry of activity and knew someone in another room was in crisis.

Dallas wasn't sleeping well, either. He knew when she was dreaming because she would clench her jaw, or she would start crying in her sleep.

Once a nurse came in and injected antibiotics and pain meds into her IV, and another time Dallas woke up and needed to go to the bathroom. Trey rang for the nurse and then stepped out in the hall to give them privacy, taking the time to check in at the station.

Dwight answered the call. "Mystic Police Department."

"Dwight, it's me. Is everything okay?"

"Yes, sir, all except for crybaby back in the skunk cell. He swears he can smell skunk, even though I told him the thing never let loose, so I sprayed the air with Piney Woods Fresh. He wanted to make a phone call, but I reminded him he'd already had his call. He wanted to eat, but I reminded him he got arrested coming out of a restaurant, so I asked him if he wanted me to sing him to sleep. His reply was unrepeatable."

Trey chuckled. Dwight was a character, but smart as they came. Mutt Judd was mistaking a Southern drawl for ignorance, while he was the stupid one who'd fucked up his life.

"Feds are coming to pick him up, supposedly sometime tomorrow afternoon," Trey said. "Tell Earl the paperwork is ready."

"Yes, sir, I will," Dwight said. "How's Dallas?"

"Hurting. Scared. She still can't hear."

"You tell her my daddy had the same thing happen to him during the war in Vietnam. A shell exploded over his head. He couldn't hear shit for a couple of days, but his hearing came back fine."

"I'll do that. It will make her feel better. Call if you need me. I have to get back."

"Yes, sir."

Trey broke the connection, and then glanced at the time. Just after 3:00 a.m. Tomorrow—today—was his day off, but he'd taken time off for the funeral, so he would be in and out of the office anyway. He needed to pack a suitcase to take out to the farm, but he could do that after he got Dallas home and settled.

There was so much they needed to know: the results of the autopsy and the rabies test on the dog, who the hell had killed Dick Phillips, and were other people in danger? Until they knew why Dick had been murdered, they wouldn't have a clue about that last answer.

"You can go back, Chief," the nurse said, as she came out of Dallas's room.

"Thanks," he said, and when he walked in, Dallas was awake and waiting for him.

"I wasn't sure you'd still be here when I woke up before," she said.

He rolled his eyes, as if to tell her that was a stupid thing to think, and then pointed to her shoulder and frowned.

"Yes, it was hurting, but it's easing up."

He nodded, then mimed going to sleep and turned out the lights. He heard her sigh as she tried to find a comfortable position, then stood and watched until her eyes were closed and her breathing was steady.

There was a knot in his belly that had been there for years and an ache in his heart so familiar he'd forgotten what true joy even felt like. He had given up believing he would have a second chance, and now here she was, asleep in a bed right in front of him. And she'd said she loved him.

Damn it! Damn it all to hell! What the fuck good was that going to do him if she walked out on him again? Well, if she tried, she was in for a surprise and just didn't know it yet.

"I know you can't hear me, and maybe that's for the

best because I think you would argue. But I'm giving you fair warning. I stood back the first time and let you go because I loved you enough to put your happiness first. But I'm older and wiser now, and I am going to pull out every cheap trick I know to keep you. I'll make love to you until you beg me to stop, and then you'll cry when I quit. I swear to God, Dallas Ann, before I'm through, you won't want me out of your sight. I am going to ruin you for ever wanting another man."

She sighed.

Tears burned the back of his throat as the years of pain he'd been living with, ignoring, rejecting, finally boiled up and over.

"You heard me, woman. Your ears didn't, but your heart did. Now sleep on that, damn it."

The hunters who'd gone looking for the feral dogs were gone all night. It wasn't the first time they'd hunted after sundown. They knew the woods like the backs of their hands, and they knew dogs. It was most likely that the dogs would hunt at night, too, and they were right.

They trailed the pack by the sounds it made, the barking and yipping, the frantic screams of their prey in its death throes. They knew when they finally ran the dogs down that they were part of the fighting ring. The animals' bodies were mapped by thick, ropy scars. Some were missing parts of ears; others were running on broken legs that had healed wrong. All of them were deadly animals ruined by the people who'd owned them.

By the time all four hunting parties checked back in at daybreak, they had accounted for nine dogs, six of which had charged them just like the dog that had attacked Dallas. Killing them had been a grisly task, but one they considered a necessity. Removing the hazard of the pack would keep their families safe.

To a man, they all agreed that the real criminals were the people who'd turned the dogs into killers, but there was no way to rehabilitate such severely abused animals that had been taught the only way to survive another day was to kill.

There was a feeling of relief on the mountain once word spread, although they weren't letting down their guard. They didn't have a head count to begin with, so there was no way to be certain if all the dogs were gone. If there were more, they hoped they had put them on the run.

Otis Woodley called Trey early the next morning and told him that he'd done the chores and set the eggs in the cooler for someone to deal with later.

Trey was glad that task was over until evening. He needed to get Dallas home and then head into the station before the Feds came to pick up his prisoner. He'd asked his mom to stay with her until he got back, but he didn't want to impose on her for too long, and he still needed to pack a suitcase to take to the farm. There was a lot to do, but he was a man on a mission.

* * *

Dallas was going home wearing the bottom half of a pair of scrubs and a hospital gown as a shirt, because she couldn't raise her arms high enough to get the scrub shirt over her head. A nurse had helped comb the tangles out of her hair, so she no longer looked as bad as she felt. She had her purse in her lap and her shoes on the floor ready to slip on, and was just waiting for her ride home.

The door to her room was open. She watched nurses scurrying up and down the halls and people walking past on their way to visit family, and thought how strange they all looked without any sound. She was still watching the parade when someone carrying a big pot of dark red chrysanthemums walked into view, and then she saw the face above it and groaned.

Mark Dodson, the face of the evening news on WOML Charleston, came into her room with a big smile, talking as he went.

"They said you were okay, but I had to come see for myself," Mark said. He set the flowers down with a flourish, then turned and grasped Dallas's hand. "So sorry about your father. This has turned into quite a trip home, hasn't it? When are you coming back? We miss you!"

Dallas watched his face, waiting for him to pause for a breath, and when he did, she pulled her hand away and gave him the news.

"Thank you for the flowers, but didn't they tell you I can't hear?"

His eyebrows knitted. "Not even a bit?"

She rolled her eyes. "Mark! I see your mouth moving, but what part of 'I can't hear you' don't you understand?"

He gasped. "But I thought… I guess I—"

Dallas sighed. He was still talking. She knew he was a bit dense behind the pretty face, but this was ridiculous.

"Tell everyone I said hello. I'm still on leave, but I'll let the boss know what's going on as soon as I figure stuff out."

Mark reached for her hand again just as Trey walked into the room.

Trey saw the flowers, the suit and the pretty face, then Dallas's frustration.

"Hey!" he said, as he headed for the bed.

Mark Dodson flinched. He saw the badge first and then the man wearing it, and was trying to figure out if the visit was business or pleasure when Trey sailed past him, leaned over and kissed Dallas on the lips, then turned around and gave him a go-to-hell look.

Mark bristled. "I work with Dallas. I just came to check on her."

"I would have thought the news crew I ran off this morning had already filled you in. She will give a statement when she is able."

Mark blinked. "And you're a local cop?"

"Chief of police, actually."

"Are you here for her in an official capacity?" Mark asked.

Trey smiled for Dallas's sake, but when he spoke, the tone of his voice could only be called challenging. "Dallas Phillips is officially mine and has been since the age of six. Wave goodbye and leave her alone."

Mark heard the warning loud and clear.

Dallas knew Trey far too well to think the two men were just having a polite chat. She could tell by the shock on Mark "I'm the hot stuff" Dodson's face that he might have just met his match.

"Trey, what's going on?" she asked.

Trey whipped out his pad and pen and quickly wrote: "Your friend is just leaving and says he'll be in touch."

He shoved the note in Mark's face long enough for him to read it, then smiled and handed it to Dallas.

She read it, then looked at Mark.

"Oh! Well, thank you again for the flowers, Mark. Have a safe trip back to Charleston."

"Sure, no problem. We look forward to seeing you back home," he said, and then glared at Trey.

Trey grinned. "She's already home, and she still can't hear you."

Mark Dodson left Mystic with far less optimism than when he'd arrived. He knew all about the film crew getting the boot and had envisioned himself as the one to get the scoop on the near scandal surrounding one of WOML's top on-the-scene faces. Not only had he failed, but he now knew why Dallas Phillips had always been romantically unavailable.

* * *

When Trey drove into the front yard, the release of tension Dallas felt was physical. Even though this was where she'd nearly lost her life, it was also the place where she would heal.

"It feels so good to be home," she said.

Trey patted her knee and motioned for her to wait, then circled the cruiser and helped her out. The sky was clear even though there was a nip in the air. When he glanced down at her, it was obvious she was exhausted and in pain. He'd feared the ride home would be tough, and it obviously had been.

He slid an arm around her waist and gently pulled her close, urging her to lean on him for support as they went into the house.

The house smelled faintly of cold coffee. Dallas remembered she'd made a pot just before going out yesterday morning to do the chores. Everything looked the same—her Dad's recliner sitting at the perfect angle to watch TV, the quilted throw draped over the arm of the sofa, her parents' wedding picture hanging over the mantel.

Home.

"I'm going to change clothes. I'll be back soon," she said, and headed down the hall.

Trey started to ask if she needed any help and then remembered she couldn't hear him, so he went into the kitchen, rinsed out the coffeepot and set a fresh pot to brewing, then looked in the refrigerator to see what might be lacking that he needed to bring back later.

He made a mental list of what to buy, then stepped out onto the back porch.

The place looked idyllic, the beautiful old farmhouse with porches running the length of both the front and back, good grass on clean pastureland with a small herd of cattle in the distance, and just for a little visual drama, the mountain in the background. The chickens were clucking and pecking, with an occasional squawk coming from inside the coop. He could hear a squirrel scolding in one of the trees down by the barnyard, and birds were chirping all around.

He thought about what it had looked like yesterday, and how close he'd come to losing her, and could hardly breathe for the emotion that surged through him.

He felt a hand at his back, and then Dallas was standing beside him wearing gray sweatpants and what looked like one of her father's long-sleeved, button-up-the-front plaid work shirts.

"I need help," she said, holding up a pair of tube socks.

Instead of taking the socks, he cupped her face and moved closer, then closer still. And when he could see his reflection in her eyes, he kissed her as if it were the first time, tentatively, with so much restraint he thought he would die from want.

The moment he touched her, Dallas lost the ability to think for herself. She'd been emotionally barren without him, and now that he was back in her life, however long it lasted, she awaited his pleasure. Whatever he wanted from her, all he had to do was take it.

His lips were warm, his jacket smelled like cold air and leather, and she remembered what it felt like to be naked beneath him. How had she walked away from this? What the hell had she been thinking?

When his hands moved from her face to her backside and pulled her close against his groin, against his rock-hard erection, she groaned.

Trey heard the groan and took it for what it was—pure, unadulterated need. Exactly what he had been waiting for. He broke the kiss and pulled back, then held out his hand for the socks.

She shuddered.

Why did he stop? What the hell just happened?

He took the socks, then led her back into the house, shutting the cold air out, and set her down in a kitchen chair.

When he knelt at her feet, for one crazy moment she imagined this was how it would be if he proposed, but he only picked up one foot and put on the sock, then did the same to the other one, before he got up and winked as he walked away.

She watched as he took out two coffee cups and then realized he'd made fresh coffee. They were going to drink coffee *now*? *Really?* Her body was wound so tight it was humming, and he wanted caffeine?

Lord, have mercy, turn me off before I explode.

Trey saw desire and confusion in her eyes. Bingo.

And then he heard a car coming up the drive and guessed it was his mother.

He took the pad out of his pocket and wrote: "Mom's here. She'll stay with you until I get back. Rest if you can. I won't be gone long."

Dallas's shoulder was throbbing, and she was desperately trying to stop thinking about being naked with him, as if it were a thought his mother would be able to read.

"Do I have any pain pills?" she asked.

He hurried out of the kitchen, retrieved her purse from the living room and then jogged back and handed it to her before letting his mom in the house.

Betsy came in smiling, carrying a small stew pot. "I made vegetable beef soup."

"Sounds good. She'll enjoy that. Thanks a million for doing this," he said.

"Honey, I'm happy to help. I brought a pad and pen like you suggested. What do I need to do first?"

"She needs to take a pain pill, and I need to get back to the station. I have a prisoner due to be picked up today," he said, as he led the way back to the kitchen.

Betsy smiled at Dallas as she set the stew pot on the stove.

Trey went back to the table, leaned over and kissed her, then mouthed the words *love you*.

Dallas nodded and tried not to stare as she watched him walk out of the room with that long-legged swagger, but he was sexy as hell and she might be in serious trouble here. He'd said he wouldn't attack her, but she hadn't promised him anything. She was suddenly curious as to how shacking up with him, however temporary, was going to go. All she needed was to get better.

It was after 2:00 p.m. when David, aka Mutt Judd, left their fine city handcuffed in the back of a government-issue vehicle and escorted by two agents from the FBI, and he'd gotten a phone call from the Health Department about the rabies test on the dog. It was clean. Dallas was in the clear.

Trey turned the paperwork over to Earl and headed for his apartment to get some clothes. He was pulling into the parking lot when his cell phone rang. It was the county sheriff's office.

"Hello?"

"Chief Jakes, this is Sheriff Osmond. Do you have a minute?"

"Yes," Trey said, and pulled into a parking space and killed the engine. "What's up?"

"I have news that will corroborate Miss Phillips's belief that her father's death was not a suicide."

"The coroner verified the injured shoulder?" Trey asked.

"Not yet. He just x-rayed the body before beginning the autopsy. Both of Dick Phillips's ankles were broken, and in the same fashion."

"What do you mean?"

"The breaks weren't horizontal. The bones were literally pulled downward out of their sockets."

Trey envisioned the body as he'd seen it, and all of a sudden, it hit him.

"Oh, my God. The killer hung him, and when it didn't immediately break his neck—"

Osmond finished the statement.

"He grabbed his legs and gave them one hell of a pull. No way could Dick Phillips have broken his ankles and then hanged himself. He was already hanging when the breaks happened. I have officially opened a murder investigation. If you would pass the message on to Miss Phillips, it would be appreciated."

"I'll be happy to do that. This is good news for her, being able to clear her father's name. Oh…did she tell you that her father also told Otis Woodley he was coming into big money?"

"No."

"Well, he did, and I'm wondering if that could have had something to do with his death."

"I'll add that info to the file. Now all I need to do is figure out who had a grudge against him, or some other motive, and go from there," Osmond said. "I'll be in touch."

Trey disconnected, then slapped the steering wheel in silent jubilation. Finally some good news.

He packed quickly, then picked up his mail and took it with him as he drove out of town, anxious to get back to Dallas.

Once the pain pill kicked in, Dallas felt antsy just sitting around. She could watch TV, but she still wouldn't be able to hear it, and her dad's set was old enough that she didn't know how to activate the closed-captioning. She finally talked Betsy into going with her to the barn to clean and sort the eggs Otis had gathered. At first Betsy objected, saying Dallas needed to be resting. But once Dallas convinced her, with some amusement, that dog bites on her shoulder and bruised ribs did not impact the movement of her feet, they set out with Dallas talking, and Betsy carrying the pad and pen.

When they approached the chicken coop and Dallas saw the darker, blood-soaked earth where the dog had attacked, she walked around it without comment. Once inside the egg room, she directed Betsy to get the basket of eggs out of the cooler, and then she began cleaning and sorting them with Dallas's input. By the time they were finished, Dallas had three dozen fresh eggs to add to the cooler, with a couple left over to go into the next carton. Betsy dated the cartons and then set them to the back of the cooler.

"And that's the egg business. Guaranteed to make you rich in no time," Dallas said, as they walked out into the breezeway.

Betsy giggled, then wrote: "Money isn't everything."

"Agreed," Dallas said. "But it can make life easier."

Betsy wrote: "You can't take it with you, and it won't make you happier."

Dallas nodded, and that ended the money conversation, although she was still puzzled about her father's claim to be coming into big money soon. Now that the stress of the memorial service was over, she decided to go back through the house again, this time looking for any clue to what he'd been talking about, although it had already occurred to her that the expected windfall could have been what got him killed.

Once they got back to the house, Betsy heated up the soup and got one of the pies from the memorial service out of the freezer for dessert and put it in the oven.

Dallas watched Betsy moving about the kitchen as if it were her own, seeing bits of Trey in the way Betsy's head tilted when she was listening and her calm demeanor as she worked.

"The soup smells good," Dallas said.

Betsy gave her a thumbs-up and a nod, and began dishing it up as Dallas got crackers out of the pantry and silverware from the drawer.

When they finally sat down and Dallas took her first spoonful, she groaned with delight.

"This is sooo good. You'll have to teach me how to make this sometime. I love vegetable beef soup."

Betsy nodded and smiled, hoping that meant Dallas wasn't leaving again.

When Dallas's phone began to ring inside her purse, Betsy jumped up and dug it out, then handed it to her. Dallas glanced at the caller ID and frowned. It was her boss.

"I don't know what's wrong with the people at WOML, but what part of 'I can't hear anything' don't they understand? How does he think I can take this call?"

Betsy wrote: "Text him back and remind him."

Dallas rolled her eyes. "Yes, of course. I'm so anxious for my hearing to return that I didn't think of the obvious."

She quickly texted him a series of terse sentences.

Don't call. Text! I can't hear. Remember? I'm not coming back anytime soon. I can't hear. I can't hear. I can't fucking hear.

A few moments later a text popped up.

Sorry. My bad. I'll put someone else on it.

The fact that he was about to give someone else what would have been her assignment didn't bother her nearly as much as it would have a week ago. The events of the past few days had quickly put life into perspective.

Eleven

Trey came in the front door with his suitcase and a giant bouquet of red roses.

Dallas knew Mark Dodson's appearance at the hospital had irked him, and now she had proof. His bouquet of roses was far bigger than Mark's potted mum. She stifled a grin. A case of "mine is bigger than yours" syndrome.

Betsy gasped when she saw them. "Oh, Trey. They're beautiful! I'll put them in water for Dallas," she said, admiring them as she left.

Trey dropped the suitcase by the sofa, took something out of his pocket and leaned down to kiss Dallas hello.

She closed her eyes, expecting that hard, sexy mouth on her lips. She got a kiss, but it was chocolate, a Hershey's Kiss to be exact.

She blinked.

He dropped another little foil-wrapped candy in

her lap, along with a note: "Another kiss from me for when you're lonely."

She didn't know whether to be enchanted or irked.

"Thank you," she said, and set the extra one on the table beside her elbow.

He held up a finger to indicate he would be right back and took his suitcase to the room he would be using. He'd already decided to sleep in the extra bedroom. Dick's bedroom still belonged to Dallas. She would have to go through his things at her leisure, when her shoulder was better.

The bedspread in the guest room was bright yellow and a little too cheery. The color wouldn't have been his first choice, but it wouldn't damage his masculinity or his sleep. The curtains were sheers, more for effect than for privacy, but the venetian blinds would suffice. He unpacked his clothes, then returned to his cruiser and came back with an armful of clothes on hangers, waving at Dallas as he passed.

He could tell she was intrigued. And the second piece of candy was gone, which made him grin. She'd always said the next best thing to sex was chocolate. He'd already introduced the notion of renewing their sexual relationship, but so far she'd had to settle for the next best thing.

He changed out of his uniform and then hurried back just as Betsy set the flowers on a table where Dallas could see them.

"Mom, thanks for staying," he said.

"It was my pleasure. Call me anytime you need help."

"You're the best," he said, and gave her a quick kiss on the forehead.

Betsy was beaming as she gathered up the empty stew pot and the rest of her things.

"I'll walk you out," he said. "There's something I need to tell you."

"Thank you for coming, Betsy!" Dallas said, as Trey and his mother headed for her car.

"What's going on?" Betsy asked, as she put her things in the backseat.

"Sheriff Osmond called me. I still have to tell Dallas, and I'm only telling you this because you found his body, so keep it to yourself until you begin to hear it on the streets."

"You're scaring me," Betsy said.

"Dick did not commit suicide. He was murdered."

Betsy moaned, then leaned back against her car and covered her face.

"Oh, my God. How do they know? Was it the shoulder injury? Dallas told me what Otis Woodley said about that."

"No. The coroner x-rayed the body before beginning the autopsy. Both of Dick's ankles were broken. He wouldn't have been able to even stand up, let alone hang himself."

"Should we be afraid?"

He gave her a quick hug. "I don't know what to tell you. Right now there's no motive and there are no suspects. I need to get back inside, though. Drive safe going home, okay?"

"I will," she said, and drove away as Trey returned to the house.

Dallas was in the kitchen, so he ran down the hall to get his laptop, returning as she was settling back down onto the sofa with a cold drink.

"Your mom made sweet tea if you want some," she said.

He nodded, then sat down beside her and powered up the laptop.

"What's going on?" she asked.

He began to type: "We need to talk. I have good news. The dog that attacked you did not have rabies."

"Thank God," Dallas said.

He continued to type: "There's more."

Sensing a certain tone, she asked, "What's wrong?"

"Sheriff Osmond called me. They've officially ruled your father's death a murder."

Dallas gasped.

"Was it the shoulder injury? I didn't know they'd done the autopsy."

"No autopsy yet," he wrote. "Coroner x-rayed body first. Both your dad's ankles were broken. No way would he have been able to stand up, let alone hang himself."

Dallas's eyes went wide with shock, and when she spoke, her voice began to shake.

"I don't understand. Why would someone break

his ankles? Were any of his other bones broken? Was he beaten?"

Trey sighed. Now it was a case of how much to tell her and how much to let her figure out for herself.

"Coroner said it was consistent with a sharp jerk from below."

He could almost see the wheels turning in her head as she went through the process of how that could have happened, and he knew when she figured it out, because her face lost all expression.

She went limp and sagged back against the sofa, her voice completely emotionless as she said, "He didn't die fast enough. The killer grabbed him by the ankles to break his neck."

"Probably." Trey tapped the keyboard.

"My poor daddy," she whispered, and covered her face.

He put the laptop on her knees. "I'm so sorry, baby. I'm so sorry."

She read the last line, then leaned against his shoulder and once again began to weep.

Trey moved the computer onto the coffee table and gently scooted her into his lap. Long after the shock had passed and the tears were gone, she lay sleeping in his arms. He hated to wake her, but he had to begin the evening chores, so he cradled her in his arms and kissed her awake.

Dallas opened her eyes, blinking slowly as she realized where she was and wondered why she was in his lap. And then she remembered.

"That wasn't a dream, was it?" she asked.

He shook his head.

"Is this nightmare ever going to end?"

He opened up the laptop. "We'll figure it out, honey. Just give it time," he wrote, then added, "I'm going to do chores. I won't be long."

"Okay. I'll clean and sort the eggs tomorrow."

He nodded, then closed the laptop and kissed her forehead before heading out the back door.

Dallas sat motionless, staring out the front windows, but her thoughts were churning. Her father had been murdered. According to Otis, he'd expected to come into a lot of money. Where would it come from? What was he doing that she hadn't known about?

The only thing on the whole farm that seemed out of place were all the large plastic storage bins in the cooler at the barn.

Frustrated, she went to the kitchen and began poking around, looking for inspiration for supper. Without knowing what he'd had at noon, she didn't have any idea how hungry he was. She had been satisfied with Betsy's soup, and there was some left, but not enough for two.

A few minutes later Trey came in the back door carrying a carton of eggs.

"Supper?" she asked.

He nodded.

"Sounds good. I'll make a fresh pot of coffee."

When he frowned, she waved away the objection.

"I have to start using my arm some or the muscles will get worse, not better."

She didn't wait to see his reaction. She didn't need ears to make coffee.

An hour later the omelets had been eaten and the dishes were in the dishwasher. Trey took a phone call from the dispatcher that had him making a quick trip into Mystic, leaving Dallas on her own. He'd been gone for a good half hour when she thought to check her cell phone for text messages.

She had two, both from friends at the station wishing her well, and two missed calls, also from friends at the station who either hadn't heard the word about her latest injury or were as oblivious as their boss. She sent texts back to all of them and put the phone on the charger. She was done with all that for the night.

She thought about the evenings she and her dad used to spend out on the back porch, watching night come to the land, and had a sudden urge to revisit that. She grabbed the throw from the sofa and carried it out the back door, then put it around her shoulders as she sat down in the swing.

If it had been summer, there would have been fireflies by now. She might have heard one of the calves calling for its mama, or hunters up on the mountain with their hounds. She looked, but she didn't see any lights.

The longer she sat, the more frightening the silence felt. She had to fight back panic, trusting that the doctor had it right. Please God her hearing would return.

When she saw headlights shining on the trees beyond the house, she guessed it was Trey coming up the drive and abandoned the back porch. She was coming in the back door as he entered through the front, and it occurred to her how grateful she was not to be out here alone, deaf to everything but her fears.

Trey came home with movie rentals, a six-pack of Coca-Cola, a gallon of rocky road ice cream and a box of microwave popcorn.

The brilliance of the movie rentals was that they were old black-and-white Laurel and Hardy comedies. Silents. No need for sound to understand what was going on. For that reason alone she fell a little harder for Trey.

Trey had already plowed through a bowl of ice cream and a can of Coke when she threw back the quilt over her legs and started to get up.

He reached for his laptop and quickly typed: "What do you need?"

"A pain pill. I haven't had one since this morning, but my shoulder is really hurting."

"Have you looked at it today?" he wrote.

"No. I was afraid I couldn't get the bandages fastened back down."

"I'll help. I'll have to unbutton your shirt, so chill."

"Do you want me to stand up?" she asked.

He shook his head as he turned sideways on the sofa and reached for the first button.

He noticed her take a quick breath as his fingers

worked the button through the hole and made a point of accidentally on purpose raking his fingertips across the soft flesh of her breasts, then down her belly, until the last button was undone.

He paused, giving her time to think about what came next, and then he eased her good arm out of the sleeve so that he could more easily remove the shirt from the bandaged shoulder.

He looked at her and winced, mouthing the word *sorry* as he undid the tape and pulled the bandage back. Several of the puncture wounds were seeping and had stuck to the gauze. When she winced, he stopped, then leaned forward and brushed a kiss across her lips.

Even though he knew she wouldn't hear him, he had to say it to ease his conscience for causing her pain. "Sorry, so sorry, baby."

"How is it?" she asked.

He shrugged.

"Not infected-looking?"

He shook his head.

"I never even asked, but can the wounds get wet? Will I be able to shower?"

He grabbed the laptop. "Don't use a washcloth on them, and don't soap them. The water from the shower shouldn't hurt. Leave them open to dry, and I'll put a bandage back on them after. Do you want to shower now?"

She nodded.

"Need any help? ☺"

Dallas rolled her eyes. "No, thank you."

"I had to ask."

"Of course you did. I'll be back in a bit. Don't make the popcorn until I get back." She started to get up.

He nodded, and then handed her the blouse he'd taken off a minute ago.

"You loved doing that, didn't you?" she muttered.

He grinned.

She punched him lightly in the belly as she left.

He flopped back down on the sofa, still smiling.

"I think that went well," he said.

Trey stayed smug right up until the moment Dallas came out of the shower wearing nothing but a big bath towel, then handed him gauze pads and tape as she plopped down beside him.

Score one point for Dallas. This topped his sexual tease all over the place.

"I really appreciate this," she said.

Trey took a deep breath, checked that her skin was dry and made quick work of the bandage, then patted her knee to indicate he was done.

"Thanks. I'll get dressed. Are you going to make popcorn?"

He leaned forward and typed: "Only if you're still hungry."

She looked past Trey to the empty recliner and all of a sudden she was done.

"I'm going to get dressed. I'll pass on the popcorn," she said, and left.

Now Trey was confused. Then he turned around to see what had distracted her, saw the recliner and sighed. Of course, her dad, a very important man in her life, gone too soon.

"Damn it."

He got up and carried the dirty bowls and glasses to the kitchen, then put them in the dishwasher and turned it on. After that he stepped out the back door for one last check.

The sky was dark, the stars hidden by cloud cover. The blue-white security light down by the barn left a moon-shaped swatch of light on the ground below. Off to the right, he heard someone driving too damned fast on the blacktop and said a prayer that they got home in one piece. He wasn't in the mood to be called out to an accident. He glanced up at the mountain and caught a glimmer of light just before it disappeared. Probably hunters, although he didn't hear any hounds baying.

"Is everything okay?"

He turned. Dallas was silhouetted in the doorway, her hands twisted against her stomach. He hurt, knowing she was scared. Too many bad things had happened to her here, and it scared him to death to think that would be what drove her away.

He walked toward her, smiling and nodding, and watched her relax as he locked the door behind them.

"Can we watch the last movie? I don't want to go to bed. Too many bad dreams."

He cupped her cheek, then rubbed a thumb across her lower lip.

"Yes," he said, then stood back to let her lead the way.

The dog was growling, its teeth bared as saliva dripped onto the ground below.

Dallas had a gun, but it wouldn't fire. She kept pulling the trigger over and over, sobbing helplessly.

The dog crouched.

She took a step backward, and when she did, the dog leaped.

She screamed.

Moments later her room was bathed in light and Trey was running toward the bed.

"It was a dream, just a dream. I'm sorry," she said, and combed the hair away from her face.

Trey scooted onto the side of the mattress, then touched her shoulder and mimed taking a pill.

"No, I don't hurt all that bad. I don't want a pain pill. When I take them, I can't wake up."

"Son of a bitch," he muttered.

Dallas saw his lips moving and guessed from the look on his face that he wasn't happy, but then, neither was she. They were as close to naked together as they'd been in six years, and she was too damn injured to do a thing about it.

She sighed. "Go back to bed. I'm fine."

He sat for a few moments without moving, watching, then finally nodded and got up.

He waited as she lay back down, covered her up and turned off the light as he left.

Dallas lay in the dark, staring at the ceiling and remembering all the bad dreams she'd had in this room as a child. Then it had been her mom or dad who'd rushed to comfort her. Tonight it had been Trey.

She closed her eyes against welling tears and wished for daylight. Eventually she fell asleep, and when she woke again, her wish had come true.

Dallas woke to the scent of fresh-brewed coffee, threw back the covers and made a quick trip across the hall to the bathroom before getting herself dressed. She forced herself to use her left arm, then groaned as sore muscles pulled and wounds that had begun to scab over broke open.

"I will put on my own damn socks," she said, and did, then stepped into the old tennis shoes from her closet. The Velcro closings made them simple to fasten. She called the job done.

Trey's cruiser was still parked in the yard, but the house was empty, so she managed to put on an old jacket and went out the back door. She could see the herd grazing about halfway between the barn and the mountain, and guessed the cows and calves were in the feed lot behind the barn.

The chickens were already in the lot. She could see them fussing and running, trying to head each other off or claim a certain spot to feed. It was strange to see their antics without accompanying sound, and she realized how she'd come to enjoy the simple task of taking care of the chickens.

Knowing there were eggs waiting to be cleaned and sorted, she headed for the barn.

Trey had already fed the cows and was in the egg room cleaning and sorting when Dallas walked in.

"Hey!" he said, and then realized she couldn't hear him, so he gave her a quick good-morning kiss instead.

"I'll sort and fill the cartons," she said, and got to work.

She was stiff and sore, but it felt good to be doing something useful. They worked side by side without trying to talk, and when they were finished she wrote the date on the cartons, moved the freshest to the back of the shelf and called it done.

Trey looked around, trying to see if he'd left anything undone. He saw a new padlock and key still in the package, and the big storage bins, and pointed at them with a question on his face.

"Beats me," she said, and took his hand. "We're through here. Have you had breakfast?"

He shook his head.

"How much time do you have before you need to leave?" she asked.

He glanced at his watch and then tapped a number.

"That's over an hour," she said. "Enough time for

pancakes. I'll tell you what goes in the batter if you'll cook."

"Deal," he said, nodding his head.

The house still smelled like pancakes long after Trey was gone. Dallas refused Betsy's offer to come over but promised if she needed help, she would text. She wanted the house to herself again. Today she was going to go through the place again, looking for anything that would give her a lead on her father's big-money project.

But she still had practicalities to consider, so the first thing she did was put a sign on the front door for her egg customers.

I cannot hear your arrival.
If you need eggs, you know where they are.
Help yourself and leave the money on the table in the egg room.
Thanks,
Dallas

She had her cell phone on vibrate and put it in her pocket in case she got a text, especially a text from Trey, and once again began going through the house. When she got to the bedroom Trey was using, she hesitated a moment, worried he might think she was being nosy, and then shrugged off her concerns. She had a job to do.

She looked past his clothes in the closet and his underwear in the drawers, trying to find something that said "big money," but she found nothing. Finally the only place left was her dad's bedroom.

She'd already been through his room once, but then she'd been looking for a reason why he might have wanted to die. Now she was looking for a reason why he would have wanted to live.

She still felt like a trespasser as she entered his room, but she needed answers, and if he had any, this would be where he hid his secrets.

Without sound to distract her, her ability to focus entirely on sight was amplified. She saw beauty in the slice of light warming the corner of the bedspread, felt a tug of sadness at the sight of her parents' wedding picture hanging over the bed. The John Deere tractor alarm clock she'd given him one Christmas many years ago was centered on an antique crocheted doily covering the top of the dresser. Her grandfather's cherrywood armoire was in the corner of the room opposite the bed, and there was a small cherrywood table and chair beneath the double windows on the south side of the room. The curtains were faded; the room felt forlorn.

What secret were you hiding, Dad? Show me where it's at.

She started with the dresser and went through every drawer, looking for something that didn't belong. Then she moved to the armoire, poking in the nooks and crannies without success. When she opened the closet and saw the array of boxes stacked on the floor beneath the clothes and on the shelf above the bar, she groaned. If she was going to move all of that around, it was time take a pain pill.

She was in the kitchen getting a glass of water when the landline began to ring, and while the sound was faint, the fact that she heard it was so startling that she dropped the glass and broke it.

She didn't care. She'd heard the sound!

She was so overjoyed that she started to cry, then cupped her hands over her ears and danced around the room like a crazy woman, even though it hurt her ribs. When she remembered the mess, she grabbed a broom and a dustpan to clean up the broken glass, and she didn't even mind that sweeping made her shoulder hurt like hell.

It took another half hour before she got the pain pill taken, but by then she was trying out all kinds of sounds. She used her cell phone and called her dad's number over and over just to hear it ring, and then she turned on the electric mixer to see if she could hear it. It was faint, but she heard the buzz. Then she tried the timer and banged drawers, and while some sounds didn't register, she smiled wider with each one that did.

She went outside, curious to see how different surroundings affected what she could hear. The first place she went was to the chicken house, because she knew they were always making noise. She wanted to see how close she had to get before she heard them. It was obvious her hearing was still defective, but the fact that it *was* coming back was an answered prayer. She continued to test it, moving from one point to another outside in near-manic mode, and when she finally got back to the house, she sat down on the steps and cried again.

"Thank you, God, thank you," she said, and cried some more at the sound of her own voice.

Twelve

It took an hour for Dallas to calm down enough to get back to exploring her father's room, and a couple of hours more to go through all the boxes. She found interesting things, but nothing that shouted "money." The only thing on the desk, besides a cup of pens and pencils and a pad of paper, was a small stack of books with diverse subject matter ranging from dousing for water to raising ginseng. At first curious as to why he would have such a strange assortment of books, she soon realized why he'd kept them.

The names on the flyleaves belonged to members of the very first Phillipses who'd claimed the land and built this house. These weren't only antique editions but family heirlooms. She put them back the way she'd found them and kept on searching.

It was after 2:00 p.m. when she ended her search with no more answers than when she'd started. She'd skipped lunch and her belly was growling, but instead of making herself something to eat, she grabbed a cold can of Dr Pepper and a handful of peanuts, and headed for the porch swing out back.

The day was clear, the sky more white than blue. She ate the peanuts one at a time, taking joy in hearing the crunch every time she bit down. And as she ate she swung, satisfied in the moment and grateful for the sound of the creaking chain.

When her phone vibrated, she quickly grabbed it, guessing the text would be from Trey, and it was.

Just making sure you're okay. Do you need anything? I need you.

Her smile stilled. The past few days had given her a whole new perspective on what mattered. He had never denied his feelings, and he'd never quit on her. She reread the message and then sent him one back.

I'm fine. I cannot lie. I need you, too.

He fired back an answer so fast it made her laugh.

Tonight. You. Me. Dinner in Mystic.

Deal. Me. You. A night on the town.

The little heart he sent back made her smile.

She took the phone off vibrate and dropped it back in her pocket, then finished off her pop. She had a hot date and her hair was a mess, but doing it herself wasn't happening when she could only raise one arm above her head. She thought of the Triple C Salon and went into the house to get the phone book. She'd gone to school with the owner. Maybe someone there could work her in.

The Triple C Hair Salon—the *C*s stood for *curl*, *cut* and *color*—was a red metal building between a small boutique and a bakery just off Main Street. Dallas had made the call with some difficulty and finally had to ask them to shout so she could hear, but they'd assured her they would work her in as soon as she arrived, so she'd headed for town.

She didn't tell Trey. He would have insisted on taking her himself. But she didn't need a babysitter. She just needed a hairdo and a little more time to get well.

She took the backstreets into town, hoping Trey wouldn't see her, and parked in front of the salon. Someone honked as she got out. She barely heard it but turned to look. An old friend from church waved as she drove past. Dallas started to wave and then winced. She'd horsed around enough today; she needed to ease back and give her body time to heal.

As soon as she walked into the salon she was inundated with greetings and condolences, most of which she barely heard. It was apparent that voices were going to be tricky.

Bonnie Glass, the owner, met Dallas at the door. Dallas quickly explained why she was there.

"Thanks for taking me on such short notice, but today is the first day since the dog attacked me that I've been able to hear anything, though what I hear is faint. My shoulder is really sore, too sore for me to do my own hair. It's a mess, and I need help."

Bonnie ran her fingers through the strands, then raised her voice and spoke slowly and distinctly.

"What you need is a good shampoo and a little styling. Your cut is great. Okay?"

Dallas smiled. "Yes, very okay."

"Then come with me and I'll get you started," Bonnie said.

It took a few minutes and some extra padding behind Dallas's shoulder so she could lean back in the chair at the shampoo station, but Bonnie finally began.

Relaxing beneath the gentle massage of Bonnie's fingers as she soaped and then rinsed, Dallas felt the first twinge of normalcy since the day she'd come back home.

It wasn't until Bonnie seated her in the styling chair that she spoke to Dallas again.

"Before we begin, I want to tell you how sorry I was to hear of what happened to your daddy. I can't imagine the shock of something like that, and I wish you grace and peace."

Dallas knew she was referring to what everyone still assumed was a suicide. Today seemed like a good day to rearrange that story.

"Thank you, Bonnie, but I won't find peace until they find Daddy's killer."

Bonnie froze, then met Dallas's gaze in the mirror in front of them. "Killer? But I thought—"

"Suicide? Oh, no! I never bought that story," Dallas said. "That wasn't my daddy's style, and it seems I was right. The sheriff contacted Trey yesterday to tell him that they've ruled Dad's death a homicide. They're already investigating."

"Oh, my God! Murder! How did they know? I mean—"

"Without going into details, I'll just say it was the coroner's findings that proved I was right."

Everyone in the hair salon had been listening, and now the shock of Dallas's revelation rolled through the room. Someone in their midst was a killer! The cell phones came out and the texts began flying. It wouldn't take long for word to get out, which was fine with Dallas. Somewhere there was a killer thinking he'd got away with murder. He was about to learn he'd made a costly mistake.

By the time Dallas left the hair salon, she looked like her on-camera self. She got in the car and quickly left town, unwilling to reveal the news that her hearing had returned to Trey until she was back on her own territory.

Trey and Earl were on their way to serve a protection order against a guy named Joe Hanson. Trey had grown up with Joe and was saddened by the turn his life had taken.

When they drove up to the auto repair shop where

he worked, they both got out. Sometimes people didn't take to being served and tried to cause trouble. In the police business, it was always better safe than sorry.

Both bay doors were open and cars were up on all three racks. Trey saw Joe at the far end of the garage.

"He's down at the third car," he said, and started walking with Earl beside him.

"Think he'll cause trouble?" Earl asked.

"If he's been drinking, maybe," Trey said. "Just pay attention."

Earl nodded.

"Hey, Joe, got a minute?" Trey called out.

Joe Hanson turned around, and the minute he saw Trey's face, he visibly paled.

"Yeah, what's up?" Joe said, and grabbed a rag to wipe the oil off his hands.

"This is for you," Trey said, and handed Joe the order. "You've just been served, so consider this as serious as it seems. If you violate this order, not only will you get arrested, but you will go to jail."

Joe scanned the paper quickly and then looked up at Trey in disbelief.

"Julie did this? This means I can't go home. I can't see her. I can't talk to her. I can't even put my boy to sleep at night?"

"That's what it means," Trey said.

Anger flashed behind Joe's pain. "What the hell? How does she get off pulling something like this?"

"You broke her nose. You fractured her cheekbone. She has to have reconstructive surgery, you jackass.

She's afraid of you now. This is what happens when you beat the hell out of your wife every night, and don't deny it. You're not fooling anyone."

Joe flinched as if he'd just been slapped. "I don't mean to. I just—"

Trey handed him a card and a flyer.

"These are the times and locations of A.A. meetings in the area. Go. Quit drinking. Get your act together. You're better than this."

Joe started to cry, but Trey ignored it.

"Julie asked me to tell you that she's packed a couple of suitcases with your clothes. They're at your mom's house. She's expecting you."

Joe frowned. "My mom? I'm twenty-seven years old. I'm not living with my mom."

"I don't care where you live, and I suspect Julie was trying to do you a favor. You won't pay rent at your mother's house, but you *will* still be paying rent where your family lives, so get that straight now."

"But that's not—"

"Look, Joe. My job was just to serve the court order and leave, but I always considered you a friend, so I'm giving you some friendly advice. Just because you fucked up your life doesn't mean you get to fuck up your family's life, too. Unless a judge tells you otherwise, you're still at least partly responsible for the welfare of your wife and child. Stop whining and take responsibility for what you've done. Don't make me have to arrest you. That would piss me off something fierce."

He glanced at Earl, and then they walked off, leaving Joe Hanson with the problems he'd caused.

"That's tough," Earl said.

Trey frowned. "What? Getting kicked out of his home? It's nothing compared to making his wife afraid to *go* home. He got exactly what he deserved."

They stopped at a gas station to fuel up before heading back to the station. Trey would be heading out to the farm soon, and there were no words for how happy he was to know Dallas was there waiting.

"I'm gonna get me a cold pop and some chips. You want anything, Chief?" Earl asked.

"Bring me a cold Coke, but in a bottle, not a cup, and ice, please," Trey said, and handed him a couple of dollars.

"Will do," Earl said, and went inside while Trey began filling up the car.

The high school football coach was on the other side of the pumps filling up his truck, and when he saw Trey he started talking.

"Hey. I heard the sheriff is treating Dick Phillips's death as a homicide. Is that true? Did someone really murder the guy?"

Trey wasn't really surprised that word was spreading, but this was the first time he'd been asked.

"Yes, they ruled it a homicide."

The coach shook his head in disbelief. "Does that mean someone in this town is likely the killer? Why do you think they did it? I mean, it's not like he interrupted a robbery, 'cuz nothing was stolen, right? So it's not like they killed him to keep him from identifying them."

Trey frowned. "Uh…I wouldn't speculate on anything at this point. Sheriff Osmond is in charge of the investigation."

"Right," the coach said, and then the fuel pump kicked off. "Well, that's me. I guess I'm full up. See you around, Chief."

"Yeah, see you around," Trey said.

Earl came out as the coach drove off and handed Trey the cold Coke.

"Thanks," Trey said. He unscrewed the lid and took a big drink, then screwed the lid back on the bottle and set it in the console just as his pump kicked off. They drove back to the station.

Trey was finishing up some paperwork when the phone rang. "Hello."

"Hi, honey, it's me."

"Oh, hi, Mom. What's up?"

He heard her sigh and frowned.

"What's wrong?" he asked.

"I can't get over knowing Dick was murdered. I keep asking myself why. What did he know? Who did he make mad? What was going on in his life that would make someone do this?"

"I understand. I'm as puzzled as you are, but I'm not in charge of the case. I don't know any more than you do, okay?"

She sighed again. "I know. I'm sorry I bothered you."

"You didn't bother me, Mom, not at all. I just don't have answers, understand?"

"Yes, you're right. I understand. We'll all have to wait and see what turns up in the investigation."

"Right," Trey said. "Uh, I'm taking Dallas out to eat tonight. Just to the steak house here in town. I don't think she's up to anything else."

"Well, I don't know about that," Betsy said. "Trina said she saw her coming out of the Triple C earlier this afternoon. Said she was all dolled up, so she must be excited about the date."

The hair stood up on the back of his neck, imagining all kinds of dire situations in which she would be hurt again.

"She drove to town?"

"Obviously," Betsy said. "Look, honey. She's tough as they come. She saved her own life, and she's trying to come to terms with losing her dad, so if she wants to drive a car, I would be the last person to argue."

"I didn't say it was a problem. I was just surprised, that's all."

"Well, at any rate, have a nice evening at the steak house."

"Thanks, we will," he said, and hung up the phone.

His eyes narrowed as he glanced at the clock. If she was already driving herself around, then what kind of an excuse was he going to use to stay at the farm with her a little longer?

* * *

Will Porter left the high school, but he wasn't ready to go home to a drunk wife and no dinner, so he stopped off at Charlie's for a cup of coffee and a piece of pie.

Gregory Standish was already ensconced in a booth in the corner and waved him over as he walked in.

"Will! Come join me," Standish called out.

Will smiled, glad for the company.

"Thanks," he said, as he slid into the booth just ahead of the waitress. "Coffee and pie. Do you have any coconut cream?"

"Yes, sir. Coming up!" she said, and went to fill the order.

Gregory leaned forward. "So, what's up at Mystic's magic high school?" he asked.

The old nickname made Will smile. "Nothing magic happening there. Just more of the same stuff that went on when we were in school. What about you? Still giving away money to the rich and famous?"

"Lending, Will, lending. Nothing is free in banking these days."

"Nothing is free anywhere," Will muttered, then smiled. He didn't want anyone to know his life was anything but perfect.

At that point Marcus Silver walked in the door, looked around the room, and then saw Gregory and waved before heading over.

Will suddenly realized Marcus and Gregory had planned to meet here.

"Oh, hey! I didn't know you were here for a meeting," he said.

"It's not that kind of business," Gregory said. "Stay. Marcus won't care."

Marcus slid into the booth. "Will, how's it going?" he asked.

"Oh, great, thanks. Look, I didn't know you guys had business. I'll move."

"No, no. Stay where you are. Yes, it's business, but nothing secret," Marcus said.

The waitress showed up with Will's pie and coffee and then looked at Marcus.

"Just coffee, please," he said.

Will took a bite of pie as Marcus leaned back in the booth.

"It's good to see you guys," Marcus said. "We don't hang out anymore. We should do this more often."

"We're all too busy," Gregory said. "And you, man. You're about to make your life even crazier."

Will swallowed as he glanced at Marcus. "What are you about to do?"

Marcus smiled. "I'm thinking of running for the state senate. The incumbent is retiring, so the seat is up for grabs."

Will grinned. "Really? I had no idea you had political aspirations."

Marcus shrugged. "It's been in my head for years. This seemed like a now-or-never moment, you know?"

Gregory knew what now-or-never felt like. He'd

had his back pushed against the wall before, but never like it was now.

Will also thought about now-or-never. The only thing left standing in his way was Rita. "Well, I for one think that's great. Is this for public knowledge?"

"Not yet, if you don't mind," Marcus said.

Will nodded. "My lips are sealed." He took another bite of pie.

They were deep in discussion about the cost of campaign managers and the fact that, due to social media, there was no such thing as a private life anymore, when Marcus's son walked into Charlie's.

"Hey, T.J.! Over here!" Marcus called.

T.J. saw his dad, smiled and waved as he began to weave his way between tables, stopping along the way to speak to some of the other diners.

"Look at him. He's working this room like a pro," Gregory said.

Marcus smiled.

"And he's as pretty as some Hollywood actor," Will said, and then punched Marcus's arm. "Good thing he took after his mother, right?"

"Oh, that's for sure. Can't argue with the truth," Marcus said, and then laughed. Being rich made up for not being pretty. He'd never suffered from being on the wrong side of handsome.

T.J. finally reached the booth and slid in beside his father. "Are we eating here tonight?" he asked.

Marcus shook his head. "No, I have that dinner meeting later. I'm interviewing another campaign manager. It's hard to know what to look for. Want to join me?"

T.J. smiled. "Yes, I would, thanks."

The waitress came back one last time. "Anything for you?" she asked T.J.

"Just coffee, black," he said.

"Coming up," she said.

The conversation lagged as they waited for her to return, and as it did, they couldn't help but overhear what a woman was saying at the table across the aisle.

"Yes, I was at the Triple C and heard it straight from Dallas Phillips's mouth. She didn't say much except that it had to do with the coroner's findings. But it's the truth. Her daddy didn't commit suicide. He was murdered."

T.J.'s eyes widened. "Dad, did you hear that?"

Marcus nodded.

Gregory looked shocked.

Will was pale.

T.J. leaned forward, whispering, "There's a killer among us. What the hell is this world coming to?"

They all looked at each other, and then turned and stared out across the room, looking intently at the people who were eating, trying to see if one of them looked like a killer.

Trey was thinking about chores when he drove into the yard, and then he saw Dallas coming out of the barn and realized she was already through. She was driving. She was doing chores. He was no longer needed. Well, hell. But he wasn't the kind of man to give up without a fight, so he got out of the car and went to meet her.

"Hi," Dallas said.

Trey waved, touched her hair, gave her a thumbs-up, then cupped her face and gave her a lingering kiss that rocked her all the way to her shoes.

"Wow. I missed you, too," she said softly, when he finally pulled back.

Before he could say anything, his phone began to ring.

"Better get that," she said. "It might be important."

"Yeah," he said, and actually had the phone in his hand when he realized what she'd said. He stopped, stared at her in disbelief, and then started to grin. "You can hear!"

She nodded. "It's coming back. Some things are easier to hear than others."

"Thank the Lord," Trey said, letting the call go to voice mail. "I want to hug you, but I'm afraid I'll hurt your shoulder."

"I would rather hurt and have a hug than do without," she said.

So he obliged.

Enfolded within his arms, she laid her cheek against his chest and closed her eyes. Home. That's what it felt like to be standing here, on this land, in his arms. It was home.

"Your hair looks and smells beautiful," he said.

"I wanted to look good for our date. We haven't had one in forever."

"Six years, four months, three weeks and two days," he said. "But who's counting?"

She looked up as shock washed through her. "Seriously?"

"Seriously."

She was obviously stunned that he'd shamelessly admitted how much he'd missed her, and he didn't want to push the issue. Instead of following up, he reached for her hand.

"Let's get back to the house. I still need to clean up, and we have a reservation for seven."

They walked back together, both of them lost in thought.

Thirteen

It was a minute shy of seven o'clock when they reached the parking lot of Cutter's Steak House.

Dallas was nervous, which was silly. She'd grown up in Mystic, and she wasn't anxious about being seen with Trey. It wasn't like he had another woman in the wings. And then, the moment she thought it, she wondered.

"Are you hungry?" Trey asked, as they headed for the door.

"Yes. I had peanuts and a Coke for lunch."

He frowned. "Seriously, Dallas Ann? Taking pain pills on an empty stomach?"

She rolled her eyes. "Seriously, Trey. I do not need a keeper. I'm not swinging from the chandeliers. I haven't passed out, and I'm not taking off my clothes in public."

He grinned. "I admit to some regret for the last part."

She laughed, and that was how they walked in the door, arm in arm, laughing.

It turned heads. It started gossip. She couldn't have cared less.

The hostess was a cute twentysomething blonde wearing a soft knit dress that hugged every curve she had. She flashed a smile at Trey that lit up her face, and then eyed Dallas with something more than curiosity.

"Good evening, Trey. Dallas, it's been a while."

Dallas gave her a second look. "Cherry? Is that you?"

Cherry Adams smiled. "Yes, it's me, minus about fifty pounds. You haven't been in for a long time." Then she picked up two menus. "This way, please," she said, and led them to the table Trey had reserved. She laid down the menus, gave Dallas one last look and left.

Dallas glanced up at Trey. "Cherry seems quite taken with you."

His eyes narrowed, but he didn't comment, and that bothered Dallas more than it should have.

"I suppose in the past six years, four months, three weeks and two days you've had plenty of girlfriends to occupy your time."

It was the sarcastic tone of her voice that ticked him off, and it showed in his response.

"You have no right to an answer to that question, Dallas Ann. You're the one who walked out on me, remember?"

She blinked. "I didn't mean to—"

He sighed. "Let's just say that I spent the first three years of that time trying to forget that you existed. It didn't work. I'm so happy to be here with you right now. Don't mess it up."

It was the pain in his voice that shamed her.

"I'm sorry. That was the bitch in me asking. For that faux pas, *she* does not get dessert. I, on the other hand, will be enjoying it for her."

He grinned, grateful she'd let the subject go. He slid a hand across the table, palm up.

She grasped it and squeezed. "Truce."

He nodded. "Truce. Now, what sounds good to you?"

"Almost anything. Peanuts as a food source are yummy. Peanuts as an entrée do not suffice."

He laughed out loud, which made heads turn again, and the gossip rebounded. It appeared the two of them were back to being an item.

Five tables back, and in a corner, Marcus and T. J. Silver were entertaining their guest, yet another man vying for the job of managing the proposed Silver campaign. They saw the couple walk in, and then heard the laughter a few moments later. Marcus thought nothing of it, while T.J. was admiring the cut of Dallas Phillips's clothes and her sense of style. A woman like that would look good on the arm of a politician. Pretty, smart and witty to boot. She was too young for his dad, but not for him. However, it looked like she was already taken. No matter. There were thousands like her and he was nowhere ready for a relationship. First his daddy needed to get elected. Then he could begin figuring out the easiest way to step into Daddy's big shoes.

After a few minutes Dallas discovered it was difficult to hear Trey over the undertone of the other diners' conversations. Frustrated to the point of tears, she finally had to confess.

"I know my responses to your witty conversation seem a little empty, but I promise I'm not pretending you're interesting, because I could write a book about your skills and exploits all by myself. But with all the other voices in here, I'm having a very hard time understanding what you're saying. I'm sorry."

Trey saw the tears in her eyes and was on his feet in seconds. Before she knew what he was doing, he'd moved his chair so that he was sitting next to her, not across the table. He proceeded to move his food and utensils, even the condiments, then picked up her hand and kissed it.

The waitress came running, thinking there had been a spill. "Is everything okay, Chief?"

He smiled. "Everything is fine, Lisa. I just wanted to be closer to my girl."

Lisa breathed a sigh of relief and grinned at Dallas.

"Lucky you," she said. "I'll be right back with more coffee."

A thousand thoughts about her career went through

Dallas's mind, and not one of them came close to making her want it more than what she had right now. Maybe it was time to redefine who she was.

"Trey?"

"What, baby?"

"Thank you for waiting."

The smile on his face froze. His heart leaped, then caution set in. *Don't make this about more than it is*, he told himself.

"You're worth waiting for," he said softly, and this time he leaned over and brushed a kiss across her lips.

Dallas's head was still spinning when Lisa came to top off their coffee. She saw a local businessman right behind the waitress, his gaze fixed on Trey.

Trey saw him and sighed. "Well, crap," he muttered.

"What's wrong?" Dallas asked.

"You're about to get a dose of the downside of my job."

The businessman all but pushed the waitress aside. "Chief, I'm glad I caught you tonight," he said. "I want to fill you in on—"

"George, you caught us in the middle of dinner. Do you know Dallas Phillips?"

Caught off guard at the interruption, George glanced at Dallas.

"No, I don't believe I do. Nice to meet you, Miss Phillips. I'm George Lowrance. I own Lowrance Shoes on Main Street."

Before Dallas could respond, George was back on

a mission. "My morning papers are still going missing and I know it's that man who owns the bakery next door. He comes to work at 3:00 a.m., free to swipe it without a soul to witness."

Trey sighed. "Have you seen him do it?"

"Well, no, but—"

"Has anyone else witnessed the thefts?"

George sputtered in frustration. "No, I told you, it's 3:00 a.m. But he—"

This time, it was Dallas who interrupted.

"Stuff like that happens all the time in Charleston. You should put up a security camera, Mr. Lowrance. You'll catch the thief in the act, whoever it may be."

Trey rolled his eyes, kicking himself for not thinking of that earlier.

George opened his mouth as if to disagree, then paused and didn't.

"Good idea. I'll do that. And when I get proof, I want him arrested. Have a nice evening, Chief, and sorry to bother you."

He left as grandly as he'd arrived.

"Why didn't I think of that?" Trey asked.

"All that fuss for a paper? Maybe it's because you were busy with real problems," Dallas said.

He grinned. "Nice save, honey, and thanks. Are you about ready for that dessert?"

"Honestly, I don't have room. We could eat rocky road ice cream at home later."

"Deal," he said, and waved the waitress over for their check.

The September air was cool as they walked across the parking lot to the car, a reminder that winter wouldn't be far behind. Trey helped her into the car, and when he reached in to buckle her up, he felt her breath on his cheek. He shuddered, thinking how close he'd come to losing her.

"Okay?" he asked, testing the seat belt to make sure it wasn't rubbing against her shoulder wounds.

"Yes, it's fine."

The drive home was quiet. Dallas dozed, exhausted by the day and the dinner, but it was a good tired.

The headlights of the car revealed brief glimpses of the passing scenery: a quick image of a deer leaping across the road; a fox slipping through weeds along the ditch; a skunk waddling along the verge of the road.

Trey drove with caution, knowing how fast a wreck could happen on a rural road from colliding with an animal. He saw a brief flash of lightning off to the west and wondered if the building storm would come this far. When he took the turn off the blacktop onto the gravel road leading up to the farm, Dallas woke and sat up.

"We're already home?"

The fact that she thought of him and home in the same breath made him smile.

"Yes, we are, and this was the best evening I've had in a long, long time. Thank you."

"Thank you for the wonderful meal," she said. And then she, too, saw the lightning. "Ooh, is it supposed to rain?"

"I don't know," Trey said. "Haven't seen news or weather all day, but we'll find out soon enough."

He parked, then got out and ran around to help her into the house.

Dallas looked up at him and smiled, and then glanced over his shoulder. Her smile slipped.

"There are those lights on the mountain again," she said, pointing.

Trey turned to look, judging where they were in conjunction with her property.

"I don't think they're on your side of the property line."

"I know, but they're not far off. I can't hear hounds. Are they running hounds?"

"Not that I can hear, but I don't think there's anything to worry about. There's nothing up on the whole side of the mountain but trees."

"True. I guess I'm just paranoid. Someone killed Dad for a reason. Otis said he was coming into big money. I can't help wondering if there's a connection between the two things."

"We'll figure this out, but for now, let's go in. The night air is chilly," he said.

Dallas led the way, unlocked the door and went in, turning lights on as she moved from room to room, leaving Trey to lock up behind her.

He went to change clothes and then headed into the kitchen to make coffee. He could hear Dallas banging around in her room and guessed she was changing clothes, as well. He wanted her to love him enough to stay this time. He wanted to mean more to her than her dreams of fame and glory. But he knew he might be wanting more than she was ever going to give.

And so he stood in a house as familiar to him as the one he'd grown up in, remembering the dreams they'd had when they were young, and reminding himself that *that* was then and *this* was now.

Dallas couldn't hear him anywhere and wondered if he'd gone outside, or if her hearing was fading out again. A little uneasy, she walked down the hall, through the living room into the kitchen, and caught him unaware.

Her first thought was what a handsome man he'd turned out to be. And then she looked at his face and it broke her heart. He was staring at the floor with a look of such sadness, and knowing it was because of her was almost too much to bear.

"Don't," she said.

Trey looked up. "I didn't hear you," he said, noticing that she was barefoot.

She started to cry, and felt like that was all she'd done since the day she'd got the phone call from Trey about her dad.

Trey ran over to hold her, one hand on her shoulder, the other beneath her chin. "What's wrong? Are you in pain? What can I do?"

The tears came faster.

"I hurt you. All you do is give, and all I do is take. I hate myself. I hate what I did. I'm sorry, Trey. I'm sorry. I was so damned selfish, and I can't bear it anymore."

He groaned and wrapped his arms around her.

"I wish to God you weren't hurt. The one thing we had going for us was how good we were together. I want to make love to you again, without promises, without expectations, until you beg me to stop and then beg me for more."

Dallas was shaking. "And I want you, too, Trey. I remember how it was. I want that magic again, the kind that happens when we make love."

He swung her off her feet and into his arms, and then carried her down the hall to her bedroom without saying a word, turning lights off as he went.

The room was dark, lit only by a small night-light. He kicked the door shut as he carried her inside, and then gently stood her up and stripped her with the precision of a master. It wasn't until she felt the slight chill of the room against her skin that she realized she was naked as the day she'd been born. He was faster at this than he used to be, and better. She wouldn't think of how many women he'd had to undress to increase his expertise. Like he'd said, she didn't have the right to ask.

By the time he took off his clothes she was shaking. Everything about him seemed exaggerated from what she remembered, but time can turn a grown man into a beautiful sight to behold, and that was what the six years, four months, three weeks and two days had done for Trey. His shoulders were massive. His belly was washboard-hard, and there was a scar on his side that hadn't been there before.

Trey was hard, and he was ready, but the bandage on her shoulder was daunting. He laid her down, then slid into bed beside her, thinking her skin smelled like flowers. No, maybe that was her hair. He wanted to drown in the scent and die in her arms, so he kissed her like he meant it, waiting for the catch in her breath and then the groan. When he heard it, he knew he was home.

He kissed the back of her ear and then ran his tongue along the curve of her chin, murmuring softly against her ear. "Don't move. Tonight I make love to you."

Dallas sighed. She'd had this dream so many nights in Charleston she could hardly believe this was real. Don't move? She could barely breathe.

Trey stayed true to his word. He used every dream he'd had of her for inspiration, touching her body, then her heart, bringing her to a climax with his tongue, then his hands. Then, when she was still gasping for breath, he slid his rock-hard penis between her legs and sent her flying.

He caught the scream coming up her throat with a soul-sucking kiss that made the world spin. He'd turned her on in ways she never knew existed, pushing and shoving her senses all the way to a peak just shy of climax, and then dropping her back to the bottom—only to do it again. By the fourth time she was in such sensual torment that she was begging him to stop. So he did, leaving her trembling with an ache that wouldn't ebb.

"I ache… I need… Oh, my God, I want this…"

His hands were on either side of her head, bracing his body as he hovered above her, his knee between her legs as he waited for her to beg.

"What do you need?"

She sobbed. "You, I need you."

He lowered his head until their mouths were so close he could feel the heat coming off her body.

"And what do you *want*, Dallas Ann?"

She sighed. Check and checkmate. She was done.

"You. I want you," she whispered, and closed her eyes, waiting for the release he'd kept just out of reach.

And then all of a sudden he was inside her, and in four hard driving thrusts he'd pulled her back into the game and set her on fire. The climax came without warning. One moment her whole body was throbbing, her nerves humming like a stretched-too-tight wire, and then it hit.

The wash of heat that went through her was a flash fire, spreading in one overwhelming rush. She went from unable to move to weightless, grabbing on to his arms to keep from floating away, then followed the pulsing tremors back to an aftershock that made her lose her breath.

Trey knew her body. He knew how she ticked. And so he watched, waiting for that telling moment when her eyes lost focus. It took every ounce of self-control he had to keep from losing it, waiting, waiting, and all the while he kept thinking, *Come on, baby, let it go. Let it go.*

And when she did, he went with her.

Dallas fell asleep twice, and both times Trey woke her up making love. She would laugh and reach for him, and each time he would gently push her back, unwilling for her to suffer one moment of pain. Then he would play her body like an instrument until he wiped the smile off her face.

It was daybreak when she woke again. After their night of lovemaking, the sight of Trey standing naked before the window shouldn't have turned her on, but it did. She thought of all the years she'd lived without this man in her life and knew she couldn't face another six years, four months, three weeks and two days without him. Whatever it took, she had to find a way to be productive and happy in his world, because he would never fit into hers.

"Trey?"

He turned around.

She was sitting up in bed with her kiss-swollen lips and her sleepy eyes, completely nude, with sleep-tousled hair, and she looked as happy as he'd ever seen a woman look.

"Good morning, beautiful."

She crawled out of bed, still favoring her wounded shoulder, and walked into his outstretched arms.

"Good morning, magic man. I don't think I ever thanked you for dinner last night."

He threw back his head, and laughed and laughed until she began to giggle, but when he didn't stop, she finally poked him in the belly.

"It wasn't that funny," she said.

Still chuckling, Trey grabbed her hand and lifted it to his lips.

"Yes, ma'am, it was. I nearly killed myself last night for your pleasure, and you thanked me for dinner."

She shrugged. "I thought it would be a bit gauche to just thank you for rearranging my molecules."

He was still grinning when he picked her up in his arms and took her back to bed.

"You can't possibly have any more tricks up your sleeves," she said.

"As you can see, I have no sleeves, no sleeves at all. But I do have tricks." He crawled on top of her, straddling her legs, and swooped down to steal a kiss. "Plenty of tricks," he said softly, and stole another kiss. "Magic tricks for the lady in my life."

"I love you, Trey Jakes. So much it makes me hurt."

The smile slid off his face. "I love you, too, baby. Forever and ever."

Ignoring the pull in her shoulder, she cupped his face with both hands. The bristle of black whiskers was rough against the palms of her hands, tough like him. Even though she didn't deserve it, the trust on his face was just like the first time they'd made love, everlasting like the man himself.

Very few people got a second chance at anything. That she was getting a second chance at love seemed like a miracle, and the best gift she could give him in return was to wipe away all doubt.

"I promise before God and the love my parents had for each other that I will never leave you again."

Trey flinched as if he'd been slapped. He hadn't seen that coming. And then her face blurred and the words wouldn't come.

"Oh, my God, you're going to make me cry again," she said.

He sat up and pulled her across his lap, then buried his face against her neck.

"Six years, four months, three weeks and two days. Thank you, Jesus," he whispered.

They held each other while they cried.

Trey went to work late with a smile on his face and a mental note to stop by the jewelry store. He had an engagement ring to buy.

Back at the farm, with the chores done and still feeling somewhat incapacitated, Dallas was at loose ends. For lack of anything else to do, she got her laptop from her luggage, set it on the kitchen table and plugged it in, guessing it would need a charge.

She checked her email and, horrified by the number of unanswered messages, started going through them, deleting some, answering others.

An hour later she got up to make herself something to drink, then stepped out on the back porch as she waited for the coffee to brew.

Out of habit, she glanced toward the mountain, and

as she did, she saw a flash of light, like sunlight reflecting off something metal. It was in the same area where she'd been seeing the night lights, and she tried to figure out what it might be. That was government land, part of a wildlife preserve, with rules against hunting and camping, not that people always paid attention to them. She didn't hear gunshots or hunting dogs, but she couldn't assume there weren't any. Her hearing was getting better, but it still wasn't as acute as it had been. She watched for a bit longer and then went back into the house, guessing her coffee would be ready.

She had just poured herself a cup and was heading back to her laptop when the home phone rang.

"Hello?"

"Hello. May I speak to Dick Phillips, please?"

It took Dallas a moment to be able to say the words. "I'm sorry, but my father is dead. Who's calling?"

The gasp of shock was unmistakable. "No! Oh, no! I am so sorry for your loss. Uh…my name is Marsh Webster. I spoke to him ten days ago about the sale. I wonder if you would be willing to honor the deal we had."

Breath caught in the back of Dallas's throat. She was about to find out about the big money deal, she just knew it.

"What deal is that, Mr. Webster?"

"I buy ginseng. He'd promised his whole crop to me."

Dallas flashed on that old book in her dad's bedroom, the one she'd assumed was nothing but a family heirloom.

"I didn't know he was growing ginseng. Do you know if he was in business with someone else?"

"Not that I know of, why?"

"Because he was murdered, and we don't know why."

"Oh, my Lord! That's terrible."

"Did he ever say where the crop was planted?"

"Not specifically, but from a couple of things he said, I took it to be up on the mountain behind the house."

"Was there a lot of it? Enough that it would be worth a lot of money?"

"Well, of course I told him I'd have to judge the quality for myself, and he was going to sell green rather than dry it himself. But he said it hadn't been dug in probably forty or fifty years, back in his grandfather's time. He also said I needed to bring a bag full of money."

"From what he told you, what kind of money were you preparing to pay?" she asked.

"Anywhere from eighty thousand to a hundred and fifty thousand dollars."

"You're not serious?" Dallas said, and dropped into the nearest chair in disbelief.

"Oh, yes, ma'am. Completely."

"Dear Lord. What does ginseng go for per pound?"

"Wild ginseng, green-dug with good roots, and anywhere from ten to forty years old with a neck anywhere from one to four inches long, will bring two hundred and fifty to five hundred dollars a pound."

"Dear God."

"Yes, ma'am. And the same, dried, can bring eight hundred to twelve hundred dollars a pound. But drying it is tricky and time-consuming, and you can lose the whole crop if you don't know what you're doing."

Her thoughts were in free fall. "If I can find the patch and get the crop dug, you'll still buy it?"

"Yes, ma'am, but I want to caution you. If you don't know what you're doing, you can ruin the plants. Dig them up whole, shake off the dirt, but don't wash off the roots or they'll rot, and store them in covered plastic boxes in a dark, cool place that's anywhere between thirty-five and thirty-eight degrees, and avoid freezing them."

Dallas thought of the egg cooler and the big plastic boxes, and kept making mental notes as he talked.

"And one other thing," he said. "The leaves are valuable, too. I'll buy them, as well. Do you know what they look like?"

"Yes. I grew up here. I've seen plenty growing wild."

"So those little red berries are seeds. When you dig up a root, plant a seed back in the hole. It ensures new growth for future harvests. If you're uncertain about anything, look it up on Google. The information online is good enough. I'll give you my number. When you've got the crop dug, give me a call. I'll be in the area until October 1."

Dallas wrote down his information, and when she hung up, she was shaking. She'd seen those plastic boxes countless times and hadn't understood. Still in shock over what she'd learned, she got up from the table and went outside.

The sun in the east, moving on its eternal westward arc, cast long morning shadows from the trees onto the ground. She looked up at the mountain, stunned that the money to save the farm was growing wild beneath the ground.

The hair rose on the back of her neck; she was in awe of the enormity of what she'd learned. Something her ancestors had established when they'd first come upon this land was not only still here but was proving paramount to keeping the land in the family. Emotion welled. All this time the answer had been right in front of her.

"Oh, Daddy, you did it, didn't you? You weren't going to lose the farm. You had already figured out a way to save it, and I'm going to make sure it happens your way. Yes, I could have bailed you out, but you were a prideful man, and I won't take that away from you, ever. Future generations will learn what you went through, because I won't let them forget."

She went back inside, turned on the laptop and looked up harvesting ginseng on Google, and then began to take notes.

She thought about calling Trey and then changed her mind. There wasn't a lot to tell until she found the ginseng, which meant a trip up the mountain. But the memory of the feral dog was still painfully fresh, so she loaded the shotgun before she got a trowel and an old pillowcase to put roots in, should she find the patch to dig, and changed her shoes. The day was sunny, but the wind was brisk. Up on the mountain beneath the trees it would most likely be chilly, so she added a jacket.

Knowing Trey would worry if he came home and found her gone, she wrote him a quick note and got the keys to her dad's truck, which was still parked in the open shed on the back side of the house. She couldn't drive her car up through the pasture without scraping the underside on the high center between the old ruts, and driving this truck over the rough road was going to make her shoulder hurt like hell. But there was no other way short of walking, and she didn't want to be on foot that far away from the house should she encounter trouble.

Fourteen

The moment Dallas opened the door of the pickup she was assailed with scents that reminded her of her father. As soon as she slid behind the steering wheel and started the engine, she imagined him riding beside her, tickled that she'd discovered his secret and ready to point out the way. She backed out of the garage and drove toward the barn, then took a sharp left onto the road leading to the pasture. Driving across the cattle guard made her wince with every jolt, but once she was over it, she followed the trail through the pasture to the mountain beyond.

The windows were down. The sun coming through the window behind her was warm on her neck. A grasshopper had hitched a ride on her windshield, and she marveled at its tenacity. The speed of the pickup, the force of the wind and the slick surface of the glass were as nothing to it. The grasshopper was along for the ride.

She looked at the road in front of her and then up at the looming mountain. It looked like a lush green cone rising from the earth, but she knew the wildlife there, not to mention the mountain itself, could be deadly.

When the cattle saw the pickup, some of them began bawling, as if calling out, *Here we are, here we are.* She knew her dad had used this pickup to haul hay out to the herd in the winter. They probably thought they were missing a treat.

The road ended at the fence, which was about thirty yards from where the incline began. Out of habit, she pocketed the keys, although she knew her dad would have left them in the truck, confident that none of his neighbors would ever steal from him. And while that had never happened, most likely one of them had killed him. She wished they'd just taken the truck and left her daddy behind.

The sun was hot on her face as she got out, but she was all about the business at hand. She felt her pocket to make sure she had her phone, picked up the old pillowcase and the trowel in one hand, and the shotgun in the other, and headed for the fence.

Ordinarily she would have bent over and crawled through the four strands of barbed wire, but she was afraid of injuring her shoulder, so she shoved her things beneath the fence and crawled under. It hurt to bend over and it hurt to lift, but not enough to make her quit, so she picked up her things and began looking for a path, something that would tell her where to start.

"Where is it?" she muttered. "Come on, Dad. Show me. Where is it hidden?"

Within seconds she heard a rustling in the brush off to her left. Imagining a threat, she dropped the pillowcase and swung the gun in that direction with both hands. The rustling continued and leaves were still moving as a lizard shot out from beneath a bush, running from whatever was behind him. Her heart was pounding, her hands shaking. She could feel those vicious bites on her shoulder all over again.

When an old tortoise came ambling out of the underbrush and into the sunlight moments later, relief was so strong that she laughed. She was still watching it go when it hit her. Her dad's favorite saying was "Slow and steady wins the race." She'd asked her dad for a sign, and there it was.

She rushed over to where the tortoise had emerged, pushed through the low bushes and looked up, and just that fast, she was in the forest. The sun was evident here only in small, scattered patches where it found a break in the canopy, and as she'd expected, it was at least ten degrees cooler in the shade. She stood for a moment to acclimate herself to her surroundings and then began to look for signs. The ground was rocky where she was standing, so she began to move forward, and within the first forty yards she saw it: a faint but definite path worn in the dirt and leaves, and leading up the mountain.

With her first step onto the path, a slight puff of

breeze moved across the back of her neck, like the breath of someone walking behind her.

"I know, Dad. I found it, thanks to you."

She started up, careful to listen for sounds that didn't belong, but was soon aware that there were sounds she was still missing. She saw a squirrel up in a nearby tree and knew it was scolding her as she passed, but she didn't hear it. A bird darted across her line of vision, which told her she should be hearing bird calls, but what she heard was so faint as to be indistinguishable. She shuddered. As long as her senses were at half-capacity, she was vulnerable.

She checked her watch. It was almost noon. She had about five hours before Trey would be back, so there was no time to waste. She wanted to finish what her dad had started, to pay off the farm with money from *his* plan, not from *her* bank.

She hadn't been walking more than five or ten minutes when she caught a glimpse of something red and moved closer before dropping to her knees.

Ginseng!

Then she rocked back on her heels and looked up; scanning the forest from left to right, and as far as her eyes could see, she saw clusters of tiny red berries and the trademark long, pointed shape of the ginseng's green leaves. Some were growing beside a nearby outcropping of rocks, others were nearly hidden beneath deadfalls and brush, and still more were growing right out in plain sight, like diamonds in the rough.

Dallas was in shock. Maybe the ginseng had already been here when the first Phillips came, or maybe this place was the result of a pioneer woman's need to provide. But however the ginseng got here it was going to save the farm.

"Oh, my God! Oh, Daddy, oh, wow!"

She laid down the shotgun, then dumped the trowel out of the pillowcase and began to dig, applying what she'd read on Google to the task at hand.

The first plant she dug up took a long time, because she was uncertain how far down to dig, and how to get it out with damaging the neck and roots. The second and then the third became easier as she figured out how they grew and the best way to extract them. She brushed off excess dirt with her fingers and then dropped each one into the pillowcase, remembering to put a red seed back in each hole and cover it up to ensure the proliferation of the plants for years to come.

The work was tedious. Her ribs were aching and her shoulder was throbbing, but she kept thinking each root she dug up was money in the bank, and that was enough to keep her moving. About two hours in she began to get thirsty and wished she'd thought to bring water. She would know better next time, she thought, and kept working.

Once she thought she heard a dog on the far side of the mountain, and sheer panic went through her before sanity prevailed. She'd been hearing hounds all her life. Almost everyone had some. They didn't really howl. They bayed, and that was all she'd heard. She pictured big-headed, short-haired dogs with floppy ears and long legs. The blueticks and the redbones were the most popular breeds, but hounds of all kinds and sizes were a hunter's most prized possessions, and they were as thick in the mountains as the people who owned them.

She dug for another hour, crawling from one place to another without ceasing. When her phone signaled a text, she stopped to read it, smiling when she saw it was from Trey. It was what she called a welfare check, and since he didn't need a call back, she sent him a quick text that she was fine, saving all her news for a face-to-face conversation, and kept digging.

Finally she stood up to stretch her legs and look around. It felt like she'd been digging forever, but from the looks of the area she'd barely scratched the surface. Now that she knew the ginseng was here, along with the enormity of the task of harvesting it, the fear that it would be stolen became real.

People were killed over the rights to a found patch of ginseng, which immediately made her think of her dad, and she knew thieves would steal it right off private property every season, even taking the chance of trespassing on state or federal land, willing to risk going to prison for the big money that "sang," as the locals called it, brought.

She couldn't imagine how this patch had stayed hidden for so long, why someone hadn't found it and poached it years ago. But there was another way to look at it. If the Phillips family had never brought roots to a buyer, then people would assume they had none to sell. And if fifty years had gone by since this had been harvested, two generations of people would have forgotten it ever existed. She couldn't tell anyone but Trey what she'd found until the harvest was over.

She thought of the lights she'd been seeing up on the mountain; most of which had been off to the north from where she was standing. They could have been poachers stealing ginseng, not hunters as she'd assumed. This was harvest season. There could be people all over this mountain looking to make some much-needed extra money. It made her antsy about getting this all dug before someone discovered it. And on another note, she was so thirsty she barely had spit enough to swallow. It was time to go home.

The pillowcase was full of ginseng, so she carried it and the trowel in one hand, and the shotgun in the other, as she started down the mountain. It was getting late, and she kept her eye on the trail and planted her feet firmly. The spots of sunshine were fewer and farther between, and the air was a little bit cooler. Remembering she still had chickens to tend, she hastened her step.

She could see the old pickup through the trees as she reached the bottom of the path, but she stopped and scanned the pasture and the horizon before she walked out of the tree line. No need advertising where she'd been.

Confident she was unobserved, she crawled back under the fence and headed home.

Still riding the elation of discovering her Daddy's

secret, she barely noticed the bumpy ruts. She drove straight to the barn, got out with the pillowcase and made a run for the cooler.

She pulled out one of the empty plastic bins and shook the roots from her pillowcase into it, then popped on a lid and set it beneath a shelf. According to Google, the temperature in here was just right to keep green roots fresh. And now that the cooler held more than eggs, the new padlock and key on the shelf also made sense.

She padlocked the cooler, added the key to the ring of keys she carried, and drove the truck back into the shed.

Her fingers were shaking as she entered the house and walked straight to the cabinet for a glass. She filled it with water straight from the tap and drank it empty, then filled it up and drank it empty again. No more digging without water.

She passed a mirror in the hall and caught a glimpse of her reflection. She barely recognized herself. Her hair was windblown, and peppered with bits of grass and leaves. Her jacket was awry, and her eyes were narrowed and secretive. Conscious of the time, she made a dash for the bathroom. The least she could do was brush the bits of the forest out of her hair before she went to do chores. She would deal with the rest of her appearance when she finished.

Trey's day started out as perfect as a day could get. He'd made mad, passionate love to the woman he loved for a good portion of the night and arrived at the station to find Avery's birthday cake in the break room.

"Morning, Chief. Help yourself to a piece of cake. It's carrot."

"That sounds great. Happy birthday, Avery," Trey said, and took a piece of cake and a cup of coffee into his office to begin the day.

By ten o'clock he was headed to the town hall for a meeting with the mayor and the city council. There had been complaints for more than three years about the availability of handicapped parking during the annual Halloween Fair held in the city park, and they wanted Trey's input on location and traffic control. He was getting ready to wrap up when he got a text.

Two men fighting at the feed store. One of them pulled a knife.

"Sorry, gentlemen. Duty calls," he said, and left in a hurry, then ran hot all the way to the site.

He turned off the siren as he drove up on the fracas, noting with disgust that it had now spilled out into the street, along with a gathering crowd of onlookers.

He jumped out on the run with his gun drawn and quickly realized the two men fighting were brothers, Walt and Stuart Pryor.

"Drop the knife, Walt!" Trey ordered. "Do it now."

Walt was hunched over in a crouch, ready to lunge, his features contorted with rage. He needed Trey to understand. "He stole my sang, Chief! My own damned brother stole my sang and was going to sell it as his own."

"Drop the knife and kick it over here," Trey ordered.

Walt gauged the four yards separating him from his brother against the gun in Trey's hand and reluctantly did as he was told.

Trey eyed the crowd with disgust. "What's the matter with you people? Go find something better to do."

The people dispersed, mumbling beneath their breath. The fight had just been getting good when the chief had to show up and ruin everything.

Trey picked up the knife, holstered his gun and pointed at the brothers. "Where's the ginseng in question?"

"In the front seat of his truck. I caught him before he got inside to sell it," Walt complained.

"How do you know it's yours?" Trey asked.

"It's in my knapsack. He stole *that*, too."

Trey eyed Stuart. "Get the knapsack and bring it to me," he said, and proceeded to handcuff Walt and bag the knife as evidence while Stuart went to the truck.

Trey set Walt in the front seat of the cruiser, locked the knife in the trunk, and then stood by the open cruiser door, watching as Stuart returned.

Stuart handed Trey the knapsack, and remained silent as he was handcuffed and put in the backseat.

Trey put the knapsack in the trunk with the knife, then got into the car and called dispatch.

Avery quickly responded. "Go ahead, Chief."

"Tell Earl I'm coming in with two prisoners."

"Will do, Chief. Over."

"Over and out," Trey said, eyeing Stuart in the rearview mirror. It was telling that the man hadn't defended himself.

"Sorry bastard," Walt muttered, and then glanced out the window, still shaking his head.

It took Trey another hour at the station before Stuart finally admitted he took the sang because Walt owed him money and wouldn't pay it back, at which point Walt reluctantly admitted that was a fact.

Trey stared at the brothers, now standing side by side in adjoining cells.

"What a mess you two made, and for what? Stuart, you sneaked around and stole your brother's property instead of facing him like a man. And you, Walt, you were willing to kill your brother for money? I know your mama. She's gonna have herself a fit when she finds out what you two have done. Now the next few months of your life depend on the leniency of the judge who hears your case."

Walt sighed. "Can someone call my wife and tell her to come get my car?"

Stuart glanced at Walt and then looked at Trey with a defeated stare. "I don't have anyone to come get my truck."

"Then it will be impounded," Trey said.

Stuart glared at Walt. "None of this would have happened if you'd just paid me back."

"Well, I didn't have the money until now," Walt said.

"Stuart, how much did Walt owe you?" Trey asked.

"A hundred and twenty dollars."

"Walt, how much was that ginseng worth?"

"Maybe twenty-five hundred dollars."

Trey shook his head in disgust. "You both act like you were dropped on your heads when you were babies. Now make yourselves comfortable and don't start any shit. You hear?"

They flopped down on their bunks. It wasn't the way they'd planned to end their day.

By the time Trey logged the knife and knapsack into evidence and officially booked the men, it was after three and his belly was growling.

"Hey, Avery, I'm going to Charlie's to grab a sandwich. You want anything?"

"No, thanks. I'm pretty full of birthday cake," the dispatcher said.

"If you need me, you know where I'll be," Trey said, and headed out the door.

He thought of Dallas and wondered what she was doing. As soon as he got in the car he sent her a text.

Hey, sweetheart, just checking in. You don't need to call me back unless you need me. Love you.

Moments later he got one back.

I'm fine. Staying busy. I'll explain tonight.

Smiling, he went to eat.

* * *

The killer was coming out of the barbershop when the chief drove past. He smiled and waved as he headed to his car, taking delight in the fact that the chief waved back. He had no sense of regret for what he'd done, having learned long ago that dirty things sometimes had to happen when the end justified the means. The only downside was his carelessness. He didn't know what he'd done that gave away the fact Dick had been murdered, but he couldn't let it happen again.

His cell phone rang as he was getting into the car. He checked the caller ID and then smiled as he answered.

"Hello?...Yes, I'm on my way home. Need anything?...Okay, then. See you soon."

He dropped the phone in the console and drove away with a nice new haircut and a satisfied smile on his face.

Dallas was in the egg room, sorting and cleaning the day's eggs, when she heard a car honk. She eyed the shotgun propped near the door as she wiped her hands, and then walked out into the breezeway, where she stopped, stunned by the sight of the news crew, led by Mark Dodson.

Mark approached her with a smile and a pen and paper, obviously intending to prove he had remembered her hearing loss.

The crew was already setting up the camera when

Dallas strode out of the barn, shouting every word as she said, "If anyone turns on a camera, I'll have you all arrested for trespassing."

They froze. Mark began writing rapidly.

Dallas yanked the pen out of his hand and poked it back in his pocket.

"I'm getting my hearing back, and to save time and your ink, what the hell are you doing here?"

Mark stuttered.

"We, uh...we found out your father's death was ruled a homicide. We wanted to get a statement from—"

"Get off my property," Dallas said, and then waved at the camera crew. "All of you! I'm not talking about my father's death. I'm not talking about the dog attack. I'm not talking, period. How many times do you have to be told?"

Mark glared. No more Mr. Nice Guy. His tone turned sarcastic, bordering on demeaning. "Sorry, but you're news, baby. The public has a right to—"

"A right to what? My personal life? No, they don't, and neither do you. I'm not a wanted felon. I'm not famous. I will not trot out the devastation I feel for everyone's entertainment as they eat their supper, understand?"

"The boss isn't going to like this," Mark snapped.

"I'll call him myself," Dallas said.

"And tell him what? If you're going to give someone the story, give it to me, damn it!"

"I'm not giving *anyone* the story. I'll be giving him

my resignation. I learned a hard lesson during all this tragedy. I now know what it feels like to be on the other side of that camera, and I don't much like it. I don't want to be a part of that anymore."

Mark looked dumbfounded. "Are you serious? Why would you quit when you're on the verge of getting into the big leagues?"

"Get in the van and go back to Charleston. All of you! And don't ever come back," Dallas said.

The camera crew scrambled into the back of the van, as Mark got in the front seat. He was still staring at her in disbelief.

She stood in the breezeway, watching them leave, and never once regretted what she'd said. And the moment they were out of sight, she sent a text to her boss. Ironically, the last scoop she gave him was about herself. Dallas Phillips, WOML's hot on-the-spot journalist, had just quit her job.

Once the text was sent, she felt nothing but relief. She'd cut ties with the very reason she'd left Trey, and instead of regret, it felt like she'd finally stepped out into the light.

Fifteen

Dallas raided the freezer, digging through the food Betsy had stored for her after the service, and took meat loaf, scalloped potatoes and a peach pie out to reheat. A little while later the house smelled wonderful.

She was in her dad's recliner with her feet up and a glass of sweet iced tea in her hand, still trying to quench her thirst. After the day she'd put in, she gave in and took a pain pill. When the throbbing began to subside, her relief was huge. Today had been a day for revelations, and she couldn't wait to tell Trey.

The television was on, but she wasn't paying much attention. She kept watching the drive for Trey's car, and when she saw it, her heart skipped a beat. He was home!

When she got up to let him in, she paused by the window. He looked so tired. Today must have been a busy one. And after next to no sleep last night, she would bet money he was out like a light tonight.

"Welcome home," she said when she opened the door.

The change of expression on his face was humbling. It was quite a heady feeling to know she was loved.

"You are a sight to come home to," he said, as he leaned down and kissed her. "Lord, something smells good."

"Not my cooking. Raided the freezer from Dad's service."

"Works for me," he said. "Give me a couple of minutes to change out of my uniform and clean up. My day was crazy."

"Mine, too," she said, and headed to the kitchen as he went to change. She couldn't wait to tell him all the news, but after seeing his exhaustion, she decided to wait until after they'd eaten.

They fixed their plates from the food on the stove and carried them to the table. Eating together like this was almost more than Trey could take in, and he wasted no time in saying so.

"You have to know that this is pure heaven to me. Usually it's takeout in the apartment and falling asleep in front of the television." He leaned over and kissed her square on the lips. "Having you back in my life is my dream come true."

Dallas took the words to heart as further affirmation that quitting her job had been the right choice. No amount of personal success would ever mean more to her than this man.

"And just so you know, my years in the city were never quite what I thought they would be. It was your absence that kept me from ever being really happy, and I'm ashamed that it took Dad's death to make me see that."

Trey's shoulders slumped. "I wish he was here to see this. I think he and Mom had given up on both of us."

He got up to refill their iced tea, and then sat back down and finished the last few bites on his plate. "Hey, honey, do you remember Walt and Stuart Pryor?"

"Ella and Willis Pryor's boys?"

"Yes, that's them," he said, as he pushed his plate to the side "I arrested them today."

Dallas frowned. "What on earth for? I don't remember them as troublemakers."

"Walt pulled a knife on Stuart at the feed store in town. They were going at it when I got there. Turns out Walt owed Stuart money, and when he didn't pay it back soon enough to suit Stuart, Stuart stole Walt's ginseng."

A chill ran through her. "Really? Brothers fighting over ginseng. That's scary."

"Yes, it is. They're both in trouble with the law now, Stuart for theft, and Walt for assault with a deadly weapon."

She sat for a few moments, trying to figure out how to tell him what she'd learned without sensationalizing the ginseng angle even more.

"So you said you had an interesting day. Tell me," he said.

"I know about the big money venture Dad had planned."

"You're kidding! What is it? How did you find out?"

"I got a phone call today from a man named Marsh Webster wanting to talk to Dad. He was shocked to learn of his death and then asked if I would honor their deal. That's when I found out Dad had a honey hole of ginseng he'd promised to sell to Webster."

Trey shuddered, struck by the odd coincidence of a man being willing to kill his own brother over ginseng and Dick being involved with it before his murder. He felt suddenly anxious. He didn't like to think that Dick could have died for ginseng, or that, by association, Dallas could be in danger, too.

"And you had no idea?" Trey asked.

"No. Never in my whole life did I hear him or Mom mention digging ginseng. In fact I know they didn't. I would have seen it. But I did find a book on ginseng in Dad's room the other day. It belonged to the first Phillips to homestead this land, and build the house and barn."

"So what else did Webster tell you?" Trey asked.

"He said Dad told him the patch hadn't been harvested in forty or fifty years, which, if it's good, means top dollar in the ginseng market."

"But your dad owed fifty thousand dollars to the bank. Surely he didn't think—"

Dallas interrupted. "Oh, yes, he did. Webster said

he was prepared to pay upward of a hundred thousand dollars."

Trey flinched as if he'd been slapped. *That* was a motive to kill.

"I don't like this," he said. "This puts you in a dangerous position. What do you want to do? Are you going to try and find it?"

Dallas looked him straight in the eye so there was no misunderstanding her intent.

"I've already found it. I dug for about five hours today, and right now there's probably fifteen hundred dollars' worth of green ginseng locked up in the egg cooler, and I didn't even scratch the surface. The whole side of the mountain is covered in it. I don't know how he kept it hidden, but it's there."

He took a deep breath and mentally backed off. This wasn't his call. This was her home and her dad's honor that was at stake.

"I'll be damned," he said softly. "So how much is ginseng going for these days?"

"The older the root, the bigger the price. Green is worth less than dried, but you take a chance losing it all if it's not dried right."

"So you'll sell it green?"

"Yes, at five hundred dollars a pound."

For a moment, all he could do was stare. "You have got to be kidding me," he finally said.

"No, I'm not. But I can't quit wondering if it's what got Dad killed. What if someone else found out about his patch and killed him so they could get to it free and easy?"

"Then why weren't they already digging?" Trey asked. "What are they waiting for?"

"I don't know. Maybe because I'm still here? I told you, I keep seeing lights on the mountain. What if they didn't know where it was, either? What if they've been looking for it, too, but I found it first."

Trey was stunned. If any part of what she was suggesting was true, then she was in big danger.

"So you put the ginseng you dug up in the egg room."

"Yes, and padlocked the door."

His eyes widened. "The plastic storage boxes! That padlock and key. He was getting ready to harvest, wasn't he?"

She nodded. "I'm being up front with you, Trey. I won't ever keep a secret from you, but at the same time, I want you to accept my decisions as I make them, just like I would yours."

"I hear you. I may not be comfortable with them, but I would never presume to override what you think is right."

"There's more," she said.

He frowned. "Like what?"

"Mark Dodson and a camera crew from WOML showed up today, wanting an exclusive because Dad's death had been ruled a murder. They seemed to think my life was big news now."

"That son of a bitch is real slow to learn, isn't he?" Trey snapped.

She nodded, got up from her chair and slid into his lap, then gave him a one-armed hug that made him wonder how she'd ever dug ginseng with the shape she was in.

"I sent them packing, and then sent my boss a text and told him I quit."

"Because of us?" Trey asked.

"Partly, but also because I've had a dose of what it feels like to be on the other side of a news story, and I don't want to be that person who shoves a microphone into a grieving parent's face anymore."

Trey hugged her. "You are amazing," he said softly, and kissed her until she was groaning.

He pulled back and gave her a look, amazed by all that had gone on while he was away.

"How on earth did you manage all that climbing and digging with a sore belly and bad shoulder?"

"Oh, it hurt, but I kept remembering Dad had planned for this to save the farm, and I want the loan to be paid off his way. It's the last thing I can do for him."

He saw the passion on her face, heard the fervor in her voice, and remembered this was part of why he loved her.

"Then I'm behind you all the way. Just don't tell anyone what you've found. Not anyone, understand?"

She nodded.

"And accept the fact that I'm going to stay so close

on your heels that you'll be sick of my shadow before this is over."

She hugged him.

"I won't complain about that. It's a little creepy up there alone."

"You *did* take the gun, didn't you?"

"Yes, and my phone. If I see or hear anything weird, you'll know."

He sighed. "Then okay."

"Okay," she said. "Let's eat pie."

He laughed. "God, I love you."

She grinned. "Because I like pie?"

"No. Because you're a little bit crazy, like I am."

She arched an eyebrow. "Let's eat pie later."

"Yes, let's," he said, and picked her up in his arms.

High up on the north side of the mountain, two men sat in front of their tent, watching the smoke from their campfire rise high above the treetops and thinking about what they'd seen that afternoon, staring down at the Phillips place through binoculars. Every now and then one of them would refill his coffee cup and top it off with a splash of Jim Beam.

Snake Warren eyed his buddy, Fraser, making sure he didn't finish off the booze.

Other than the snake tattoo on his belly that had given him his nickname, he wasn't much to look at. The fact that he was missing a tooth and one eye didn't bother him much, and he dared it to bother anyone else.

"I told you if we watched that house long enough we'd find a way to get back the money we lost on Zeus," Snake said.

Fraser Pitts screwed the cap back on the bottle of Jim Beam and set it down between them.

"We'd have Zeus himself back if she hadn't killed him. I had him in my sights that night, remember? One shot with that tranquilizer gun and he would have been ours, but you had to go and fart. If you could have just held it a few seconds we would already be gone."

Snake shrugged. "What did you want me to do, blow up? Gas is gas, it has to go somewhere. If you'd pulled the trigger a few seconds sooner my fart wouldn't have made a bit of difference."

Fraser took another sip of coffee as he stared down into the fire.

"It's over and done with, and Zeus is dead, although I didn't believe it until I saw that guy bring the body in to the vet. When we told Sonny that bunch of hillbillies hunted down all the other dogs we came to pick up, he lost his mind. I'm scared to death to tell him Zeus is dead, too. The son of a bitch is crazy."

Snake shuddered. Disappointing Sonny Dalton was the quickest way to get killed, and Fraser was right. Telling him his best fighting dogs were dead *had* sent him into a frenzy. He didn't see the problem himself. They were just dogs. All Sonny had to do was get some more.

"So the bitch killed Zeus. What's your angle now?"

Snake frowned. "The woman's a looker, and worth

a lot more to some sex trafficker than what Sonny would get fighting a new dog."

"Well, you tell Sonny your plan. I'm not going to," Fraser said.

"I'll call him," Snake said. "And now that we know what she's doing up here, we don't even have to go to her house to snatch her. She'll come back up the mountain to dig up more of them damn man roots again, and when she does, we'll hike over to where she's digging and grab her. Won't be a witness around to hear her scream, and we'll be long gone before anyone knows she's missing. I think she'll bring upward of half a million on the foreign market. That would make Sonny happy."

"Whatever," Fraser muttered, then downed the last of his coffee. "I'm gonna take a piss and turn in."

"I think I'll sit watch for a while, maybe finish off that Jim Beam," Snake said.

As soon as Fraser hit the trees to do his business, Snake poured out his coffee and grabbed the whiskey. The night was cold and the whiskey would set him on fire, and he needed some liquid courage to make the call.

He took two big swigs of whiskey and walked off with his phone. He didn't want Fraser to hear him grovel.

Dallas slept on her back, favoring the shoulder that was too sore to lie on. Trey slept curled up beside her.

one arm across her belly. Even in sleep his need to protect her was strong.

Considering the six years, four months, three weeks and two days that they'd been without each other and the way they'd made love earlier with total abandon, maybe it was an unconscious desire to recoup what they'd missed.

Betsy let out a cry in her sleep that yanked her awake. She sat up in bed, her heart pounding, her body bathed in sweat.

"Oh my God, oh my God," she moaned, and rolled over to turn on the light. She stumbled out of bed, stripping her nightgown off as she went, and then moved to the dresser to get a fresh one.

But not even the change of clothes could take away the terror she'd felt in her dream. Still shaking, she went to get the journal she'd started using to keep track of her dreams. She'd read on the internet that it was helpful in controlling nightmares, though she didn't know what good it would do, writing all this down. Still, if it would help her get back to sleep, she would do it gladly.

She curled up in her reading chair, making sure to stay quiet. She didn't want to wake Trina, because she didn't want to talk about what was happening in her head. As soon as she turned on the light, she began a new page, writing down everything she could remember. Maybe when all the dreams were written down they would make sense. Right now they were nothing but a jumble of horror-filled images that wouldn't go away. She longed for the days when her sleep was restful. Now she hated for it to get dark.

Trey left the farm before daylight. The town drunk had been found dead in the alley behind Charlie's Burgers. It was a sad end to a wasted life, although in the end, everyone died. It was only the specifics of the exit that were never the same.

Trey's departure also gave Dallas an early start to her day. She was out doing chores just before daybreak. The cows were fed and already moving off toward the pasture, and she had put a new note on her door stating eggs could be purchased anytime before 8:00 a.m. and anytime after 5:00 p.m.

As soon as she was packed, she headed to the mountain. This time she was prepared. Phone. Food. Water. Her digging tools, two plastic garbage bags and the shotgun. There was more to carry up this time, but she'd used a backpack and thought she could sling it over her good shoulder and suffer the pain rather than make two trips.

She walked out to get in the pickup through fog so thick she could barely see the shed. She drove slowly across the cattle guard. Visibility was less than twenty yards, and sounds were muffled to the point that it was almost like before, when she'd been deaf. It gave her an eerie feeling, knowing how easy it would be to get caught off guard. And because she couldn't see much past the hood of the pickup, it was difficult to keep an eye on the trail.

She was thinking she was almost there, and then the next thing she knew she had just missed hitting the herd bull. She slammed on the brakes, her heart pounding as she looked out the driver's side window. If she put her hand out, the bull's nose would have been close enough to touch.

"Oh, Lord," she breathed, and then eased back into motion, going slower, watching carefully for the rest of the herd, until finally she drove up on the fence.

Now that she was here, she debated the wisdom of going up the mountain. What if she couldn't find the path? What if she wandered off her father's land? There weren't any fences on the mountain. Nothing to mark property lines except for some ancient flat rocks with surveyors' marks on them, and you had to know where to look to even find them.

Still, nothing ventured, nothing gained. She could start up, and if it appeared to be a lost cause, it cost nothing to go back.

She crawled under the fence, thankful for the flannel-lined jacket she was wearing, and leaned the shotgun against the tree to shoulder the backpack.

"Holy crap," she moaned, as the weight of the strap pulled at the muscles all across her back. She grabbed the shotgun and headed for the bushes, then moved them aside and stepped into another world.

Water was dripping from the leaves. The fog swirled eerily around her legs as she passed, like ghostly arms futilely trying to hinder her progress. There was no need to look up. The fog hid all but the faint shapes of trees and bushes. She kept her gaze on the ground, looking for the path. Just when she thought that she'd missed it, the fog swirled away and she saw it just a few steps ahead.

Thank you, God.

Breathing a slow sigh of relief, she kept walking, her gaze down and fixed on that narrow path.

Snap!

She froze. Something or someone had just stepped on a twig. The urge to turn and run was strong. She swung the shotgun up in her hands and stared into the thick gray mist.

Moments later she heard movement off to her right and swung the gun in that direction, ready to fire if necessary. She saw movement. Something was walking across the path a few yards ahead. Then she saw him, as shrouded as the trees from which he'd come, but the shape of his body and his immense rack of antlers were unmistakable. Her heart was pounding; she was mesmerized by his majesty. When he stopped and turned, she knew he'd seen her, too. She didn't move, and neither did the buck. They stared, each at the other, while time stopped.

Dallas couldn't say why, but she felt like she'd just been blessed, that her presence here had been accepted. When the buck made the first move, it was instantaneous. One leap and he was gone, swallowed up by the fog.

"Oh, my God. That did not just happen," she said, then took a deep breath and proceeded to the ginseng patch.

After a quick recon of where she'd dug yesterday, she set the backpack aside and sent Trey a text.

I'm on the mountain.

Then she dropped to her knees and went to work.

It was the drip of water onto the top of the tent that woke Fraser up. He rolled over, expecting to see Snake in the other bedroll, but it was empty.

"What the fuck?" he muttered, put on his boots and went out to take a piss, then stopped in his tracks. He couldn't see shit beyond their campsite.

The fire had long since gone out. The stack of firewood was wet from the thick, soupy fog, and Snake was flat on his back, arms outstretched. His crotch was wet where he'd pissed his pants, and his hair and face were beaded with moisture from the fog. Either he was dead or passed out drunk.

"What a fuckup," Fraser muttered, and walked away from the camp a few feet to find a tree.

He came back and dug through the tent for a can of Spam and a sleeve of crackers. He would have killed for a cup of coffee, but the wood was too wet to burn. He went back out to look around for the whiskey, and when he realized Snake had finished it off, he kicked the bottom of Snake's boot in anger, which dislodged a fart of disgusting proportions.

"Son of a bitch, Snake! That smells like something

crawled up your ass and died. Wake the hell up and do something productive, like change your pants. I didn't know we needed to bring diapers."

Snake rolled over onto the empty whiskey bottle with a jerk and a flop, and busted his lip. He came upright with his fists doubled, cursing a blue streak as he took a swing at thin air, apparently thinking someone had just punched him in the mouth.

Fraser rolled his eyes and went back into the tent to eat. At least it was dry and smelled better in there.

Between the fog and the hangover, neither one of them would be trekking through the woods today.

Sixteen

After Trey got Dallas's text, he had a difficult time concentrating on the work at hand, and got up and wandered through the jail area, making notes on things that needed to be fixed. It was almost nine when he went back to the paperwork that had been piling up. He had just begun when he heard a familiar voice.

"Oh, crap," he muttered, and then stood up just as fussbudget Lowrance came in his door. "Morning, Mr. Lowrance. What can I do for you?" he asked.

George Lowrance was good at selling shoes, but not so great on apologies. Still, he considered it his duty, since he'd made two official complaints.

"I wanted to let you know that I put that surveillance camera in like your girl suggested, and this morning I finally caught the culprit in the act."

Trey stifled a groan, hoping he wasn't going to have to actually arrest someone for stealing a newspaper.

"So who was taking your papers?" he asked.

George rolled his eyes. "A dog. That scruffy mutt that hangs around the firehouse. You know the one—a little black short-haired thing with a bobbed tail and one floppy ear."

Trey grinned. "Shorty. They call him Shorty."

"Yes, that's the one," George said. "Anyway, I went down to the firehouse and talked to the guys myself. They told me Shorty had a mind of his own and they didn't have an answer for my situation."

"Well, I do," Trey said. "Have the paper delivered to your home. You can bring it to work."

George stood there a moment and then slapped his head. "Well, good grief! I should have thought of that myself. It would have saved me the cost of that surveillance camera."

"Oh, I don't know. Extra security is always a good thing," Trey said.

"Yes, well, I just wanted you to know. Thanks again, Chief."

"You're welcome."

Avery passed the shoe salesman in the hall and poked his head in Trey's office. "Arraignment for the Pryor brothers is over."

"Already?" Trey asked, glancing up at the clock.

"Lonnie said they were the first thing on Judge Evans's docket and they both pled not guilty."

"What? Why the hell would they do that? There were a dozen witnesses to the whole thing."

"I don't know. Lonnie just put them back in their cells and said you would want to know."

"Yeah, thanks," Trey said, but he was shocked.

So on top of everything else, those idiots were planning on dragging everything out and going through a trial. He thought about what Dallas had told him about storing ginseng, so now he knew the ginseng in that knapsack was going to rot. He thought about Walt's wife and four kids being on their own if he went to jail; without money to tide them over this winter, they would go hungry.

He had an idea, and decided to see if he could get a minute to talk to Judge Evans. It might be a wasted trip, but he wouldn't be able to live with himself if he didn't try.

Trey's steps were long and hurried as he walked the courthouse hall to Evans's office.

The judge's secretary was at her computer, and looked up and smiled when he entered.

"Hello, Chief. What brings *you* here?"

"Hey, Loretta. If the judge is in I'd like to talk to him a minute."

"I'll check," she said, then rang his office.

Inside his chambers, Judge Evans put a bookmark in the legal volume he was searching to answer the phone.

"What's up, Loretta?"

"The chief is here. He wants a few minutes with you."

"Sure. Send him in," Evans said.

"You can go in," Loretta said,

"Thanks," Trey said, and entered the judge's chambers.

"Trey! Have a seat," Evans said.

"Thanks. I appreciate this. I have something I'd like to run by you. It's about the Pryor brothers."

"Quite a mess. I imagine their families aren't too happy with them about now."

"Yes, that's part of what I wanted to talk about. As you are aware, the stolen knapsack with the freshly dug ginseng belongs to Walt Pryor."

"Right."

"I know they've pled not guilty and that they want this to go to trial. The deal is, they committed or admitted to their crimes in front of a dozen witnesses as I was putting them under arrest."

"Go on," he said.

"Walt is the one who pulled the knife. His brother was unarmed, so he knows he can't claim self-defense, and basically he has no leg to stand on getting out of the assault with a deadly weapon charge."

"According to the law, you're right."

"And Stuart has already admitted to stealing his brother's property, so he can't deny what he did, because I witnessed his admission, and he got the stolen property out of his own vehicle and turned it over to me."

"Yes, right again," Evans said.

"My point is, if this is drawn out, the ginseng is going to rot. It needs to be sold now to keep it from spoiling, or at the least refrigerated to keep it fresh."

"And how is that our problem?" Evans asked.

"Other than having part of the evidence spoil on our watch, none. But I was thinking, if the brothers agreed to waive trial and let you assess their guilt and punishment, and sentence them from the bench, the evidence would then be returned, correct?"

Evans sat there for a minute, thinking, and then it hit him. "You're thinking about Walt's family, aren't you, Chief?"

"Guilty as charged, Judge," Trey said.

Evans smiled. "You're a good cop. You know your people, and you care about them. So I'm listening."

"If the brothers were willing to do as I've said, then Walt's wife could sell the ginseng today and have money to live on through the winter while Walt is in jail. If not, I know a woman and four kids who are going to have a cold and hungry winter up on the mountain."

Evans leaned back in his chair. "You know you're damn young to be the chief of police, right?"

"Yes, sir, I do."

"Well, just so you know, you're doing a fine job, regardless of your age."

"Thank you. I grew up here, and I do care about these people and what happens in this town. I intend to live and die here without one day of regret."

Evans nodded. "Okay. Here's my thought. If the brothers waive trial, and are willing to accept their sentences from the bench, then yes, Walt's wife will get his property back and be free to do whatever she chooses with it."

Trey beamed.

"Thank you, Judge. I'm going to have a talk with the brothers right now. Would you be willing to get this done today?"

"Hell yes," Evans said. "The more cases I can clear from my docket, the happier it makes me."

"I'll be in touch," Trey said.

He left the office in haste and headed back to the station.

Avery was dispatching an ambulance to the nursing home when Trey walked in.

"Where's Earl?" Trey asked, as soon as Avery finished.

"On patrol," Avery said.

"Get him in here ASAP. I need someone to witness a discussion I'm going to have with our two jailbirds."

"Yes, sir," Avery said, and quickly sent out a call for the officer to return to the station.

"When he gets here, tell him to come back to the jail."

"Will do, Chief," Avery said.

Trey headed down the hall to the back of the building where the jail cells were located. He could hear the brothers talking when he walked in, and from the sound of their discussion, they were both deeply regretting what they'd done.

"Good day, gentlemen. How's it going?" he asked.

The brothers looked at him like he'd lost his mind.

"How do you think it's going, Chief? We've fucked ourselves, and we're going to prison."

"Yes, well, you have only yourselves to blame for that now, don't you?"

They looked at each other and then down at the floor.

"Out of curiosity, what do you two hope to gain by going to trial?"

"Well, we thought one of us might get off, and then he could go home and take care of the family until the other one gets out," Walt said.

Trey shook his head. "That's not gonna happen. You know why?"

They looked crestfallen.

"No. Why?" Stuart asked.

"Walt tried to assault you with a deadly weapon in front of witnesses. He tried to cut you. Someone could say he was trying to kill you. That's attempted murder."

Walt groaned and buried his face in his hands.

"And you, Stuart, have already confessed to theft and handed over the stolen property to me from your own vehicle, again in front of witnesses. And since the value of the stolen property was over five hundred dollars, it became a felony. You're not getting off on that, either."

Stuart began to cry.

At that point, Earl walked in.

"Is everything all right, Chief? Avery said you needed me."

"Everything is fine, Earl. I want you to be a witness to what I'm going to propose to these fine gentlemen here, so that they can't come back later and claim they were railroaded into anything."

Earl took out his cell phone.

"I'll record it, Chief, and download it into evidence."

Trey nodded.

"Okay, now. Walt. Stuart. You have both committed crimes in front of at least a dozen witnesses, and have confessed your guilt in those crimes to me at booking. Is this true?"

"Yes, I did," Walt said.

"So did I," Stuart added.

"And you're both worried about Walt's wife and kids, and your mother, who will be up on the mountain alone when you and Stuart go to jail. Is this true?"

"Yes," they said in unison.

"And I assume you know that the ginseng being held in evidence, the ginseng Walt dug to sell and Stuart stole, is going to rot sitting in that knapsack in the evidence room."

"I told him that," Walt said.

"You need to know that I talked to Judge Evans on your behalf, and if you are both willing to waive your rights to a trial by jury and let him assess your crimes and sentence you from the bench, he will release the property in question to your family. Immediately."

Walt jumped up from his bunk and grabbed the bars of the cell, his eyes wide with disbelief.

"You did that, Chief? You went out of your way to help our family like that?"

Trey shrugged. "They don't deserve to suffer for the mistakes you two made."

"I'm waiving my right!" Walt said.

Stuart was standing now, too, the tears drying on his face. "I'm waiving my right to trial, too," he said.

"How quick can we do this? That ginseng isn't going to last much longer," Walt said.

Trey pulled his phone out of his pocket and made the call.

Loretta answered.

"Judge Evans's office."

"Loretta, it's me, Trey. Tell the judge the Pryor brothers are willing. They're ready when he is."

"Just a moment, Chief, while I put you on hold."

Trey waited.

"What did he say?" Walt asked.

"I'm on hold," Trey said, and then Loretta came back on the line.

"He said to tell you, get the prisoners over here. Go to courtroom eight. He'll meet you there. I'll have a stenographer waiting."

"Thanks, Loretta. See you soon."

Trey hung up.

"Earl, grab the handcuffs and leg chains. We're going to court."

"Leg chains?" Stuart cried.

"So you don't change your mind and run," Earl said.

Within fifteen minutes they were pulling up at the courthouse and escorting the prisoners into court.

Less than thirty minutes later the brothers had been sentenced and were on their way back to jail to await transport to prison. Since neither man had a record of any kind, the judge had, in Trey's opinion, been as lenient as he could be. The men would serve minimal time for their offenses, with the possibility of parole within the year.

Even better, the evidence had been released, and the minute it was back on Trey's desk he was on the phone to Walt's wife, who broke down in tears, thanked him effusively and said she was on her way.

The day was turning out to be a good one after all.

The fog didn't completely dissipate on the mountain until after noon had come and gone. Dallas was sitting on an outcropping of rock taking a much-needed break and eating the sandwich she'd brought from home. Her back was tired, her shoulder was throbbing, and her belly ached from crouching to dig, but she had plenty to show for her misery. One of the plastic bags she'd brought was almost full.

She looked down at the area in which she'd been digging and then up at what was still left to harvest, and for a moment she felt the impossibility of accomplishing such a task alone. The harvest time for ginseng in West Virginia ran from September 1 to November 30, but she didn't have the luxury of all that time. Not with the foreclosure date on the farm looming closer by the day and her buyer leaving on the first of October.

As soon as she was through eating, she quenched her thirst, found a bush where she could take a bathroom break and went back to work.

Now that the fog had lifted, she was more aware of how dense the woods were and how isolated she was. If only her hearing had been fully restored, she wouldn't feel so vulnerable. So she kept the shotgun within reach and every so often rocked back on her heels to scan the woods around her.

It was sometime after 3:00 p.m. and Fraser was dozing when he heard a commotion outside the tent. Without thinking, he jumped up with his rifle in hand and walked out to find Snake holding a chunk of firewood and arguing with a gun-toting man wearing a uniform. His back was to Fraser, so his badge wasn't visible, but Fraser was 99 percent sure the guy was a forest ranger.

His heart stopped. They were gonna get arrested, and when that happened, the outstanding warrants on his head would throw him right back in prison and he would die of old age in his cell.

He didn't even wait to hear what he and Snake were arguing about. He just took aim and shot the ranger in the back.

The man dropped facedown less than three yards

from where Snake was standing, and the shock on Snake's face quickly turned to rage.

"Why the fuck did you do that?" Snake screamed.

Fraser waved his gun and shouted back, "He was gonna arrest us, and I'm not going back to prison, that's why."

Snake threw the chunk of firewood at Fraser, barely missing his head.

"He wasn't going to arrest us. He was just telling me that there's no camping here."

Fraser frowned. "You two were yelling. I heard you. And I come out and see you holding that stick and ready to fight. What was I supposed to think?"

"We weren't yelling, we were arguing. And I wasn't gonna fight him with no damn stick. I was about to build a fire when he walked up. Now you've gone and shot a Fed. We've got to hide this body and move our camp or we'll be running for the rest of our lives."

Fraser shrugged. "What about going after the woman?"

Snake threw up his arms. "Not now, you stupid fuck. We have to get out of the area. There'll be a search party looking for this guy before daylight tomorrow, and the last place we want to be is here."

"Well, shit," Fraser said.

Snake was already throwing things in a duffel bag and cursing beneath his breath.

"Where should we hide the body?" Fraser asked.

"You killed him. You figure it out," Snake muttered, and kept on packing.

Fraser put the ranger's gun in the back of his waistband, threw the man's lifeless body over his shoulder and walked out of the camp.

It was just after 4:00 p.m. when Dallas called a halt to the day. Both the plastic bags were full, her water was gone, and all she wanted to do was get home and take a bath. She loaded up her things in the backpack, grabbed the two bags of ginseng with her good arm and the shotgun with the other, and started back down the mountain.

The wind was up, the air smelled damp, and she was thinking they might get rain tonight when she stumbled and barely caught herself before she fell. As she did, the sudden noise spooked a rabbit. It darted across the path and into the brush, and in seconds it had disappeared.

"Sorry, little guy."

She got a better grip on her things and kept moving, grateful that she was going downhill.

When she finally crawled into the pickup, the thought of what was left to be done at home made her groan. Then she reminded herself this dig was temporary. There would be plenty of time to rest when it was over.

As soon as she crossed the cattle guard, she took a left toward the barn and parked out front. She put the freshly dug roots into the cooler with the ones from the day before, and then walked up to the chicken house.

The little hens were chasing down the occasional

bug, and any other hen that got too close to their spot of ground, clucking to each other and squawking their disapproval of imagined infractions. The henhouse hierarchy was her entertainment as she went about refilling feeders and putting out fresh water.

The old broody hen was still sitting on her ceramic egg, but the peck she aimed toward Dallas's arm was halfhearted.

"You missed," Dallas said, as she got the still-warm egg from underneath the hen, leaving the ceramic one behind.

Dallas noticed that one hen in the flock had a bloody place on the back of her head, a sign she was being pecked by some of the others. As tired as she was, she spent minutes trying to catch her so she could doctor the wound, then more time trying to hold the hen still to smear a nasty purple salve on the sore.

"Poor little girl," Dallas said, as she turned the hen loose.

It wasn't just women who gave other females in their group a hard time. Even hens could be bitchy to their own.

By the time the eggs were gathered, the wind had grown stronger and cooler. She glanced up at the dark clouds rolling in and wasted no time getting back to the barn with the eggs. Too tired to clean and sort them, she left them on the table in the cooler, then locked it up. The cows hadn't come up, and it looked like it was going to pour, so she wasn't putting out feed that would get ruined before they ate it. Obviously they'd taken cover somewhere and could wait until morning for their hay. She got back in the truck and drove up to the shed. Her feet were dragging by the time she got into the house with her gear. The door lock clicked, and for a few seconds it was the only sound in the house.

Dallas stood in the silence, absorbing the safety of her home as the first raindrops hit the roof. She was so tired she could hardly think. Her clothes were filthy, her hair windblown and, again, sporting some of the mountain's best greenery. She went into the utility room and stripped by the washer, dumping in clothes as she went. After starting the laundry, she walked bare-assed naked through the house, cradling her arm like a sling to ease her shoulder pain.

It was almost five o'clock. Trey wouldn't be home before six at the earliest. She had just enough time to clean up and then think about food after.

Trey's last text from Dallas had been just after two. She'd been fine then, and he had no reason to assume she wouldn't still be fine when he got home. Even so, he was worried. Dealing with the aftermath of the Pryor brothers' fight was a vivid reminder of the dangers of cultivating ginseng.

It started raining just as he stopped by his apartment to pick up some more of his things and then head out to the farm, suddenly anxious to see her face. He was certain she was already home, so he picked up the phone and called her. When it went to voice mail, he told himself she could be in the shower or the phone could be in another room. There could be any number of reasons why she didn't pick up, but he accelerated anyway.

The house was dark when he pulled into the yard and parked, and that made him nervous. He ran through the rain, his heartbeat going double time. And then he walked in and stopped, letting out a sigh of relief, and closed the front door.

She was sprawled out on the sofa in a pair of sweats, with an old T-shirt draped across the upper half of her body like a blanket. Her hair was still damp, and her feet were bare. It looked like she'd just sat down and passed out.

He shed his wet jacket, then moved closer to where she was lying, and saw medicine for her shoulder on the coffee table and guessed she'd left the T-shirt off on purpose, waiting for him to come home and help her doctor the wounds.

Her hands were skinned, the knuckles scraped and one a little bloody, and even though she'd obviously bathed, there was still a faint tinge of dirt beneath her nails from a long day's digging. It hurt him to see her so beat-up, but at the same time his admiration for her grew. He thought about their lives down through the years and knew that, no matter what they were dealt, she would not shy away.

He scooped her up and carried her to her bedroom.

She whispered his name and rolled over when he laid her down.

"Love you, baby," he said softly, then pulled a blanket over her shoulders and left her to rest.

Dallas woke up in the dark and for a moment couldn't think where she was. Then she smelled bacon and fresh-brewed coffee, and remembered she'd been waiting for Trey to come home, which obviously, he had.

She threw back the blanket and got up, slipped into a pair of house shoes, and took the T-shirt with her when she left. She walked into the kitchen just as Trey was taking a pan of biscuits out of the oven.

"Oh, my Lord, that smells good. I'm sorry I passed out on you."

He set the pan down and went to hug her. Even from where he was standing, she smelled wonderful, like bath powder and the lavender scent of her bedroom. And the fact that she was still carrying that T-shirt made for an interesting view.

"There you are," he said, as he slipped his arms around her. "This making out half-dressed could catch on." He gave her a quick pat on the butt. "Turn sideways for me, baby, so I can look at your shoulder."

"It hurts, and it's my own fault," Dallas said. "I carried a backpack today. The weight aggravated the wounds. Just tell me they're all okay."

"Yes, I think so. None of them look infected, but you do need the ointment. It's still on the coffee table."

She went to get it, and as soon as he doctored

the wounds, he helped her on with the T-shirt, then washed up and began putting dinner on the table.

"What can I do?" she asked.

"Sit down and eat all this food I made."

"Gladly," she said, and glanced out the window as he sat down with her. "It's still raining."

"Yes, and it's plenty cold. Even if it stops raining, you're going to have a muddy dig tomorrow."

"Don't remind me," she said, as she lifted a biscuit from the plate in front of her and took a bite. "Oh, my Lord, on a happier note, your biscuits are way better than mine."

He grinned. "You'll be pleased to know that I excel at a whole lot of things."

She rolled her eyes. "I'm well aware of the vast scope of your skills. Pass the butter, please."

When he scooted the tub of butter toward her with his fork, she laughed.

He smiled, and the meal progressed as he related the latest installment on the Pryor brothers' story, and then he listened in awe as she told about the big buck coming out of the fog.

They were almost through cleaning up when Trey's cell phone rang. Dallas was standing by it and saw the caller ID. "It's your mom."

He winked at her as he picked it up. "Hey, Mom."

"Are you home?" she asked.

"I'm at Dallas's place, why?"

"I just wondered if you'd heard."

"Heard what?"

"Bobby Ramsey is missing. He didn't show up at the ranger station, and he hasn't called home. His wife has been calling him ever since it started raining, and he hasn't answered. I heard they were organizing a search party. I thought you might be involved."

There was a sinking feeling in the pit of Trey's stomach. He and Dallas had grown up with Bobby.

"Well, hell, this doesn't sound good. Thanks for telling me. I'm sure the Park Service is in charge, but I'll find out what's happening. If there's a search party, I'm going."

"Let me know if you hear anything more. And my best to Dallas. I haven't heard from her in a couple of days. Is she okay?"

"She's fine, Mom. She's just been working around the farm, kind of reacquainting herself with everything here."

"Good for her. I don't suppose she's said anything more about her future plans?"

"Hey, Mom, I'm getting another call. Talk to you later."

He switched calls as Dallas slid underneath his arm.

"Something bad happened, didn't it?"

He nodded. "Bobby Ramsey is missing." Then he held up a finger to indicate his other call was on the line. "Hello?...Yes, I just heard. Where are they organizing the search?...I can be there in about twenty minutes, give or take....Okay. Thanks."

Dallas shuddered. "Isn't he a forest ranger?"

"Yes," Trey said. "Walk with me while I change, so we can talk."

She followed him to his room. "What was he doing when he went missing?" she asked.

"They said he went out on a call and never came back. They're organizing search teams at the ranger station on the national park side of the mountain. I don't know how long I'll be gone."

Dallas was already digging through his closet, pulling out work boots and a sweatshirt.

"I know you'll have your poncho and your coat, but put this sweatshirt on over your shirt or you'll freeze." She was trying not to panic. "It *would* have to be raining."

"Trouble doesn't wait for good weather," he said, as he changed back into his work boots. He had a winter coat back at the apartment, but there was no time to go get it, so he pulled the sweatshirt over his shirt, grabbed his heavy jacket, and put his service revolver and holster back on.

This was the first time she'd been faced with the reality of his job, and it made her anxious. "If you get a chance, call and let me know you're okay."

"Don't wait up," he said. "There's no telling how long this will last."

He gave her a hard, hungry kiss and headed for the front door, grabbing his hat off the hall tree as he passed.

"Where's your rain gear?" she asked.

"In the car. Lock up behind me, and say a prayer

that we find Bobby with nothing worse than a broken leg and a dead cell phone."

"I will," she said, and then he leaped off the porch out into the rain, and moments later he was gone.

She locked the door behind him, and as she turned around, a shiver suddenly went up her spine.

There would be no sleeping in this house tonight.

Seventeen

Trey arrived just as they were dividing the searchers up into groups. The captain at the ranger station quickly caught him up on what they knew and where Bobby had been seen last.

"He radioed in that he was heading toward the northeast side of the mountain, that someone had spotted smoke from a campfire and called it in the day before."

All of a sudden Trey was remembering the lights that Dallas had been seeing from her side of the mountain and wondered aloud, "No camping allowed there, right?"

"Right," the captain said.

"Do you know where Dick Phillips's farm is?" he asked.

"Yes, I do, actually. My son-in-law, Larry Sherman, buys eggs from him…or did before Dick's death."

"Well, his daughter is living in the house now, and

more than once she's seen lights up on the mountain after dark."

"Exactly where would that be on this map?" the captain asked.

Trey scanned the topographical map, and then pointed. "This is the location of the farm, and this is about where she was seeing lights."

"That's in the general vicinity of the report Bobby was following up on. Do you know the area?"

"Yes, sir."

"Then go with the blue team."

"Yes, sir," Trey said, and took his place with the group.

"Okay," the captain said. "You all know what to look for. Find his truck, and then spread out. He probably won't be able to hear over the rain, and any signs to lead you to his whereabouts are long gone because of it, too. It's the best we can do in this godforsaken weather until daylight. You've got your radios. Let's find him."

It took two hours of slogging through cold rain and mud before they found the government-issue truck but not the man who drove it. The searchers regrouped at that location, then fanned out from there, moving in four different directions.

Trey found the remnants of a campsite about twenty minutes into the search, and another man found a ranger's hat nearby. The fact that the campsite had been dismantled but for a circle of rocks and a stack of unused firewood was disheartening.

Trey had a sick feeling. This looked like a confrontation gone bad. The only positive thing about the search so far was that the rain was coming to an end.

The men were wet and cold to the bone, but thinking about Bobby Ramsey out in this weather with less protective gear than they had kept complaining to a minimum.

"Fan out and pay close attention. We know he was here, so he shouldn't be far," Trey said.

Their faces were grim as they set out on another search, but this time they didn't have to go far.

Trey walked up on an outcropping of rocks, flashed his searchlight down into the darkness and saw Bobby Ramsey's broken body about twenty feet below.

He keyed up his radio, shouting as he ran, "Found him! Below an outcrop about a hundred yards northwest of the campsite."

He circled the jutting rocks and followed the descent until he reached the body. His heart was pounding, and he knew before he felt for a pulse that Bobby was gone. He wouldn't let himself think about the memories he'd shared with this man, or the fact that his wife, Holly, had yet to find out she was a widow. He swept the searchlight over the body twice before he saw the hole in the back of the jacket.

Trey eased the body over on its side long enough to confirm the exit wound and the watered down blood stains on the front of Bobby's shirt. His heart sank.

"Son of a bitch."

The first of the searchers to catch up was the captain. "I can't believe he fell," he said.

"He didn't fall. He was shot. There's a bullet hole in the back of his jacket. I moved him just enough to confirm an exit wound in the front."

The shock on the captain's face was evident. "We have a crime scene."

"You have a body dump. I'd bet money the crime scene is the campsite where he lost his hat."

The captain was on the radio, calling in the searchers and sending out a message to dispatch a crime scene investigation team and notify the coroner.

Trey looked at his watch. It was almost 3:00 a.m. A long miserable search had just come to a sad and tragic end. He was heartily glad he wasn't the one who had to notify Bobby's wife.

When she wasn't pacing the floor or peering through the rain into the darkness, Dallas was trying to catnap on the sofa. Her vigil lasted all through the night and into the early morning before she gave up on sleep and went to make coffee. Too many years as an investigative reporter had given her a bad feeling about incidents like this. They rarely had a happy ending.

She had just walked back into the living room with a hot cup of coffee when she saw headlights coming down the drive.

It was almost 6:00 a.m., and the new day was here despite the lingering overcast sky.

Thank you, God, he's home.

She watched Trey park. When he began walking toward the house, his head was down, his steps dragging. She opened the door and, despite the chill air, walked out to meet him.

Trey looked up. Dallas was on the porch, and from the steam coming off the cup in her hand, whatever was in it was hot.

She handed it to him without saying a word.

He lifted it to his lips with both hands and took the first sip. Warmth from the liquid started to dissipate the chill in his body. He took another sip, and then another, until the cup was empty, before he gave it back. Then he began to undress without care for where he was leaving every sodden piece of clothing he'd been wearing in a pile on the porch. When he walked inside, Dallas was holding the quilt from the sofa. She wrapped it around him and led him to her dad's recliner, then refilled the cup and gave it to him again.

The silence stretched until Trey finally broke it. "He's dead."

Dallas moaned, and sat down at the end of the sofa beside his chair. "Poor Holly. What happened?"

"He was shot in the back."

Dallas gasped. "Another murder? This is crazy. What's happening here?"

"Someone reported people camping on the north side of the mountain. He went to investigate and never came back. We found the campsite and his hat. His body was about a hundred yards away."

"The north side? Where I've been seeing lights?"

He nodded. "Probably the same site."

"How far away from Dad's part of the mountain would you say it is?"

"On foot, at least a two-hour walk, maybe more."

She shivered, thinking how all of that had been going on and she hadn't known a thing. On a clear day, sound carried on the mountains.

"I didn't hear a shot," she said, then touched her ears. "I'm still not hearing everything. And the fog didn't help."

"It wouldn't have mattered," Trey said. "I'd guess he never knew what hit him."

Dallas waited until Trey had taken a few more sips of coffee before she took the mug out of his hands.

"Go get in the shower. It's the fastest way to get warm. We'll talk more when you're through."

"Don't go up the mountain today," he said.

She hesitated, but understood. The killers could still be up there, hiding. The authorities would most likely comb the area looking for them, and until the search parties swept the mountain, she wasn't going to argue.

She went to make breakfast, but they'd had bacon and eggs last night. This morning felt like winter, so she made a pot of oatmeal and toasted some of the leftover biscuits. By the time Trey came back, the meal was ready and waiting.

"I'm guessing you don't have much of an appetite, but I made oatmeal. At least get some hot food in your stomach."

He didn't argue and ate what she put in front of him.

"Will you stay home and sleep some?" she asked.

"I'll check in and see what's going on first," he said. "It wouldn't be the first time I went to work with no rest."

Dallas began clearing the table. She heard Trey leave the room to make his call but kept working. The horror of what had happened was beginning to soak in. Mystic was losing its sleepy mountain town feel far too fast. First her father and now this, although she doubted they were connected. Her father's murder had been deliberate. Bobby Ramsey had gone out on a random call and never came back. Still, she couldn't help feeling uneasy.

Trey slept through lunch, and when he finally woke, it was to the smell of beef stew and corn bread. He followed the aroma into the kitchen and found Dallas digging through her mother's collection of recipes.

"Something smells good," he said, as he leaned over and kissed the back of her neck.

"You woke up! Do you feel better?"

"I'm fine," he said. "Have you eaten?"

"About an hour ago. I can reheat the stew if you'd like to eat."

"I'll do it," he said, and dipped up a bowl and reheated it in the microwave, along with a couple of pieces of corn bread, then brought it to the table and sat beside her.

He took a bite and rolled his eyes. "Lord, this is good. You have your mom's touch with cooking. She always made the best meals."

Dallas smiled. "Yes, she did, didn't she? I've been going through her recipes, marveling at the legacy she left behind. There are recipes in her handwriting, and in both my grandmothers' handwriting, as well as a couple that were from one of my great-grandmothers. Some of the measurements are going to be hard to duplicate, though."

"What do you mean?" Trey asked, as he ate.

"A teacup full of sugar, a handful of flour, a pinch of salt. Think of the different sizes of teacups and the sizes of women's hands. I could end up with something good, or it could be a royal mess."

"I'll volunteer my services as the official taster," he offered.

She grinned. "So you say now, but we'll wait and see."

He watched the changing expressions on her face as she continued to go through the recipes and thought how very blessed he was to still have her, and what a sad turn Holly Ramsey's life had just taken.

Fraser Pitts and Snake Warren were in a motel room in Summerton enjoying dry beds, hot water and clean clothes. When the knock sounded at their door, Snake got up with a handful of money.

"That'll be the pizza," he said, and opened the door to trade money for food, then grabbed the first piece of pizza as he carried it back.

Fraser took a piece out of the box, folded it up like a taco and ate it in four bites, then reached for a second while Snake was chasing his with beer.

"So what's the plan?" Fraser asked, as he licked tomato sauce from his fingers. "Do we go after that woman tomorrow?"

"We can't," Snake said. "Thanks to you, that mountain is likely crawling with people looking for their missing ranger."

Fraser frowned. "Yeah, yeah, and if you hadn't farted and let Zeus get away, we wouldn't have even been there. Woulda, coulda, shoulda."

Snake gave Fraser his best glare, but it was hard to look pissed with only one eye.

Trey was getting ready to go in to work when he saw an old pickup coming up the drive.

"Hey, Dallas, company's coming. Might be an egg customer."

She looked out the window and shook her head. "If it is, I don't recognize them."

The driver parked beside Trey's patrol car. It wasn't until he got out that Trey recognized him.

"That's Teddy, the youngest Pryor brother. Something tells me he came looking for me," he said, and went out on the porch to meet him.

"Hello, Teddy."

"Hey, Chief. You got a minute to talk?"

"Sure, come in," Trey said.

Teddy Pryor ducked his head. "I'd rather talk out here, if you don't mind."

"At least come up on the porch and have a seat."

Teddy Pryor sat down in one of the cane-backed chairs, and then leaned forward, his elbows on his knees. "I heard about Bobby Ramsey this morning. Damn shame. I always liked him."

"Me, too," Trey said, watching Teddy pick at a hangnail. There was obviously something more on his mind, but he didn't push it. Best let the storyteller say it his way.

Teddy was looking at a spot near Trey's boot as he continued.

"Walt's wife sold the ginseng yesterday. She got near seven thousand dollars for it. Momma said it'll get us all through the winter just fine, and we sure appreciate what you did."

"I was glad to help, and sorry Walt and Stuart took their disagreement to such drastic lengths."

"Yeah, they never did have much sense," Teddy said, and then took a deep breath and looked up. "I heard Bobby Ramsey was looking to find some campers when he went missing."

Trey nodded. "Yes, that's right."

"So, are ya'll thinking it was the campers who killed him?"

"It certainly appears that way. Why?"

"I know who they were."

Trey's pulse leaped. "The hell you say."

Teddy nodded. "Remember that dogfighting ring they busted up some months back?"

"Yes."

"I'm ashamed to say I used to go to them dogfights once in a while, so I got to knowing pretty much all the guys who ran it."

"Most of them were arrested," Trey said.

"Not all of them, though. The boss was a guy named Sonny. Don't know his last name, but it was his gig, and he got away. And there were a few more who weren't there the day they made the bust."

"How do you know that?" Trey asked.

"Because I saw two of them up on the mountains about a week back. I saw their camp, and I think Sonny probably sent them back to look for Zeus. He was one of the first ones they turned loose when they heard the cops were coming."

"Who's Zeus?" Trey asked.

"He was their big moneymaker. Biggest damn dog I ever saw in my life. You saw him. He's the dog that attacked Dallas."

"But he's dead," Trey said.

"Yeah, and they may or may not know that."

"Do you know their names?" Trey asked.

"Yeah, I do. But I don't want anyone to know I gave them up, okay? They find that out, me and my whole family are dead."

"I understand. So who are they?"

"Fraser Pitts and Snake Warren."

"Can you describe them?"

"Fraser is big, real big. Built like a bodybuilder. Snake is ugly as homemade soap. He's got one eye and a tooth missing, and a big-ass snake tattoo on his belly. Pretty hard to miss ol' Snake."

Something Teddy had said earlier made Trey think to ask one more question.

"If they did know Zeus was dead, then why would they still be here? Why wouldn't they have left after the dog was killed?"

"I can't say. Maybe they didn't want to tell Sonny they'd failed. Sonny doesn't take to having his plans messed up. Anyway, that's all I came to say."

Trey stood up and then reached out to shake Teddy's hand.

"You did a good thing today, Teddy. You've given us what we need to solve Bobby Ramsey's murder, and that makes you a hero in my book."

Teddy shrugged. "Mama said to tell you that you're a good man."

"You tell your mother I thank her for the thought," Trey said.

"I reckon I'll just get on home now," Teddy said. "I sure hope you catch them two. Won't anybody be safe as long as they're still around."

Trey was already calling the ranger station as Teddy Pryor was driving away. Since Bobby Ramsey had been a federal employee, he was guessing the FBI would be heading up this case.

The captain answered.

"Captain, it's me, Trey Jakes. I just had an informant give me some very valuable information regarding Bobby's murder."

He relayed the information as Teddy had given it, topping it off with both names.

"This is just the break we were looking for," the captain said. "The FBI is handling the case. I'll forward all this to them, although they might want to talk to your informant themselves."

"Well, that isn't happening," Trey said. "You have names and a reason they were in the area. That's it."

"Understood, and thank you. This information is gold."

"Agreed. Good luck," Trey said. "I hope you find them soon. I won't feel good about this until they're behind bars."

As soon as he disconnected, he went back in the house.

Dallas was sitting in her dad's recliner with a clear shot at the front porch where he and Teddy had been sitting. Her eyes narrowed thoughtfully, gauging his mood as he came in the door.

"I know he told you something important. It was payback for what you did for them. That's how mountain people think. I'm just telling you right now, that as far as I'm concerned, Teddy Pryor was never here."

Trey was a bit taken aback. "I think I just had a glimpse of the investigative reporter you are."

"Was," she said.

He nodded. "I'm going to the station."

"I promised I won't go dig today and I meant it, but my digging time is limited. I'll be going tomorrow, regardless."

Trey's gut knotted. They had to find those killers fast or he would never be able to let her out of his sight.

Larry Sherman showed up just after five to buy eggs. Dallas walked him down to the barn and left him in the breezeway as she went into the egg room alone. No one knew she'd begun locking up the cooler, and she wanted to keep it that way. She came back carrying his usual six dozen eggs.

"Here you go, Larry."

"I really appreciate this," he said, handing her the money.

"You're doing me the favor," she said, as she walked him back to his truck. "Take care, and see you next time."

"So you're staying on a while longer?"

"I'm staying for good," she said.

"Oh, wow! That's great, Dallas. Your dad would be real proud to know this."

"I think so, too," she said. "Drive safe, and my best to your family."

Now that she'd said it aloud, it wouldn't take long for the news to spread, but that was good. It helped when people knew where you stood.

Betsy made pie. Baking was what she did when she was anxious or upset, and after learning about Bobby

Ramsey's fate she was sick at heart all over again. She called to make sure Dallas was home before she started that way, using the excuse that she needed eggs. No one was telling her anything, and she had a vested interest in knowing if her son's future was ever going to be bright.

When Dallas got the call that Betsy wanted eggs, she was glad for the company. It was hard to stay focused here when there was so much digging left to do. So she put on a jacket and walked down to the barn to get the eggs so they would already be in the house when Betsy arrived.

Everything was still wet. The chickens had the option of being outside, but few had taken it. Dallas could hear them clucking and fussing inside the coop, but it was nothing out of the ordinary.

She skirted the trees to keep from getting raindrops on her head and walked the gravel road down to the barn, thinking about Bobby Ramsey's murder. Mystic always had its share of trouble but never anything like this. Murder was for big cities like Charleston. Not for sleepy mountain towns.

The barn loomed as she got closer, two huge stories of storage space and granaries no longer in use. She couldn't remember the last time there were any barn cats living in the loft, or a dog lying in wait on the porch, at the ready, if needed, to protect his home.

Why had her dad given that up, too? Why hadn't she noticed? Maybe he'd lost heart for all of that when he lost her mom. And maybe it was because he thought he'd lost Dallas, too. The thought hurt all the way to her soul.

Her steps were dragging when she went into the barn, but instead of going straight to the cooler she walked through the breezeway to the other side, looking past the corral to the pasture beyond. There used to be hay stacked up in this corner, making it handy to feed during the winter. It was empty now, which meant she had another choice to make. Either sell the cattle or buy hay for the winter.

She sighed. Transition was never easy, even when it was for the best. She turned around, abandoning the future to get Betsy's eggs, and headed back to the house.

Betsy had the radio on the oldies channel. She loved all kinds of music but was still partial to the songs of her youth.

The car smelled like the apple pie she was taking to Dallas, and the sun was halfway between zenith and the horizon, bouncing off the shiny surface of the hood and into her eyes. She squinted for a better view of the road and turned the radio up until all she could hear were the drums and the heavy metal scream, and then the car hit a pothole. She flew up, then came down hard enough in the seat that she bit her tongue, and with the pain and the taste of blood came the confusion.

The music began to fade, and the smell of hot apple

pie was noticeably absent. It began to get dark, and she could hear screaming. The scent of vomit was up her nose and burning the back of her throat. Someone was crying. Someone else was praying.

She slammed on the brakes and jammed the car into Park, and just like that the darkness was gone and the sunlight was back in her eyes. She bailed out of the front seat and threw up until she was staggering and gasping for breath.

"Oh, my God. What's happening? What's happening to me," she moaned, then crawled back into her car and laid her forehead on the steering wheel, too shaky to drive.

Eighteen

Dallas was just beginning to worry when she finally saw Betsy's car coming up the drive.

"Thank goodness," she said, and went to the door to meet her.

"I come bearing gifts," Betsy said, as she carried the pie up to the porch and into the house.

"Just set it anywhere in the kitchen." When Betsy put it on the counter, Dallas handed her the eggs. "Trade you a couple dozen eggs for that pie," she said.

Betsy laughed. "I intend to pay for the eggs. The pie is a gift."

"I can give away eggs if I want to," Dallas said, and gave her a quick kiss on the cheek. "Can you stay for a bit?"

Betsy nodded. "But not for long. I promised to help with a baby shower at the church. Everybody's becoming a grandmother but me."

She gave Dallas such a look of longing that it made her laugh.

"You are less than subtle, Betsy Jakes."

Betsy plopped down on the sofa. "I'm not getting any younger," she said. "And on another note, how are you feeling? Is your shoulder still sore? What about your ribs?"

Dallas sat down at the other end of the sofa, curling her feet up beneath her as she turned to face Betsy.

"The shoulder is still pretty sore, but the ribs not so much. I won't complain. It could have been worse."

Betsy shuddered. "I still have nightmares about how you looked when they brought you into the ER. The hand of God was with you that day or you wouldn't be here."

Dallas shivered. "You're right about that."

Betsy's soft brown curls slipped down across her forehead as she leaned forward. "Slap my mouth if you don't want to answer, but what's going on with you and Trey?"

Dallas sighed. "It took losing Dad and a near-death experience to put perspective back in my life. I love your son to the ends of the earth, and you know it. That was never the issue. I thought I wanted fame and bright lights. Found out I'd rather have Trey."

Betsy started smiling.

"I quit my job," Dallas went on. "I'm staying here. I told him I'd never leave him again."

Betsy's eyes welled, and tears started rolling as she got up and gave Dallas a hug.

"This is the best news I've heard in years. Praise the Lord," she said.

Dallas grinned. "Your son is very persuasive."

"Are we planning a wedding anytime soon?" Betsy asked.

Dallas shrugged. "We haven't talked about any of that, and truthfully, I'd rather wait until Dad's murder is solved. I want to concentrate on happy stuff when I start planning the wedding."

Betsy nodded. "I can live with that. As long as I know you two are together again, I can die happy."

Dallas frowned. "I thought you wanted to be a grandmother, and now you're ready to give up the ghost because I moved back to town? We need to work on your priorities, woman."

Betsy threw back her head and laughed.

"Oh, my Lord, but you remind me of your mama. She never minced words." She glanced at the clock. "And, I've talked enough. I need to get home. Many thanks for the eggs."

Dallas walked her to the door. "And thank you for the pie. Trey is going to be a happy man when he comes home tonight."

She stood in the doorway and waved until Betsy drove out of sight, then went back inside to change shoes. It was time to do chores.

Trey spent a good part of the afternoon at the sheriff's office, getting caught up on where Dick Phillips's murder investigation was at, and if they had any leads on the whereabouts of the two men Teddy Pryor had given up.

Sheriff Osmond had just received the preliminary autopsy on Dick Phillips's body from the coroner. They were still waiting on a few results from toxicology, but there were even more findings that backed up the definition of murder.

"See for yourself," Dewey Osmond said, as he handed Trey a copy of the autopsy report.

Trey took a seat and began to read, and then suddenly stopped and looked up. "I see the coroner verified the shoulder injury," he said.

"Yes, it definitely happened prior to the day of his death, so your witness was correct in saying he could never have hanged himself."

Trey kept reading, then paused again. "A fractured skull?"

"On the back of his head," Osmond said. "It explained why the back of his clothing was dirty and the front was not. He either fell or was yanked backward hard enough to crack his skull. And one other thing of note. There was skin beneath his fingernails, but it turned out to be his own, and from the scratch marks on his neck it appears he was trying to get the noose off when they strung him up."

The image that put in Trey's head made him sick to his stomach. What a nightmare. What a horrible way to die.

"But there's nothing on here to give you any leads in the investigation?"

Osmond frowned. "Not a damn thing. And forensics didn't even find anything on the rope. Whoever handled it was wearing gloves."

"Anything unusual about the rope?" Trey asked.

"No, it was the kind you can buy anywhere. And it was new, so there weren't any traces of dirt, chemicals, or grease to lead us to a particular location where the killer might have kept it."

"Shit," Trey said.

"That's exactly how I feel," the sheriff said. "All we know is that Dick Phillips was murdered, and so far, we don't have a hint of motive. Did you find anything out about that big money he was expecting?"

Trey nodded. "Yes, but we're not advertising it. Dallas found out by accident when a man called to confirm a deal he had with Dick, then asked if she would honor it when he found out Dick had passed away."

"What was the deal?" Osmond asked.

"Ginseng. Dick Phillips had a honey hole. He expected to get over a hundred thousand dollars after harvest and was going to use part of it to pay off a loan against his farm."

Osmond whistled softly. "My Granddaddy used to dig sang. It would take an awful lot of roots to bring in money like that."

"Dallas said the patch hadn't been dug in something like forty or fifty years, so the roots would bring a higher price."

Osmond's eyes narrowed. "That's a reason to kill right there," he said.

"Yes, but as soon as Dallas heard about the deal she went looking for the patch and when she found it, it was still untouched. Dick's been dead awhile now, and if he'd been killed for the ginseng, the killer would have gone straight for the patch, trying to dig it out before he was discovered, so I doubt the ginseng had anything to do with his murder."

"I tend to agree, but we'll look into it," Osmond said.

"No one knows about the ginseng but you, me and Dallas," Trey said. "And the buyer, of course. It's safer for her if it stays that way until after harvest, okay?"

The sheriff nodded.

Trey shifted gears. "What do you know about the missing campers in the Ramsey case?"

"Not much. FBI is working that. All I know is Pitts and Warren both have rap sheets a mile long and open warrants out for their arrests. They'll go back to jail when they're located, whether they killed Ramsey or not."

"Are they still on the mountain?" Trey asked.

"The Feds don't think so, but whatever leads would have been left behind at the camp washed away in that downpour. Two murders in our area, two of our own dead and gone, and we haven't caught our killer on either one. Don't even have a lead on Dick Phillips's death. It's damn frustrating is what it is," Osmond muttered.

Trey glanced at the clock. By the time he got back to Mystic it would be time to go home.

"Let me know when they release Dick's body and thank you for the information," he said.

Osmond nodded as he shoved a hand through his hair in frustration. "We could use a miracle right about now."

"If I see any angels, I'll let you know," Trey said, and they shook hands.

A few minutes later he was in his patrol car and heading back to Mystic.

Summerton, West Virginia

There was nothing in Mystic comparable to Bailey's for Men, which was the only place to go for designer clothing in Summerton. The killer frequented the store because appearance mattered, and because it took him out of the humdrum life he had back home. He glanced up at the clock. It was almost 6:00 p.m., which was closing time. Even though the salesman was being patient, he needed to make a decision.

"How about this jacket, sir?" the salesman suggested. "It's from an Italian designer, and it's a good cut for you."

The killer slipped it on as he stood in front of the three-way mirror, eyeing his reflection and thinking about when he would wear the jacket.

"I like this one, but the sleeves are a good half-inch too long for my taste. Once those are altered, I'll be satisfied."

The salesman beamed. This would be a good commission. "Perfect choice, sir. When do you need it?"

"Next Friday at the latest."

The salesman called the shop tailor up to the front, and the man quickly pinned the sleeves.

Both men making a fuss over him gave the killer a feeling of satisfaction. It was ridiculous that a man had to leave town to get respect.

The salesman made a note on the work slip, and then helped him out of the new sport coat and back into the one he'd worn into the store.

"I'll give you a call when it's ready for you to pick up," the salesman said. "And you have a nice day."

The killer had parked about half a block down and was walking back to his car when he heard someone yell out his name from a passing car. He turned, then smiled and waved as the driver pulled up to the curb to talk.

"How's it going?" the killer asked.

"Great! How about a round of golf Sunday?"

"You're on!" he said. "I'll be in touch." He gave the driver a thumbs-up.

He was still smiling as he got back into his car. He started the engine, glanced in the rearview mirror, and then looked over his shoulder before pulling away from the curb.

He was driving into the setting sun as he left Summerton. It would be dinnertime before he got back to Mystic, but the drive would give him time to work out what he needed to do next. Everyone had skeletons in their past, but some of his had yet to be buried.

Dallas was on the computer when Trey came home. She had chicken and dumplings warming on the back burner and a fresh pot of coffee waiting. When she heard him come in the door, she called out, "I'm in here!"

He brought the outside in as he walked into the room. His leather jacket smelled faintly of pine and his cheeks were cold, but his lips were not.

"Mmm," he said, as he moved his mouth to the curve of her neck. "You not only smell good, you taste good."

She smiled. "That's the chicken and dumplings you smell. They're ready when you are."

"Give me a couple of minutes to change out of these clothes. I don't like to wear work to the table."

He winked as he left, and she thought about what he'd said about wearing work to the table. That was something she understood. She'd never wanted to bring the work part of her life home, either.

She moved her laptop and began setting the table, and by the time she finished, he was back.

Trey began filling her in on his trip to see the sheriff as they ate.

"So, there's still no timeline on when they'll release Dad's body?" she asked.

"No, I'm sorry, honey. I asked him to let me know. That's the best I can do."

She sighed. "It's not your fault. It is what it is. On another note, your mom came by. She came for eggs and brought a pie, but what she really wanted was to know if I was going to mess with her son's heart again." Dallas pushed her half-eaten plate of food aside, no longer hungry.

He rolled his eyes. "Sorry."

"Don't be," Dallas said. "I told her I was staying, and that I quit my job. She's already planning the wedding, although I told her we hadn't talked about it and I didn't want to start planning a wedding in the middle of Dad's murder investigation."

"Agreed," he said, and then got up to refill his coffee cup. He cut two pieces of pie and brought them to the table, and kissed the side of her cheek.

She felt so much love in such a small gesture that it took her breath away. She watched him digging into his mother's pie, and just for a moment she saw the little boy he had been. God, but he'd turned into a magnificent man, and the blessing of it was, he still loved her.

He caught her watching him. "What?"

"Do you remember our first day of school?"

He grinned. "I remember *you.* When I got home that day, Mom asked me what school was like. I told her it was fun. She asked me what I liked best, and I said the little girl with brown hair and blue eyes who sat across the aisle from me."

Dallas smiled. "I saw you, too. You had a black eye and a busted lip, and you winked at me."

Trey laughed. “Yeah, I was already working on my moves,” he said, and took another bite.

“You call it what you want,” Dallas said. “But you taught me something as we were growing up that I’ve never found anywhere else.”

“What was that?”

“What it means to be steadfast. That’s what you are to me, Trey. You’ve never wavered in your faith in me or your love for me. Even when I left, you didn’t let your disappointment turn to hate. You just continued to love me. I don’t deserve it, but I’m so very grateful you are in my life.”

Trey hadn’t expected this. He wasn’t prepared for the feeling that went through him. He shoved the pie away and reached for her hands.

“Some people come into this world already knowing who they are and what they want out of life. I knew I was going to be a cop and that the only girl I would ever love was you. I knew it at six. I know it now.”

Dallas tried to smile, but she was too close to tears. “I think you should probably just give up your apartment and move the rest of your stuff out here, don’t you?”

“I think that’s a stellar idea. I already think of this as home,” Trey said.

“I think we should commemorate this decision,” she added.

“But not with pie,” he said.

She smiled. “No, not with pie.”

"How about I put up the pie and start the dishwasher while you get ready to commemorate?"

"It won't take long," Dallas said. "All I have to do is strip."

She got up.

Trey started grabbing plates and putting food away as she was walking out of the kitchen.

He could hear her footsteps going down the hall as he was throwing dishes in the dishwasher and then locking up the house.

When he walked into the room she was standing in the dark near the window, her body outlined by the moon glow seeping through the blinds.

Trey grunted like someone had punched him in the gut.

"God bless America and the decision we are about to commemorate," he said softly, and kicked off his boots.

He was naked in seconds and then reached for her.

Her skin was silk against his body and when she wrapped her arms around his waist the contact was an instant turn-on. Her hands were cupped tight against his butt, and she was kissing his chest everywhere she could reach. He was hard and hurting so fast he didn't think he would make it to the bed with her, but he did. He sat as she straddled his lap and eased down onto his erection.

"Oh, baby, you feel so good," he whispered.

She wrapped her arms around his neck and moved just enough to make him groan, and then his hands were on her breasts before moving around her waist. Then she began to rock against him, and in the silence of the room they began the dance of love.

Soft gasps.

A guttural moan.

The slap of flesh against flesh.

The soft rustle of a sheet.

The slight creak of wood against metal somewhere beneath the bed.

The dance steps varied, but the end result was still the same: a climax of magnificent proportions that left the dancers spent and shaking.

Trey eased her down onto the bed, taking care to cradle her shoulder, and then started all over. When they were lying arm in arm, stroking bodies and kissing lips, they made sparks fly, but when they were one, they made magic.

When the last climax finally shattered Dallas's mind and she grabbed hold of his shoulders to keep from falling, he went with her.

She moaned. "Oh, my Lord, you're a drug to my body. Being without you could drive me insane."

"One damn fine decision commemorated," he said softly.

"God bless America—and you," Dallas added.

Morning came softly, the sun's rays sneaking quietly up over the mountain, down through the trees, and creeping over the flatlands before crossing the pasture and coming to rest on the roof of the barn. Just when it appeared the brightness was fixed there for the day, it spilled off the edge, painting the side of the chicken house and then slathering light across the ground like a knife spreading butter.

Trey was awake, watching Dallas sleep. He saw the first rays of light trying to penetrate the curtains, as if saying, *Wake up, wake up. It's time to wake up.*

He thought of the engagement ring being sized back at the jeweler's and couldn't wait to put it on her finger.

He thought of the life that lay ahead for them, the babies they would raise, the years and the love they would share as they grew old.

For six years, four months, three weeks and two days he had believed that life would never happen. He had been wrong, and he would never lose faith in her again.

He leaned down and kissed her awake.

"Good morning, sunshine," he said softly.

Dallas groaned, stretched, and then winced when her shoulder muscles pulled.

"Good morning to you," she said, and then slid a hand behind his head and pulled him back for another kiss.

"If I make omelets, all you get is a kiss. If we have cereal, you get so much more," she said.

"I'll have so much more," he said, and proceeded to work his way through the menu, leaving her too stunned to comment and too weak to walk.

He planted one last kiss on her lips. "I'm going to take a shower," he said.

She blinked. "What did you say?"

He grinned. "I'm going to take a shower."

She groaned. "How did you do that?"

"Do what?"

"You know."

His grin widened. "Did you like it?"

"Oh, dear Lord, did I like it? Did you not hear me scream?"

"Why, yes, I believe I did," he said.

"I can't feel my legs."

He ran a hand down the long slender length of one. "Feels just fine to me."

She groaned and punched him on the arm. "Go! And wash that smile off your face while you're at it."

He rolled out of bed and tried not to strut as he walked out of the room.

Trey was gone before 7:00 a.m., and Dallas was on the mountain before eight. She sent him a text to let him know she was there and picked up digging where she'd left off. The ground was soft from the rain and digging up the roots was easier, but it was more difficult to shake off the excess dirt. Soon her hands were grimy and the dark, black earth was embedded beneath her fingernails. But it was all good. The cold wet weather had moved on, and today was all about sunshine.

As she worked, it became apparent that her hearing was continuing to improve. She could hear a few birds, the breeze rustling leaves, even the slithering sounds nearby as the small lizards and animals of the forest took note of her presence and moved on. It was a continuing relief to know she was healing. Now if the bite marks, plus or minus a few scars, would get well, she would be good to go.

Fraser was sitting in their van waiting for Snake to finish pumping gas. The phone call they'd had from Sonny this morning had lit a fire under them. They now had orders: *bring back the bitch who killed my dog or don't come back at all.*

Nobody wanted to be on Sonny Dalton's blacklist. He had a bad habit of sending someone to cross them off.

Snake got back in the car, cursing.

"What's wrong?" Fraser asked.

"I got gas on my boot. Now it's gonna stink all day."

Fraser rolled his eyes. Snake couldn't smell worse if he was dead. "What's the plan? Which way do we go?"

"There's bound to be Feds still searching the mountain, so we can't snatch her and take her away like we planned. I think we should just drive up to her place and follow the same trail she takes. She lives alone. If she's on the mountain, there's no one at the house to see us go by."

"Whatever," Fraser said. "I just want this over with. I'm done with West Virginia. I wanna be back in the city before winter comes."

"Agreed," Snake said. "So we'll go back through Mystic and then to her farm."

"You know where it is?" Fraser asked.

"I know the blacktop to take, and I think I can find her place. I saw that big two-story barn plenty of times through the binoculars. It's tall enough I'm sure you can see it from the road. All we have to do is keep watch."

"Okay, then," Fraser said. "You navigate. I'll drive."

Nineteen

The FBI had issued a BOLO to police departments across the state on Fraser Pitts and Charles "Snake" Warren. Physical descriptions, mug shots and a description of a vehicle registered to Pitts were part of morning roll call all across the state.

Trey passed out copies of the information before the staff went out on patrol. Bobby Ramsey had been one of their own, and everyone wanted to get justice for his murder.

Today they had to transport a prisoner to another city, and before Trey could assign the task, Earl volunteered. So they shackled and cuffed the prisoner, then loaded him in the back of a cruiser and Earl quickly left town.

The rest of the day continued much like any other. Trey went out on a shoplifting call only to find out it was a young unmarried mother with a baby and no food or milk.

After a discussion with the store manager, punctuated by the young girl's frantic pleas for mercy as the baby cried in her arms, the manager withdrew the request for arrest. Trey gave her contact numbers for Social Services, bought her some groceries, told her she wouldn't be that lucky a second time and sent her on her way.

It was just after 3:00 p.m. when he finally stopped work and headed up to Charlie's to get something to eat.

Earl had radioed that he was on the flip-flop back to Mystic, and as he drove he let his mind wander, preoccupied with an ongoing family drama at home, so when he passed a dark blue van in the oncoming lane, it was already gone before he registered what he'd seen. He thought about ignoring the sighting—the odds of that van belonging to the missing campers were slim—but his conscience wouldn't let him. He had to check the tag, so he made a U-turn and took off to catch up.

He sped up without running lights or sirens, and quickly spotted the van topping a hill. He floored the gas pedal and within a couple of minutes he'd caught up. The minute he saw the tag number he knew he'd found the men. His heart was racing as he radioed in.

"Officer Redd to dispatch. Over."

Avery caught the call and keyed back. "Dispatch to Redd. Go ahead."

"Notify the highway patrol I am in pursuit of dark blue van, license tag NJ 337, as per the description on the BOLO from this morning. I'm going northbound on Highway 8 and just passed mile marker 223."

"Ten-four," Avery said, and quickly relayed the message as Earl hit his lights and siren, signaling for the van to pull over.

Trey was just about to order when his cell phone rang. When he saw the number that came up, he laid down the menu and answered.

"Yeah! What's up?" he asked.

"Officer Redd is in pursuit of a dark blue van belonging to a Fraser Pitts out of Tennessee. They're northbound on Highway 8 and just passed mile marker 223. Highway patrol has been notified."

Trey was already out the door and heading for his car.

"Tell Earl to keep relaying locations, and contact Sheriff Osmond."

"Will do," Avery said.

Once again Trey headed out of town with lights flashing and the siren screaming. At his best guess, he was four miles behind, maybe more.

Snake was the first to spot the cop car behind them.

"Shit! Fraser, are you speeding?"

"Yeah, so what?"

"There's a cop car behind us."

Fraser glanced in his rearview mirror and then frowned. "That's not highway patrol. That's a city cop car."

"It's still a cop," Snake said, and then the cop suddenly hit the lights and turned on his siren. "He wants us to pull over."

"Like hell," Fraser said, and floored it.

The van shot forward like a blue bullet out of a gun, widening the gap between them and the cop.

The cop responded by coming up on his bumper without breaking a sweat.

"Shoot him!" Fraser yelled.

"I can't hit a goddamned thing at this speed. I only got one eye, you know!" Snake yelled.

"Just get the gun, and when I swerve onto the center line, start shooting. You'll have a bigger target and you might get lucky."

Snake was cursing at a remarkable rate as he rolled down the window and leaned out. As soon as Fraser swerved the van to the left, Snake found himself staring straight into the windshield at the cop in pursuit. He emptied the clip.

Earl was scared. He didn't want to be in this position, but he couldn't back away or he'd lose them. He was driving so fast the car was shaking and he wasn't sure the tires were on the ground. The only positive aspcct of the chase was the erratic squawk of radio traffic indicating other police departments were en route. He was driving with his thumb on the call button, and every time he passed another mile marker, he called it in.

* * *

The siren in Trey's ears became a high-pitched whine. He was driving so fast that the view from his passenger window was little more than a blur. He could tell by the sound of Earl's voice that he was scared, but he was staying with the van.

Suddenly he heard panic in Earl's voice and the sounds of gunfire, followed by skidding tires, breaking glass and crushing metal. The silence afterward was sickening.

Highway patrol dispatch was trying to raise Earl, but with no response, and Trey had no option but to keep driving.

"You got him!" Fraser crowed, as he watched the cop car careen across the highway into the oncoming lane, and then skid onto its side as it began to roll.

"We gotta get off the highway!" Snake shouted. "They're likely to drive up on us from both directions any minute. We're less than half a mile from the turnoff to that bitch's farm. From there we can get onto those dirt roads and they'll never find us."

Snake was good as his word. A minute later he pointed, and Fraser barely hit the brakes as he took the turn off the highway, then quickly disappeared over a hill. They were less than three miles from the Phillips farm.

Trey drove up on the wreck while the wheels were still spinning. The police car was upside down between a ditch and a stand of trees, with smoke coming out from under the hood.

He radioed for an ambulance as he slid to a stop angled across the southbound lane, and followed up with the information that the van was no longer in sight. He grabbed his fire extinguisher and jumped the ditch, reaching the vehicle just as the smoke turned into flames and began reaching through the dash inside the cab.

Earl was still buckled into the seat, upside down, bloody and unconscious. Trey kept trying to reach through the broken window to release the seat belt, but the flames were too close. He shot a burst of foam from the fire extinguisher, which gave him enough time to reach the latch, but then the catch wouldn't release.

He wouldn't think about how close they were to blowing up together, or that the flames were getting closer to Earl's face with every passing second. The only way he was going to get Earl out now was to cut him out. He grabbed his pocket knife, and just as he began sawing at the heavy nylon strap he heard a siren coming up behind him. Moments later a highway patrolman came running, grabbed the fire extinguisher and began spraying it at the fire as Trey kept slashing at the seat belt.

All of a sudden the strap gave way.

"He's free!" Trey yelled, as he caught Earl by the shoulders and began dragging him out of the car. Once Earl was free, Trey threw him over his shoulder and ran.

The patrolman emptied the fire extinguisher into the flames, and then bolted only seconds before it blew, sending fire and burning shrapnel into the air.

"Is he alive?" the patrolman yelled, as he reached the ditch where they'd taken cover.

"I've got a pulse," Trey said.

The explosion had caused a fire that quickly began threatening the wooded area nearby, and the patrolman raced back to his car, requesting assistance from the fire department. The last thing they wanted was to start a forest fire.

Now that he had a better view of Earl's body, he could see a bullet wound to the shoulder and a deep cut on his forehead. He packed gauze pads on top of the bullet wound and kept applying pressure in a desperate race to stop the bleeding. Because there was no exit wound, he had to accept that internal bleeding was not only possible but probable. He kept calling Earl's name and asking him questions, afraid if he stopped, Earl would never come back.

And then all of a sudden help was on the scene and paramedics had taken over. They stabilized Earl for transport, and just as they were leaving, the fire trucks arrived.

The highway patrolman had also radioed in for assistance and was directing traffic on the highway as the ambulance departed.

Within minutes a half-dozen patrol cars pulled up from two different directions, all with the same bad news. They'd never seen the van. It had exited the highway, taking any one of a number of side roads that wound up into the mountains.

Trey knew those roads as well as he knew his own name and put a call in to tell dispatch where he was headed, then quickly left the scene.

From the scene of the wreck, the closest exit off the highway was the blacktop that led to both his mom's house and the Phillips farm. He knew the sheriff and his deputies would be combing the rural back roads, so as soon as he knew his mom and Dallas were safe he would get back to town and check on Earl.

He called his mom as he drove, and when she answered, he began filling her in, describing the men and the van, and then he told her to make sure all her doors were locked.

Betsy had been a cop's wife too long to panic, but she didn't like the news.

"I'll pay attention," she said. "You stay safe. Have you told Dallas yet?"

"Just about to. You spread the word to the neighbors, okay?"

Moments later he took the turn and accelerated. It was only three miles to the farm, but Dallas wouldn't be there. She was even farther away, up on the mountain, and he wasn't sure where. He called her number, then waited impatiently for her to answer.

Fraser spotted the big barn on the Phillips property as they topped a hill.

"There it is!" he yelled, pointing off to the right.

"I see it," Snake said. "Now start watching for the driveway." They drove a quarter of a mile farther before he saw a mailbox. "There's the road," he said.

As soon as Fraser took the turn, he was forced to slow down to negotiate the narrow gravel drive through what felt like a tunnel of trees.

"Nice place," Fraser said when they arrived, eyeing the house and all the outbuildings.

"We're not window-shopping," Snake growled. "Look for a road that will take us up through the pasture to where we saw her parked."

Moments later Snake spotted the cattle guard. "There!" he yelled.

Fraser winced. "Stop screaming in my ear. I got both my eyes. I can see, damn it."

Snake cursed and tried to backhand him.

Fraser fended off the blow with one hand and slapped Snake on the back of the head. "Keep your damn hands to yourself," he said. "We got a job to do."

"Then don't make fun of how I look," Snake said.

They aimed for the old pickup at the far end of the pasture and didn't talk until they were getting out of the van.

"Get the tranquilizer gun," Snake said. "We won't have to chase her down if we can dart her."

Fraser made sure the gun, which they'd originally got to help with the dogs, was loaded and pocketed the extra darts as he went over the fence. Snake crawled through it. The ground was soft, and it was easy to follow her tracks. They stepped into the forest and within a few yards were deep in the trees.

Dallas had one bag almost full and had stopped to get a drink when her cell phone began to ring. She saw the caller ID and smiled as she answered.

"Hey, good-looking," she said, expecting Trey to answer in kind.

Instead, she heard the tension in his voice when he asked, "Where are you?"

"I'm still at the patch. What's wrong?"

"Earl spotted the two men suspected in Bobby Ramsey's murder and gave chase. He took a bullet in the shoulder and rolled the car, and we lost the van. We're guessing they took one of the side roads off the highway, and yours was the nearest one. For sure they're in the area somewhere. I need you to get home and lock yourself in, understand?"

"Yes! I'm gathering up my things as we speak," she said, and headed for her backpack, carrying the sack of roots with her as she went. The moment she stopped for the backpack, she thought she heard something. Sound carried on the mountain, but Trey was still talking.

"Trey," she whispered sharply. "Stop talking. I think I hear voices."

Trey's pulse jumped. That was the worst thing she could have said. He stomped the accelerator.

Dallas took a few steps to the right and then moved up about a yard. From where she was standing she could see a long way down the trail, and within seconds two men come into view.

She crouched and ran for the shotgun, talking softly as she went.

"Two men coming up the trail right toward me. Why here? Why me?"

Panic shot through Trey so fast he couldn't think.

"I don't know, but the why doesn't matter. I want you to run."

She moaned. "They're between me and the truck."

"Then go another direction! I'm almost at the house. Get out of their line of sight, then find a way to get off the mountain. I'll find you. You still have the shotgun, right?

"Yes."

"If you shoot, aim for the waist down. Buckshot in their legs and balls will slow the bastards down. I'm not far behind. Don't talk, but don't hang up on me. If you need help, I'll be listening."

She dropped the phone in her jacket pocket and headed west at a dead run, leaving everything behind but her gun.

Trey put his phone on speaker and dropped it in his pocket, then grabbed his radio and began calling for backup.

They had a possible sighting and a woman in jeopardy.

Snake slipped on a wet patch of moss and fell down on one knee, slamming it hard into a rock.

"Son of a bitch!" he yelped, as he scrambled back to his feet.

"Shut the hell up or she'll hear us coming," Fraser snapped. "She's gotta be somewhere close."

Snake rolled his eyes, but shut his mouth and followed in Fraser's tracks.

Fraser was on the alert, listening to every sound while scanning the woods above them. All of a sudden he caught a flash of dark blue moving west through the trees.

"She's running! She spotted us!" he yelled, and took off running in the same direction, but at an angle so he could intercept her, with Snake right behind.

Dallas caught a glimpse of movement down the slope and realized that not only had they spotted her, they were running parallel to her trail. Now she couldn't go down without getting caught. It was an instinct for survival that made her pivot and run up the slope. She ran until she was out of their sight, then backtracked east as fast as she could go. When she saw the trail, she took it down. Ignoring the steep incline, she ran at full speed, knowing at any moment she could go head over heels. She just kept telling herself that Trey was coming, that any minute Trey would be here.

Within seconds Fraser had lost sight of her. His heart was pounding, and he was already out of breath. He didn't know where she'd gone, but the only way she could have made it out of their sight was to go up, so they ran up as well, with Fraser cursing Snake for lagging as they went.

The next time he caught sight of her, he was standing on a rock scanning the trees, and she was a hundred yards or more below them and descending at an unbelievable pace.

"There she goes!" he yelled, pointing down the trail. He leaped off the rock onto the path, confident his long legs and greater strength—not to mention the fact that he was going downhill—would quickly lessen her lead.

Dallas heard them coming, but she couldn't look back for fear she would stumble. At the speed she was running, it took every ounce of her concentration to stay upright.

When the first tranquilizer dart flew past her and thunked into the tree beside her head, she panicked.

She might outrun them, but at this distance they could still put her down like a mad dog, and she wouldn't even see it coming.

She only had one chance, and she knew without looking that now was the time, because he would be reloading the gun as he ran. She clenched her jaw, planted her feet and then crouched as she spun. Allowing for the incline, she aimed for the middle of his body and unloaded both barrels.

She saw the surprise on his face as the buckshot hit. When he grabbed at his legs and crotch, she turned and ran.

* * *

Fraser staggered as the buckshot pierced clothing and flesh, and let out a roar of pain and rage as his body began to burn. The pain was piercing , like having fire ants in his jeans with no way to relieve the fury of their bites.

"She shot me!" he screamed, as his hand came away bloody. "She fucking shot me!"

Snake didn't stop to visit. She was getting away, and Sonny Dalton would kill them. He ran past Fraser with his eye on the prize and a skinning knife in his hand.

Trey flew up the drive, fishtailing in the barnyard as he took the turn across the cattle guard, continuing to radio in the final details of his location. When he saw the blue van parked at the far end of the pasture beside Dick's old pickup, he floored it. The ruts were muddy, but he was going too fast to get stuck.

He slid to a halt behind the van and jumped out on the run with the rifle clutched tight in his hand. It was easy to see the footprints, and like Fraser and Snake, he followed them up the mountain, with the sounds of approaching sirens coming fast behind him.

He was less than a hundred yards up the trail when he heard a shotgun go off somewhere above him and shifted direction, ignoring the men's tracks. From the sound he knew she'd fired both barrels, so wherever she was, she was almost certainly unarmed now. Fear lent speed to his feet as he lengthened his stride.

* * *

Dallas's legs were shaking. She knew someone was still in pursuit, and the extra ammunition for the shotgun was back at the dig. Her only hope was Trey.

No sooner had she thought his name than she saw him running up the trail toward her with a rifle in his hand. For a heart-stopping second she thought she was hallucinating, and then their gazes locked.

She caught a flash of joy on his face just before she heard him yell. When he motioned for her to drop, she took a fast dive forward, doing a belly flop in the moss and mud.

One moment he'd been on the trail alone, and the next she ran into view, coming toward him at breakneck speed. The fact that she was still free and breathing, with at least one man still in pursuit, was a miracle.

Then she saw him, and the look of fear on her face stopped his heart.

"Get down!" he shouted, and motioned for her to take a dive.

She went belly first onto the ground without stopping, and she was still sliding when he took the first shot.

Snake Warren feared two things: going blind and dying. Now they both happened all at once.

Trey's shot went through his good eye. He was dead before he hit the ground.

Fraser Pitts was in a pain-filled rage but he was

still moving, and the minute Snake was no longer in front of him, he swung the tranquilizer gun up, aiming straight at Trey's face.

Trey fired the rifle again.

The bullet shattered Fraser's right knee and sent him tumbling over Snake's body like a semi rolling over a skunk. He came to rest facedown, screaming in pain.

Trey's relief was instantaneous.

He dropped down beside Dallas, who was still belly down in the mud.

"Are you hurt? Did they hurt you!" he kept asking.

"I hurt myself," she moaned, as she rolled over onto her back, holding her stomach.

"One's still alive. Don't move," Trey said, and ran up to where Fraser was lying, confiscated the tranquilizer gun and Snake's knife, then patted Fraser down and removed the other darts from his pocket.

Fraser rolled over onto his side, clutching his knee with both hands.

"She shot me up with buckshot. My legs are on fire, and my pecker hurts. You busted up my knee. I'm bleeding to death. Someone get me a doctor. I don't wanna die."

Trey yanked the big man into a sitting position and handcuffed his hands behind his back while Fraser continued to curse him and scream.

"Did Bobby Ramsey beg for his life?" Trey asked, as he locked the second cuff around Fraser's wrist.

"I don't know who that is. I don't know what you're talking about," Fraser insisted.

Trey yanked the handcuffs. "The ranger, you fucking coward. You shot him in the back."

"No, no, no, we didn't do that," Fraser moaned.

Trey aimed his rifle at the other knee.

"I'm going to ask you again. Why did you kill him?"

Fraser shuddered, rocking back and forth in mindless pain.

"He shouldn't have been there. If he'd minded his own business it wouldn't have happened."

Trey felt sick. It had happened to his father like that—dying between one heartbeat and the next just because he'd been in the wrong place at the wrong time.

He pointed at Dallas. "Why were you chasing this woman? What does she have to do with you?"

Fraser moaned.

Trey pushed the barrel of the gun down on Fraser's injured knee.

Fraser screamed.

"I asked you a question," Trey said. "I want an answer. Why were you chasing this woman?"

"She killed Sonny's dog, damn it! She killed Zeus, and Sonny said since his dog was dead, he wanted her in return. Please! I need a doctor. Don't let me die."

Dallas had been sitting there listening, and when she heard the man tell Trey why they'd been after her, she thought her hearing was playing tricks. She crawled to her feet, screaming out in fury as she started toward him.

"All of this happened because I killed a dog to save my life? Are you *serious*?"

Before Trey could stop her, she swung a fist and punched Fraser in the face. He fell backward, bawling, as he rolled from one side to the other.

"She broke my nose! She broke my nose!"

"Whoa now!" Trey yelled, and sat Fraser back up so he wouldn't drown in his own blood. Then he grabbed Dallas around the waist and swung her out of harm's way. "You can't hit an unarmed felon, even if he deserves it," he said.

Dallas was shaking with rage. "Yes I can! I'm not a cop!"

Trey grinned. "Well, just don't hit him again, okay?"

She was mud from her chin to her knees, and there was a bleeding cut over one eye, but the fury on her face was clear.

"Whatever," she muttered, then sat down with a thump, suddenly too weak to stand.

The sirens they'd been hearing stopped abruptly.

"Backup has arrived," Trey said.

"You saved my life," Dallas said, and then put her head between her knees to keep from passing out.

Trey cupped the back of her neck as he crouched down beside her.

"I'm damn proud of you," he said. "You kept your head and saved yourself."

She looked up. He grinned at her and winked, just like the first time she'd seen him.

"I was so scared," she said, and then she started to cry.

He gave her a quick hug, and as the sound of running feet came closer, he laid the rifle at his feet and stood up. Moments later, plainclothes FBI and uniformed officers from the county sheriff's office reached them.

Trey held up his arms and his badge, standing between Dallas and the chaos.

While the FBI were taking Dallas's statement, Trey went up looking for the ginseng patch, and when he found it, he could only stare in disbelief. From where he was standing, dark leaves and red berries dotted the side of the mountain as far as the eye could see. It was a miracle it hadn't been poached.

Then he remembered what he'd come to do and began gathering up her things. On his way back down he got a phone call from Lonnie Doyle, with an update on Earl.

"He's out of surgery," Lonnie said. "He'll be off work for at least six weeks. He had a bullet in his shoulder, broken ribs and a pretty severe concussion. But Carl said Earl woke up and knew him."

"That's great," Trey said. "I tried to call the station earlier to check, but no one answered the phone. Did you shut the place down?"

Lonnie chuckled. "No, but Dwight has the runs.

Said it was something he ate. He's kept the path hot between the dispatch desk and the bathroom, that's all."

Trey had to chuckle. "Oh, okay. I know the schedule is all messed up right now, and it'll be tomorrow before I can go in and work it out. Just consider everyone on duty until further notice, okay?"

"Yes, sir. I wanted to ask, is your girl okay?"

"She's still in one piece. If I can keep her that way long enough, she's bound to heal up one of these days."

"Tell her we all asked about her," Lonnie said.

"I'll do that, and thanks for holding down the fort. If a big emergency comes up, just call. I can be there quick."

"Yes, sir," Lonnie said, and hung up.

Trey dropped the phone into his jacket, anxious to get back to Dallas and take her home.

By the time he got back down to the scene, she was sitting off to one side with her head resting on her knees. From where he was standing he could see her body shaking, most likely from the adrenaline crash.

After a quick confirmation from the lead investigator that she could leave, he helped her up.

"Think you can walk, baby?"

"You mean I can go home?"

"Just hang on to me," he said, and started leading her away.

Dallas clung to him all the way down the mountain. When he loaded her into his car, a couple of agents helped them get her old pickup home. One parked the pickup in the shed and then hitched a ride back with his buddy, who'd followed in his own vehicle.

The hens were scratching and squawking as Dallas hobbled up onto the back porch. "My poor little chickens," she said.

Trey kissed her forehead and then tucked a wild strand of hair behind her ear.

"I'll feed them and shut them up, and I'll put the ginseng in the cooler. You can fix it like you want tomorrow," Trey said. "For now, you need to go soak in a long hot bath."

She was watching his lips move, but she couldn't focus on a word he was saying. He was her anchor to sanity, and all she wanted to do was latch on and never let go. Her head was spinning as she leaned against him, pressing her muddy cheek against his chest.

"You saved my life."

He pulled her close, resting his chin on the crown of her head, and focused on a spot on the wall to keep from crying.

"I waited a long time for you to come back to me. I couldn't lose you again."

"They had nothing to do with Dad's murder, though, did they?"

"Unless some revelation happens at a later date, I don't think so."

He felt her body wilt and understood her despair. She needed all this to be over.

"Do they have enough to arrest the boss who caused all this hell?"

"You mean Sonny Dalton?"

She nodded.

"Then I would say yes. Fraser Pitts was offering up all kinds of testimony against Dalton in trade for a lesser sentence."

"But he murdered Bobby!" Dallas said.

"And West Virginia doesn't have the death penalty," Trey reminded her. "Go take your bath. All of that will happen without us."

"I'm filthy," she said, as she unlocked the door.

"Leave your clothes in the utility room. I'll put everything in the washer after I come back inside."

"Thank you, Trey…more than I can say." She stopped inside the utility room and stripped. It was beginning to become routine.

"Oh, totally my pleasure," Trey said, as he watched her jacket, shirt and bra hit the floor. He paused a moment longer to admire the scenery and then went out to do her chores.

Twenty

They ate leftovers in the living room, watching the televised news conference regarding the murder of Bobby Ramsey. The FBI spokesman announced that they had identified the two men responsible, and stated that one man had died during the arrest and the other was in custody.

At Trey's request, no mention had been made of his part in the event, or of the Mystic police in general. No one needed to know that his officer was the one responsible for locating their whereabouts, or that he was the one who'd taken them down. He wanted Sonny Dalton behind bars without him ever knowing who was really responsible.

While Trey was watching the report, Dallas fell asleep beside him eating Betsy's apple pie. The plate was sliding out of her lap when he caught it and set it aside. He cradled her hands, looking at her battered palms, and the scratches on her arms and legs, and wondered how much more she could actually take.

She moaned, and he couldn't bear it. He scooped her up and carried her to bed.

"Are you coming to bed with me?" she mumbled, her eyes already closing again as he pulled the covers up over her shoulders.

"I'll be in later," he said, as he kissed her goodnight. "I have some calls to make."

"'Kay. Love you."

"I love you, too," he said softly, and turned out the light.

He went back into the living room to clean up their dishes, but his thoughts were in free fall. He needed to find a way to help her. At this rate, her body wasn't going to hold up to digging that much ginseng alone in such a short time, and even worse, now everyone knew it was there.

He started the dishwasher and was cleaning off the cabinets when his cell phone rang. It was his mother.

"Hey, Mom."

"Hello, honey, I'm not going to waste time with chitchat. I'm calling about Dallas. I know you said earlier she was all right, and that those men didn't hurt her, but is she really okay? She looked so worn-out yesterday when I was there. Is her shoulder paining her so much she isn't getting any rest?"

"It's not that," he said, and took the phone into the living room, where he plopped down in the recliner. "We've been keeping a secret, but since the gaggle of

Feds and most of the officers from the county sheriff's office were on the mountain today, word is going to spread like crazy, which means the secret is basically out."

"What secret?" she asked.

"Long story short, Dallas found out how Dick was planning on saving the farm. He had a secret ginseng patch that hadn't been harvested in something like forty or fifty years. He was going to pay off the farm with the money, upward of a hundred thousand dollars, or so the buyer told Dallas. She's been digging it by herself, wanting to pay the bank back her dad's way, and being up there alone nearly got her killed. She's so worn-out right now she can barely move, and the kidnap attempt today about finished her off. I put her to bed like a baby, but I know she's planning on getting up tomorrow and doing it all over again."

His mom was crying, and Trey heard it.

"God bless her sweet heart. Dick and Marcy raised themselves a real good girl. So how many days does she have left before the loan comes due?"

"Less than twenty, I think, and that's if we don't have a bunch of poachers getting into her crop. I think the park service has someone watching the patch tonight out of gratitude for our help in catching Bobby Ramsey's killers. But that's a onetime thing."

"I think I can fix this," Betsy said. "You tell Dallas not to leave the house in the morning until she hears from me, okay?"

Trey was leery. His mom could come up with

some real harebrained schemes. "What are you going to do?"

"Don't worry. It'll be fine. Just make sure she doesn't leave."

Trey was already gone, and Dallas was dressed and waiting for Betsy's call when she heard a car coming up the drive. She sighed; it was likely someone wanting eggs, which would delay her even more. She went out on the porch to wait for their arrival, then recognized Betsy's car as it came into sight. And then she saw another car right behind her, and another one behind that one, and another and another, plenty of them pickups and SUVs, so many that she lost count and simply stared in disbelief.

Betsy got out with a smile as Dallas came to meet her.

"It is so good to see you're still in one piece," Betsy said as she hugged her carefully.

"What on earth?" Dallas asked, watching woman after woman getting out of their vehicles, people she'd known all her life, coming into the yard.

As soon as they had assembled, Betsy made her announcement.

"We came to dig with you, girl. You're trying to move a mountain a teaspoon at a time to honor your Daddy's memory, and that kind of thinking sits good with us. Every woman here knows what to look for and how to dig. Most of them dig their own sang every year, and we're not leaving your place today until yours is out of the ground."

Dallas was stunned. Her eyes began welling.

"I don't know when I've ever been so grateful," she said, and then went through the crowd one by one, personally hugging everyone and thanking them for what they were about to do.

"You'll want water," she added.

Betsy threw up her hands, laughing. "Oh, honey, we came prepared. We brought bags, digging tools, first aid kits, and enough food and water for a picnic. You get your stuff and give us a few minutes to shift our loads. We'll leave the cars here and pile into the pickups and four-wheelers. All you have to do is lead the way. You've got girl power behind you today."

Dallas flew into the house, grabbed her water bottle out of the refrigerator and dropped it in her backpack as she went out the kitchen door, heading for the shed. The house was locked, the chickens and cows had been fed and she was on a mission.

She tossed her things in the pickup, then drove down toward the barn as vehicles began lining up and following behind her. She took them across the cattle guard and through the pasture with a joyful heart and the blue sky above her promising a clear day.

They joined Dallas in parking along the fence. Then they began helping each other through the wire, shouldered their gear and waited for her to show them the way.

Dallas eyed the weathered faces of the older women

and the clear-eyed gazes of the younger ones, and felt a kinship with them that she had never felt in Charleston.

"It's about a fifteen-minute walk up," she said.

"Lead the way," Betsy said. "We're right behind you."

Dallas pushed past the clump of bushes and started walking. She heard the women talking and chattering behind her, and for the first time since her father's death, she felt a promise of better days to come.

When she reached the patch she moved through it to where she'd stopped digging, then waited for the last of them to catch up.

One by one, as the women saw the honey hole, their chatter stopped, and by the time the last few reached the destination, the only sounds to be heard were the rustling leaves above their heads.

One voice came out of the crowd that said it all.

"Sweet Lord have mercy. I have never seen such a sight."

"Pick a spot and start digging, and if you please, plant a seed back in the hole as you go," Dallas said.

The women dispersed themselves across the patch in a long even row so that they would move up the slope in unison without missing any plants.

Dallas dropped her backpack, grabbed her trowel and one of her bags, and knelt in front of the nearest plant. She worked the blade carefully downward into the dark, rich dirt and then thrust her fingers in behind it, feeling for the neck and the roots of the plant hidden deep in the earth below. And when it finally came free in her hand, she threw back her head and laughed.

The women heard and understood.

The last ginseng root went into a bag at fifteen minutes after five. The woman who'd dug it made a little whoop of delight, and then she stood up and let out a rebel yell that made the hair stand up on the back of Dallas's neck.

She took in the sight of the work-weary women scattered about the mountain; they all looked as tired and dirty as she felt. But it was done.

"It's over. You did it. *We* did it!" Dallas said.

And then she put her hands in the air and did a little celebratory dance that had the women hooting and laughing in pure joy.

And then, just as quickly as they had celebrated, the reality of the moment hit them. They still had to get all that ginseng home. They began gathering up their things and started the long trek down.

Someone started singing, and then someone else joined in. They trooped down the mountain, singing the truth of their day as they went.

"'Mine eyes have seen the glory of the coming of the Lord…'"

Dallas was walking blindly, her vision so blurred with tears of relief and gratitude that she could hardly think.

"'He is trampling out the vintage where the grapes of wrath are stored.'"

One by one, with long weary steps, they went, their voices blending in song just as their hands had joined together on this day to right the world of one of their own.

And just when Dallas thought she'd seen it all, they walked out of the forest to their cars and found a dozen armed men with Trey at their head, waiting.

Betsy began to explain. "You're not done yet, honey. Taking this to sell on your own would be like asking to be shot. We're taking this to town together, all of us."

Trey could tell she was in shock, but he was heartily glad that this was almost over. He gave her a quick kiss and a hug.

"Did you know about all this?" Dallas asked.

"Not at first," Trey said. "But when word got out what the women were doing, some of their men contacted me, wanting to help. What you have here is an armed escort to the buyer, who is waiting for your arrival. And even though it's almost closing time, our fine banker, Gregory Standish, has two employees waiting with him inside the bank to make sure the money you receive tonight is locked up inside his vault before you go home. So hustle your backsides, ladies! We have sang to sell!"

"What about the ginseng I had in the cooler?" Dallas asked.

"I put it in your truck." He shifted his attention to the women behind her. "Are you in it until it's over?" he asked.

"Yes!" they said as one.

"We want to watch this sell!" another shouted.

"We just helped make history," Betsy said. "The size of this crop is something that's never been seen around here. Of course we're going."

Trey called out to the men, "Break out those empty boxes so they can unload the bags."

The men lined up the plastic boxes as the women began dumping in the roots and fastening the lids before the men started loading them into Dallas's truck. When hers was full they began filling up the next truck, and the next and the next, and when there were still bags of ginseng but no more boxes, she made a quick decision.

"Put the bags in the pickup beds in a single layer. Given that we're not going far, they should be fine."

When the last bags were loaded, she turned and shouted, "That's it! We're ready to go, and we have an escort all the way back to town. Lead the way, Chief. We're right behind you."

They followed Trey back through the pasture and across the cattle guard, and then Dallas remembered her little hens.

"Oh, no! The chickens need to be fed and put up."

Betsy reached for her phone. "I'll call Otis Woodley. He'll be happy to help, and he knows what to do."

"I am going to owe so many favors to so many people that I'll grow old and gray before I can pay them all back," Dallas said.

Betsy grinned as she began making the call while

women spilled out of the pickups and SUVs and began moving to their own vehicles to follow the crop into town.

When Trey reached the blacktop he hit the lights and siren for the hell of it and headed for the highway with a long line of vehicles bringing up the rear. He'd done this countless times leading a funeral procession to a cemetery, but he'd never escorted a group like this.

The drive into town turned into a parade. Everyone in Mystic had heard about the dig, and when they found out Dallas Phillips was bringing her ginseng in to sell under police escort, they began lining the streets from the bank all the way to the feed store.

The buyer was waiting there with his own armed guards, a suitcase full of money and a refrigerated truck to haul away not only what was coming in, but what he'd been buying all month.

Betsy was in the seat beside Dallas when they hit the city limits.

"What on earth?" Dallas asked, as she saw the people lining both sides of the street.

Betsy laughed. "You, my sweet girl, are making history here in Mystic. Just wave and smile."

"It's all because of you," Dallas said.

"No, baby. It's because of you. Anything would have been easier than what you chose to do. You have to know that today you made your daddy proud."

The mention of her dad made Dallas teary, but she was too happy this was over, and too damned tired, to cry. People were shouting and waving and taking videos and pictures as they drove through town, and when they pulled up at the feed store, the drivers all began looking for a place to park.

A tall, skinny man with a thick head of dark hair got up from the steps of the feed store and started walking toward Trey's police car.

"I'm Marsh Webster," he said, as he shook Trey's hand.

"Pleased to meet you, sir," Trey said, and pointed at Dallas, who was coming toward them. "That's the lady you're waiting for."

"Mr. Webster, I'm Dallas Phillips."

He'd heard everything there was to know about this woman while he'd been waiting. From her success in front of a camera to the heartache of her father's murder, her near-death dance with a vicious dog and yesterday's attempt to kidnap her. He saw the dark circles under her eyes and the crowd of women behind her, and for one of the few times in his life, he was in awe. He held out his hand.

"Pleased to meet you, ma'am."

Dallas grasped his hand firmly. "I'm pleased to meet you, too. I understand you buy ginseng."

He grinned. "Yes, ma'am, I do. And I was given to understand you had some to sell. The scales are in the feed store. If you'll bring in your harvest, we'll start getting it weighed."

"It'll take a bit," she warned, and then waved at the women. "Start carrying it in."

The armed men formed a protective line between

the crowd on the street and their women and what they were carrying.

Trey stood on the top step of the feed store with a watchful eye on the crowd. He spotted Officers Lonnie and Carl Doyle watching it from the back.

Marsh Webster smiled when he saw what was coming in and began examining the ginseng with growing delight. As Dick Phillips had promised, both the age of the roots and the quantity were staggering, and the women had brought the crop in fine condition. He began weighing and marking each lot, and just when he thought he was through, they would bring in another box, and another and another, and then they began handing him bag after bag. The silence inside a room filled with this many people was unusual, but every woman wanted to be present, to be able to tell the tale down the years of how they'd saved a family's heritage with a honey hole of sang.

Dallas lost count of time and pounds, and was leaning against Trey for both strength and moral support when Marsh Webster jotted down the last weight and looked up.

"Is that it?" he asked.

"Yes, sir," Dallas said.

Marsh shook his head. "Glory be," he mumbled. "Give me a minute to total up these weights. I believe we talked about four hundred dollars a pound," he said.

"No, sir. We talked about five hundred dollars a

pound," Dallas said. Her expression was firm, her gaze locked on his, and she wasn't backing down.

He grinned. "Maybe we did," he said, and pulled out a calculator.

A slight murmur began rolling through the crowd as excitement grew.

Dallas watched him punch in every amount, and as he did, he checked it off with a neat red mark to prove he was keeping things honest. When the total came up, he whistled softly under his breath.

Dallas's nerves were shot. She was tired and dirty and as hungry as she'd ever been, and yet standing here in this place at this moment was something she would never forget.

Trey watched Webster multiply out the weight times five hundred, and when the buyer's eyebrows went up, he watched him do it up again.

Finally Webster was done.

"Monroe! Bring me the money," he yelled.

One of his guards went running and came back quickly with a big brown case.

Webster gave Dallas a copy of his work sheet, then wrote out a bill of sale for the total amount and handed that to her, as well.

"You set a record in West Virginia history that I doubt will ever be broken," he said. "As of this moment, I owe you one hundred and thirty-two thousand dollars for two hundred and sixty-four pounds of prime green ginseng."

The room erupted in chaos. Women were laughing

and crying as Dallas stood beside the table watching him count out the money. All she could think was that this day should have been Dad's.

When Trey saw the sadness on her face, he put a hand on the back of her neck to remind her she wasn't alone.

Dallas picked up one of the boxes Webster had emptied, and when he was done counting out the money, she put it into the box, one stack at a time, and then snapped the lid shut.

The click was a signal of the end of their transaction.

"Thank you, Mr. Webster."

"Thank *you*, Miss Phillips. It was a pleasure doing business with you. Keep me in mind now, you hear?"

"You won't be seeing me here again. The Phillips ginseng saved the farm. I think we'll just let it be."

"Tell me something," Marsh said.

"If I can," Dallas said.

"How the heck did you manage to keep a patch like that untouched?"

"I don't know that myself," she said.

And then one of the older women who'd been digging with Dallas stepped out of the crowd, waving her hand.

"Oh, I can answer that," she said. "Anyone who's ever been up on that side of the mountain knows that the poison ivy is solid from the survey marks on the Phillips property outward and up all the way around to the other side. It's so thick we used to joke how someone must have let it grow to hide a still back in the old days. Didn't any of us question the reason or want to wade through nearly a quarter of a mile of it to see if the story was true."

Finally Dallas smiled. Her ancestors had been brilliant. Poison ivy, a barrier that kept growing and spreading with every passing year.

"We need to get going," Trey said. "We're keeping a banker waiting. Dallas, honey, if I may, I'd be happy to carry that money for you."

"Much appreciated," she said, and followed him out.

The crowd saw them emerge, and with so much money for their harvest that they were carrying it in a box. People erupted in cheers. Once again the procession reformed as the women drove all the way back to the bank with Dallas, determined to see the deal through.

Gregory Standish knew he, too, would become part of history and was planning how that would fit into his campaign for mayor when he finally saw them coming. He began shouting orders.

"They're coming! Get ready. Get her account pulled up."

The tellers were at their stations, ready to receive and deposit the money into Dick Phillips's checking account.

But when the chief and Dallas came in the door, the tellers were taken aback by the swarm of bedraggled women who came in with them, then a little uneasy at the sight of the armed men who stood barring the door.

Gregory Standish put a hand under Dallas's elbow and urged her forward.

"Right this way, Miss Phillips. These are my two best tellers. They will be counting out your money and depositing it into your account."

"Count it all," she said, "but I want the exact loan amount paid to your bank today. When I go to sleep tonight, I need to know my land is free and clear of any debt."

"Yes, certainly," he said, and went to work right along with the tellers, pulling up the loan amount and then waiting for them to total and deposit the whole, before they could deduct the amount she owed.

Finally the counting was done, matching Marsh Webster's total, and the money was deposited. At that point they began a series of debit and credit actions that made her lose count of what was going on.

When Gregory Standish finally handed her the loan paper marked Paid In Full, she turned and thrust it in the air.

"We did it! We saved the farm! My dad would be so proud."

The women began laughing and cheering, while Standish and the tellers grinned from ear to ear.

Trey stood by smiling, struck by the power of the female bond.

When they began to leave, Dallas suddenly remembered what she'd intended to do and began calling them back.

"Wait! Wait! I want to give each—"

They answered en masse with a resounding "No!"

"We did this for you. Not for the money," Betsy said. "Just live a long and happy life on that land, and make me some pretty babies to spoil. That's what we want."

"No, Mom. That's what *you* want," Trey teased.

The women were still laughing and joking as they walked out of the bank. It had been a long hard day, but they were satisfied with their work and the final outcome.

As for Dallas, her reward had become more than paying off the loan. As of this moment, she was almost eighty thousand dollars to the good and had the deposit slips from the tellers to prove it. And today Dallas and all those women had done more than dig up a mountain of ginseng. They had forged a bond of kinship that would never be broken, something no amount of money could buy.

"Thank you for this. Thank you for giving me time you would have spent with your families."

Gregory Standish just kept beaming. "It was my pleasure…our pleasure to do this. Dick was a friend."

Standish followed everyone out, and then locked the bank doors and remotely reset the alarm before going home.

Night had come to Mystic while Dallas was putting

her world back together. She paused at the curb for a quick word with Trey. "Are you done for the day?"

"I sure am, baby. You and Mom head home. I'll bring up the rear."

Dallas climbed slowly back into the truck and then glanced over at Betsy as she started the engine. "You do know that you're working your way toward being the best mother-in-law on the planet, right?"

Betsy giggled. "I do what I can."

As Dallas pulled away from the curb, she felt like the weight of the world was gone from her shoulders. She also felt like she wanted to sleep for a week.

After all the elation, the drive home was oddly quiet. All the energy that had followed their success had been used up. As soon as Dallas drove into the yard, Betsy started gathering up her things.

"Just let me out here, honey. I'm ready to go home, too." She leaned across the seat and gave Dallas a kiss on the cheek. "Welcome to the family, sweet girl."

"Thank you again for everything," Dallas said, then sat and waited until Betsy transferred her things to her car and drove away. Dallas drove around to the back of the house and was putting the pickup in the shed when Trey pulled in.

The night air was chilly, the black sky ablaze with stars to infinity, the kind of night for making love, but she was almost too weary to stand.

Trey met her at the porch, walked her in the back door and once again pointed at the washer.

"Strip for me, honey."

"Don't bother with my clothes, Trey. Just leave them on the floor and I'll deal with them in the morning. Come wash my back and talk to me. I don't want to cry again."

Trey locked up as she walked naked through the dark house. He heard her in the shower. The scent of her shampoo drifted out across the hall. He put up his weapon and began to undress.

By the time he entered the bathroom, she was standing beneath the jets with her eyes closed and her arms braced against the wall in front of her, letting the water run down her back.

"Coming in," he said softly.

She reached back and clutched his hand, needing an anchor. Her head was spinning. She had been trying to count the number of days since she'd left Charleston, but she kept losing track. In the short time she'd been home, life had given her a crash course in gratitude. Some would say she'd reconnected with Trey out of fear and grief. But she knew better. Her crash course in life hadn't scared her into commitment. All it had done was to show her what had been missing.

He slid his hands around her waist and then traded places with her. Now he was the one under the pelting spray and she was in the lee, just out of range.

She watched the water flatten his hair like a silky black cap, and then drip from his eyelashes and down onto his cheeks. She might have thought he was crying except for the heat of passion in his eyes.

"Make love to me, Trey."

He hesitated even as he pulled her to him. "You look so hurt. I don't want to make it worse."

Her hand was splayed across her breasts. "The worst pains are in here, and I think only you can make those better."

His nostrils flared. "Standing up or lying down?"

"Here and now," she said.

"We can do that," he said. "Put your arms around my neck."

So she did, then responded to the pressure as he cupped the backs of her hips and lifted her up.

"Put your legs around my waist," he said.

She settled on the jut of his erection with a grateful sigh. This was what it felt like to belong. This was what it felt like to be home.

"Hold on tight, Dallas Ann. You are going for a ride."

And she did, riding him straight up to glory, wrapped in his loving arms. The pulse of the water jets was a tease to the blood pulsing through their bodies. And as he began to move inside her, her body became supersensitive to touch. Everything she felt turned her on, from the pelting flow of the water to the rough brush of his unshaven cheek against her breast, then the hard thrust of his body as he drove her need for a sudden and mind-shattering climax.

Dallas lost focus on everything except what Trey was doing. Every kiss he gave her seared her skin, marked her soul. She wanted to catch fire in his arms. She could never get enough of this man. And when the feeling finally came upon her, she gave up to the blood rush and died the little death in his arms.

Trey felt her climax coming and finally let go, spilling his seed until his body was weak and his legs were shaking.

She unlocked her legs and slid down, then took a washcloth and washed every inch of his body until he was as clean as she felt.

He turned off the water, and as they stepped out together he grabbed a towel to dry her off. She stood motionless beneath his care until he was satisfied.

Then he kissed her healing shoulder and whispered in her ear, "Go take your medicine, baby. Your body has been through a whole lot of hell, and what we just did didn't make it better. I sure don't want you sick."

Dallas glanced in the mirror. So much had happened since the dog attack, and in such a short span of time, that it felt as if it had happened to someone else.

She went through the house to get the antibiotics and took them in the kitchen, standing naked in the dark as she took them. Then she dug the loan paper out of her backpack and carried it with her to her room.

Trey walked in behind her as she laid it on the desk and then, without saying a word, fell into bed as he crawled in behind her.

He waited until she'd fallen asleep, then got up to retrieve the engagement ring he'd picked up earlier and went back to bed.

She slept with the abandon that only total exhaustion can bring, and Trey brushed a kiss along the curve of her cheek that she didn't feel while he told her a story she didn't hear.

"For six years, four months, three weeks and two days I went to bed thinking this moment would never come, and yet here you are, so beautiful, and yet so beaten and worn by what life has done to you that I can't say this to your face without coming undone. I love you more than my life, Dallas Ann. Thank you for wanting to be my wife."

Slowly he slipped the ring onto her finger, and when it went all the way without effort, it felt like a sign.

"Perfect fit, just like us," he said, then stretched out beside her and closed his eyes.

Trey was in the kitchen making coffee when he heard her scream. He grinned at the sound of running feet as she came up the hall.

She flew into the kitchen buck naked, holding her hand out as if it had turned to stone, her eyes wide with disbelief.

"Did I forget this happened? Is this a dream and I'm still asleep? Talk to me, damn it! Am I engaged?"

"Well, you are naked," Trey said, "and you have an egg customer down at the barn, and yes, ma'am, you are engaged to me with a promise to wed."

She slapped her hands across her breasts.

"Oh, son of a bitch," she muttered, and flew back down the hall to get dressed and then ran out the door to deal with her customer.

Trey threw back his head and laughed, and he was still laughing when she came back with the money and a smile.

He swung her up in his arms, kissing her soundly before he sat down at the table and pulled her into his lap.

"You had a need to know this land was free and clear before you went to bed last night, and I had a similar need to officially put my name in the bright lights of your life before I closed my eyes. And then you passed out and I couldn't sleep, so I engaged you to me. I didn't think you would mind."

She started laughing and crying, and then she threw her arms around his neck and proceeded to kiss him on every inch of his face. After which she stopped, looked at the ring and did it all over again.

"It's so beautiful," she breathed.

"Just like you," he said.

"Oh, Trey, oh, honey, I am so proud to be marrying you," Dallas whispered, and then buried her face against his neck and hugged him.

"You're not crying, are you?" Trey asked.

"No. I'm just taking this all in. I came home to bury Daddy and thought I'd lost everything that mattered. Instead, I find out everything that mattered was just waiting for me to come home."

He saw her face, and just for a second, instead of the smile, he saw the terrified look from yesterday as she came running down the trail.

"Life is precious, baby. I don't want to waste another minute of it without you. So, now that you're wide-awake and listening, will you marry me, Dallas Ann?"

And just like that, everything that had been in turmoil within her slid into place.

She touched her forehead to his.

"Yes, I will marry you, and thank you for asking."

Epilogue

Fall had come in all her glory to the mountain, turning the leaves to burnished gold and crimson red and citrus orange, sending animals into a shopping frenzy to shore up the larders in their dens with food enough to get them through winter's cold.

Life for Trey and Dallas had found its level, save for the unsolved mystery of her father's death. The untidy shrine she'd made of her father's room was also gone, packed or given away, save for that precious stack of antique books from the ancestors who'd established this farm. She had everything that mattered stored close within her heart.

The decision to keep the cattle had been Trey's, so there was now a big stack of new hay in the far corner of the barn. The chickens still ruled the roost in their own coop, confident that food, water and heat would be furnished in return for the tidy sum of one egg apiece each day. The broody hen had finally abandoned the nest, disgusted with the ceramic egg that never hatched. And the day Trey came home with a cat for the barn, Dallas knew life had truly begun anew.

She had her own plans for the future and was in the midst of working on a book she'd begun years earlier, about a forever kind of love. She had another book on the back burner about the mystery surrounding her father's murder. She knew part of the story, but not the rest. It would have to wait until the mystery was solved.

Once in a while she would get a text from an old friend back at WOML Charleston, still giving it the old college try to persuade her to give up her story. But that was hers to tell, in her words, in her own way, and not with a thirty-second sound bite on the ten o'clock news.

The only thing still in limbo was laying her father's body to rest, and when that day finally came it was just her and Trey at the grave site, holding hands as his casket was lowered into the ground next to his wife.

"It's a real nice day for this," Trey said, and pulled her a little closer against him for her comfort.

Dallas glanced up at the cold, clear sky and then at the beauty of the changing leaves around them. He was right. It was a real nice day.

"Fall was Dad's favorite time of year. He would love this," she said.

The grave digger came forward with a scoop of fresh earth and handed her the shovel.

Despite her best intent, tears welled as she cast the earth down on the casket.

"Rest well, my sweet daddy. You'll never be out of my thoughts."

Then she handed the shovel to Trey.

He shoved it into the freshly dug earth and then moved closer to the edge as he tossed in the dirt. He heard it land, but he didn't look down. Instead, he was looking out across the countryside, remembering the ride he and Dick had taken the day Dallas first left home.

"I miss you, man. I know you were worried about Dallas, but look how great she turned out. Remember I told you she could take care of herself, and that no matter how far she went, she would never forget the way home? I was right. She came back for you, but she's staying for me. Rest in peace, my friend. God knows you've earned it."

Dallas was in tears when he turned to face her.

"Hey, no more tears, love," he said. "Let's go home. Your job here is done."

They walked hand in hand back to the car, and while neither one of them said the words aloud, they were both thinking the same thing.

The job would never be over as long as the killer was walking free.

* * * * *

Look for
the next book in
New York Times *bestselling author*
Sharon Sala's
SECRETS AND LIES *trilogy,*
COLD HEARTS
coming in September
from
MIRA Books.

Discover the pulse-pounding psychological suspense debut that has everyone talking, from

MARY KUBICA

A shocking twist you won't see coming.
And neither did she...

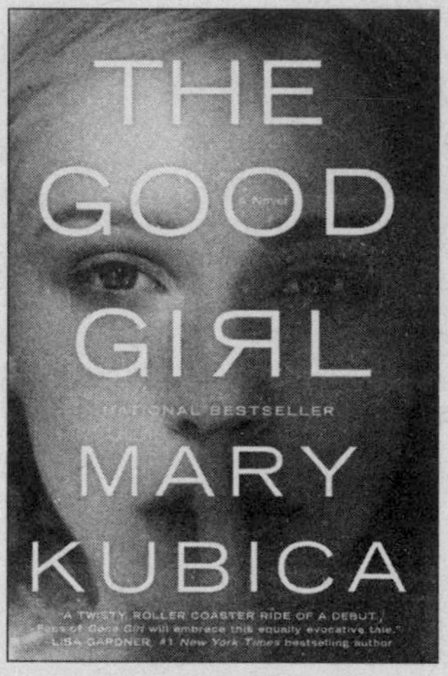

One night, Mia Dennett enters a bar to meet her on-again, off-again boyfriend. When he doesn't show, she unwisely leaves with an enigmatic stranger. At first Colin Thatcher seems like a safe one-night stand. But following Colin home will turn out to be the worst mistake of Mia's life.

When Colin decides to hide Mia in a secluded cabin in rural Minnesota instead of delivering her to his employers, Mia's mother, Eve, and detective Gabe Hoffman will stop at nothing to find them. But no one could have predicted the emotional entanglements that eventually cause this family's world to shatter.

An addictively suspenseful and tautly written thriller, *The Good Girl* is a propulsive debut that reveals how even in the perfect family, nothing is as it seems.

"A twisty, roller coaster ride of a debut. Fans of *Gone Girl* will embrace this equally evocative tale."
—Lisa Gardner, #1 *New York Times* bestselling author

Available now, wherever books are sold!

Be sure to connect with us at:

Harlequin.com/Newsletters

Facebook.com/HarlequinBooks

Twitter.com/HarlequinBooks

www.MIRABooks.com

MMK1776

From #1 *New York Times* bestselling author

LISA JACKSON

come two of her finest stories that have earned her the title "Queen of Romantic Suspense."

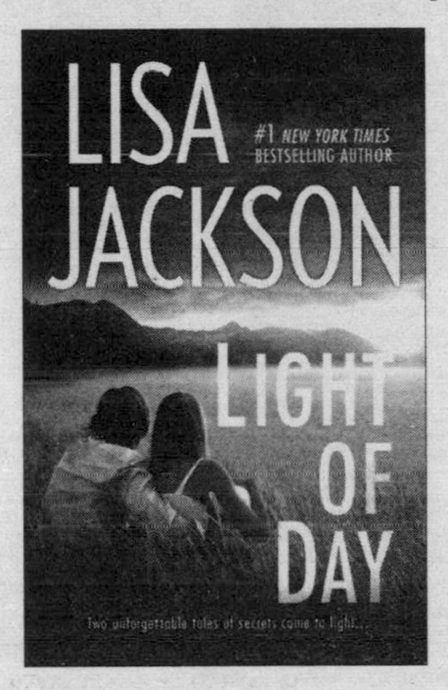

Pick up your copy today!

Be sure to connect with us at:

Harlequin.com/Newsletters
Facebook.com/HarlequinBooks
Twitter.com/HQNBooks

www.HQNBooks.com

PHLJ965

REQUEST YOUR FREE BOOKS!

2 FREE NOVELS FROM THE SUSPENSE COLLECTION PLUS 2 FREE GIFTS!

YES! Please send me 2 FREE novels from the Suspense Collection and my 2 FREE gifts (gifts are worth about $10). After receiving them, if I don't wish to receive any more books, I can return the shipping statement marked "cancel." If I don't cancel, I will receive 4 brand-new novels every month and be billed just $6.24 per book in the U.S. or $6.74 per book in Canada. That's a savings of at least 22% off the cover price. It's quite a bargain! Shipping and handling is just 50¢ per book in the U.S. and 75¢ per book in Canada.* I understand that accepting the 2 free books and gifts places me under no obligation to buy anything. I can always return a shipment and cancel at any time. Even if I never buy another book, the two free books and gifts are mine to keep forever.

191/391 MDN F4XN

Name (PLEASE PRINT)

Address Apt. #

City State/Prov. Zip/Postal Code

Signature (if under 18, a parent or guardian must sign)

Mail to the **Harlequin® Reader Service:**
IN U.S.A.: P.O. Box 1867, Buffalo, NY 14240-1867
IN CANADA: P.O. Box 609, Fort Erie, Ontario L2A 5X3

Want to try two free books from another line?
Call 1-800-873-8635 or visit www.ReaderService.com.

* Terms and prices subject to change without notice. Prices do not include applicable taxes. Sales tax applicable in N.Y. Canadian residents will be charged applicable taxes. Offer not valid in Quebec. This offer is limited to one order per household. Not valid for current subscribers to the Suspense Collection or the Romance/Suspense Collection. All orders subject to credit approval. Credit or debit balances in a customer's account(s) may be offset by any other outstanding balance owed by or to the customer. Please allow 4 to 6 weeks for delivery. Offer available while quantities last.

Your Privacy—The Harlequin® Reader Service is committed to protecting your privacy. Our Privacy Policy is available online at www.ReaderService.com or upon request from the Harlequin Reader Service.

We make a portion of our mailing list available to reputable third parties that offer products we believe may interest you. If you prefer that we not exchange your name with third parties, or if you wish to clarify or modify your communication preferences, please visit us at www.ReaderService.com/consumerschoice or write to us at Harlequin Reader Service Preference Service, P.O. Box 9062, Buffalo, NY 14269. Include your complete name and address.

SUS13R

New York Times **bestselling author**

LINDSAY McKENNA

brings you into the line of fire with a gripping new *Shadow Warrior* tale.

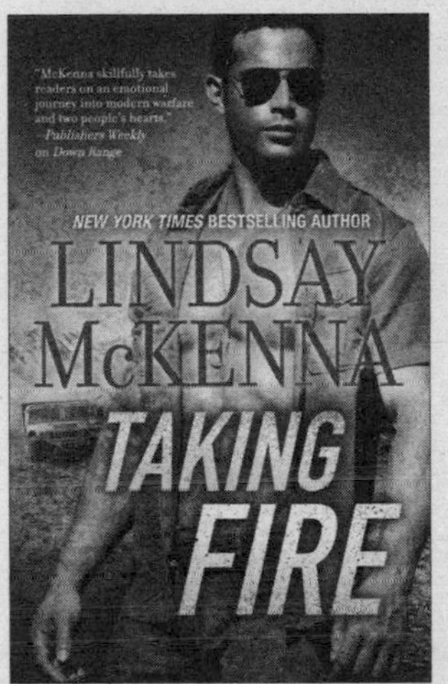

Not all are meant to walk in the light.

Marine Corps sergeant Khat Shinwari lives among the shadows of the rocky Afghani hills, a Shadow Warrior by name and by nature. She works alone, undercover and undetected—until a small team of US Navy SEALs are set upon by the Taliban…and Khat is forced to disobey orders to save their lives.

To go rogue.

Now, hidden deep in the hills with injured SEAL Michael Tarik in her care, Khat learns that he's more than just a soldier. In him, she sees something of herself and of what she could be. Now duty faces off against the raw, overwhelming attraction she has for Mike. And she must decide between the safety of the shadows…and risking everything by stepping into the light.

Pick up your copy today!

Be sure to connect with us at:

Harlequin.com/Newsletters
Facebook.com/HarlequinBooks
Twitter.com/HQNBooks

www.HQNBooks.com

PHLM505R

SHARON SALA

32792	TORN APART	___ $7.99 U.S.	___ $9.99 CAN.
32785	BLOWN AWAY	___ $7.99 U.S.	___ $9.99 CAN.
32677	THE RETURN	___ $7.99 U.S.	___ $8.99 CAN.
32633	THE WARRIOR	___ $7.99 U.S.	___ $7.99 CAN.
31659	GOING GONE	___ $7.99 U.S.	___ $8.99 CAN.
31592	GOING TWICE	___ $7.99 U.S.	___ $8.99 CAN.
31548	GOING ONCE	___ $7.99 U.S.	___ $8.99 CAN.
31427	'TIL DEATH	___ $7.99 U.S.	___ $9.99 CAN.
31342	DON'T CRY FOR ME	___ $7.99 U.S.	___ $9.99 CAN.
31312	NEXT OF KIN	___ $7.99 U.S.	___ $9.99 CAN.
31241	BLOOD TRAILS	___ $7.99 U.S.	___ $9.99 CAN.

(limited quantities available)

TOTAL AMOUNT $__________
POSTAGE & HANDLING $__________
($1.00 for 1 book, 50¢ for each additional)
APPLICABLE TAXES* $__________
TOTAL PAYABLE $__________
(check or money order—please do not send cash)

To order, complete this form and send it, along with a check or money order for the total above, payable to MIRA Books, to: **In the U.S.:** 3010 Walden Avenue, P.O. Box 9077, Buffalo, NY 14269-9077; **In Canada:** P.O. Box 636, Fort Erie, Ontario, L2A 5X3.

Name: ______________________________
Address: ____________________ City: ______________
State/Prov.: ____________________ Zip/Postal Code: ______________
Account Number (if applicable): ______________________________
075 CSAS

*New York residents remit applicable sales taxes.
*Canadian residents remit applicable GST and provincial taxes.

www.MIRABooks.com

MSS0415BL